ENTER SIR JOHN

ENTER SIR JOHN

CLEMENCE DANE AND HELEN SIMPSON

ISBN: 978-1-963956-44-3

Contents

Sir John could enter—and did.

FOREWORD

There should be a third name added to the two which stand at the head of this story: that of Mr. C. S. Evans, the publisher and friend of the writers. He it was who communicated to them the plot, with regrets for his own lack of leisure, and encouragement to do with it whatever they pleased. The reader must be the only judge of their success in a form of writing unfamiliar to both; but in any event they owe Mr. Evans gratitude for the happy weeks spent in developing his story, and here, with respect and affection, pay him some part of their debt.

CHAPTER I So Early in the Morning

Knock! knock! knock! Never at quiet? What are you?, But this place is too cold for hell. —Macbeth

Knock—knock—knock!

The gray dawn was filtering into the sky, and the church clock was striking three, when the knocking began.

The rambling up-hill street of the little mining town was startled by the knocking. Peridu went to bed early, and without candles, for the incessant eruption of red-hot slag from a black, cone-shaped hilltop kept the town cozily half-lighted, as a room is lighted by the flicker of a dying fire. Peridu was now on the edge of coal country, though it had had assembly rooms once, and a theater and wells. The assembly rooms had become a hotel, and the two wells were part of the town water system, but the theater still faced the town hall on the other side of the square; and its fat Doric pillars had play-bills posted round them when amateur societies performed Gilbert and Sullivan operas. Announcements of melodramas, comedies, gentilities, and farces for one night only, yellowed and decayed upon the theater walls.

Hopeful stock companies rented the theater for odd weeks between spring and summer tours, and such a company announced from walls and pillars the performance of "King's Evidence." The London cast would include Messrs. Gordon Druce, Ion Marion, Tom Drewitt, Handell Fane: and Mesdames Magda Warwick, Doucebell Dearing, and Martella Baring. Manager—Gordon Druce: Stage Manager—Novello Markham. Doors open at 6:30. Performance at 7, sharp.

No company opened later than seven for that matter, for, Shakespeare or Boucicault, Sutro, Dumas, or Paulton, Peridu went to bed early and slept the night through in such country quiet that a late drunkard, singing and stumbling through the streets, was quite enough to wake indignant householders and send up window-sashes; and the policein the pretty little police-station with the Virginia creeper would hear Peridu's opinion of them next day.

Knock—knock—knock!

Little wonder that the commotion on the doorstep of Miss Mitcham's highly recommended lodgings (ground floor back and front, coals, bath and hot water included, a minute and a half from the stage door of the Theater Royal itself, as her neat letters had informed uncounted clients for the last thirty-five years) should rouse sound sleepers and send up sashes with a rattle.

Knock—knock—knock!

The knocking broke into the slumbers of Novello Markham, stage manager for the Theater Royal's latest tenants. With a vague impression that he was once more with the Bensons, playing porter in "Macbeth," and late for his call, he sat up in bed with a start.

"Knock—knock—knock!" mumbled Novello drowsily. "I'm coming! Keep the curtain down for God's sake!" and felt for his teeth in the toothglass at his side as his wife stirred and woke.

"What is that filthy noise?" demanded Mrs. Markham, who in her more public moments was known as Miss Doucebell Dearing. "What are you doing, Nello? Stop it, dearie, can't you? Letting in the draft on me!" For Mr. Markham had pattered across to the window, pushed it up, and joined the fringe of heads that gave the little lane—the block of houses was no longer than the breadth of the theater—a fantastic resemblance to old prints of Temple Bar.

Knock—knock—knock!

"It's two doors down. They're kicking up the devil of a racket. They'll have the police—Ah, I thought so! Come and have a look, Doucie! Police on to it already. They're going to have a high old row!" And Mr. Markham half turned in the window to make room for the plump little figure in the flowered nightdress and the bathing cap. Miss Dearing invariably set her shingle with a bathing cap.

"Where's your policeman?" demanded the bathing cap, craning.

"Isn't he there? But I saw him coming round the corner just by the bakery." Mr. Markham leaned out once more.

"Rot! There's only the man knocking. He must be mad, making all that racket at this hour. Wonder what's up!" And Mrs. Markham peered to right and left: then, as a flicker from the hillside once more set the street aglow, she cried excitedly: "No, no! You're right! There is a policeman coming right enough. He's running down the square." And then: "Nello, d'you know who it is knocking? It's Druce."

"What? So it is! Look here, Doucie, I'd better go down. Damn the matches! I wish to goodness you wouldn't take the matches into the bathroom. Here, see if you can make them strike! Where's my overcoat?"

He groped and swore energetically while his wife continued:

"And I tell you what, Nello, that's Baring's digs. She has the ground floor, front and back. Here, I'm coming too. Wait for me!"

But Mr. Markham was gone; and between the desire to follow and the desire not to miss a detail of the drama, Mrs. Markham caught up her shoes and stockings and hastily returned to the window, pulling them on with blind hands as she watched.

The scene was as curious as any she had ever helped to create upon the stage. The strengthening daylight showed a constantly augmented crowd of blue-gray forms that, in each flicker from the hillside, were crisply outlined in pink and gold. The wild knocking had ceased. She could see clearly the solid policeman and the squat, gesticulating figure of the company's manager Gordon Druce. Both faces were upturned to the first-floor window, whence leaned a shawled and nightgowned shape pouring forth eloquence. Mrs. Markham put her hand to her ear, straining her sense of hearing in a fever of curiosity. The men's deeper notes were barely audible, but the landlady's voice rang out like a trumpet:

"Certainly not! I'm not going to let people come ramping and raging through my house at all hours of the night. This is a respectable house; nobody knows that better than Mr. Grogram."

The policeman's reply could not be heard, but the voice of the knocker became suddenly distinct—

"I want my wife!" it said.

"There's nobody's wife here," responded the head at the upstairs window. "I've told you and I tell you again that this is a respectable house."

"She mus' be here," the knocker insisted. "She was coming here and she said she'd be back by two. Now it'sh three—"

"We know that," said the head with a couple of threatening nods. "The lockup, that's the place for you. It's a mystery to me where you can have got it—and the pubs all shut at ten."

Mrs. Markham missed the policeman's next words; they were not many; the head cut him short.

"You take him away. I'm not going to wake my lodger, poor young lady, not for twenty wives! I wonder at you, Mr. Grogram. Wait till you're married yourself and you won't be so nosey."

From a window near-by issued a very competent imitation of

two fighting cats, which served as obbligato to the chorus of protest and inquiry that rustled from house to house.

"Whatever is it?"

"You don't go down, George—not without your trousers, you don't!"

"People ought to be ashamed—"

"Why, it's a gentleman drunk!"

"That oughtn't to be no treat to you!"

I "Gentleman, I said! It's at Miss Mitcham's!"

"Well, what of it?"

"That's what comes of theatricals."

"Come off it, Annie! Come to bed with that blanket!"

Again the murmur of male voices drowned the dwindling chorus; and as the policeman showed no disposition to continue the argument with the triumphant head, the lesser heads were gradually withdrawn, and the small crowd that had collected upon the white scoured doorstep began to straggle away. Doucebell could see her husband prominent in the thinning group, and a flicker of light showed his actual movements. He was talking to the police-man as he slipped an arm through that of the swaying figure beside him.

"Sense, Novello has," murmured Mrs. Markham as she watched. "Drunk or sober, a manager's a manager. Bet you he brings him here. I'd better get something on."

She turned back into the room, and with the quickness of a professional had in two minutes slipped into a kimono, lighted the lamp, and flung open the folding doors that divided the small parlor from the grandiose bedroom. For the house, like the rest of the block, as well as the theater behind it, had been built in an ampler day. The "front-and-backs" of the ground floors, now let out as lodgings, had once been stately dining-rooms where, protected from the vulgar gaze of passers-by by rep curtains, gentlemen talked politics and port, while the first-floor rooms were the withdrawing-rooms in which the fine ladies awaited by candle-light their lords' return.

The ground floor fireplaces were black marble caverns, and the folding doors, that still bore traces of gilding, were decorated with garlands and even mirrors. It was at such a mirror that Mrs. Markham, after twitching bedclothes into place and hurling discarded garments beneath the bed, began to restore her face to its Doucebell Dearing appearance.

She was still busily employed on this delicate operation, when a scream rang down the quieting street, and was followed by another, and yet another.

But though the little actress was back at the window in a flash, she could not see who had screamed; she could see only that the last of the diminished group was disappearing through the doorway that had been so stoutly closed against them.

Once more the windows were flung open, but the outcries were pitched in another key.

"Whatever was that?"

"Like a pig being stuck."

"Go to sleep, lovey! Mumma won't let them 'urt you. Sh, sh!"

"What was it, George? Can you see anything yet?"

"What's the police doing?"

This seemed to be the general preoccupation. The neighbors, safe behind locked doors and up a flight or so of stairs, displayed indignation, and were wondering what the police were for if not to prevent screams issuing from respectable houses, when a door of the ill-behaved house was flung open again, and Markham bolted out. His wife turned eagerly back into the room to meet him.

"Well, Novello? Well, what is it? What's happened? Can't you tell me what's happened? Why, you're as white as a sheet! What, in God's name—Why, Novello, what are you looking for? What's the matter with you, dearie?"

Little Novello Markham was fumbling in the huge Victorian sideboard with shaking hands, knocking over egg-cups, rattling cruets.

"I can't stay. Gordon Druce wants me. Collapsed. Where's the brandy?"

"Here, dearie—here it is. Is Gordon ill? What's happened?"

He said the word to which, on the familiar stage, she had so often responded with appropriate gestures of horror; but this stage was strange, and she had no gesture ready. He said the word "Murder."

"Murder? Who?"

"Magda Druce."

"But—she was having supper with Martella Baring!"

"She was," said Novello.

"But, my God! Who did it?"

"Martella Baring. Battered her head in with a poker. I've just seen it."

"I don't believe you."

"You would if you'd seen it. Where's that brandy? I've got to get back."

"Shall I come too?"

"I wouldn't let you see it, Doucie. It's—it's filthy. Miss Mitcham's looking after her."

"Looking after her!" said Doucie, horrified and indignant. "Haven't you got in the police?"

"Yes, but the girl's half-dazed. I've got to go, Doucie. I'll come back when I can. Let me go, for God's sake!"

"But—" said Doucie, "murder!"

The doors clapped together. She sat down on the bed, rehearsing dully, as a beginner might, the first lines of that colloquy.

"What's happened?"

"Murder!"

She did not go back to the window.

Her husband, hurrying along the street with his brandy, was thinking:

"Murder! I'm mixed up in a murder case; the manager's wife's been murdered, and Martella Baring's done it! That nice girl, a murderess! What do you think of that?"

He was at the dreadful house before he had time to answer his own question, halted on the steps for an instant to control himself, then squared his shoulders and went in.

CHAPTER II Murder Most Foul

Some aqua vitae, ho!—Romeo and Juliet

When little Novello Markham, the flask of brandy in his hand, returned from his own house, to the disordered chamber he had so recently quitted, he found the scene little changed. The candle still flared upon the table laden with the refuse of the meal—used cups, a loaf of bread, a dirtied wine-glass, and a stack of plates; but the living had left the room. Only the dead woman remained; she still lay stiffly across the sofa end, as if she had been flung upon it as you fling back a discarded covering. Her legs, in their pink silk stockings and high-heeled shoes, stuck out stiffly like doll's legs from her short skirt; her body was humped over the bolster, her dangling head had fallen back revealing the cause of her death; her short fuzz of hair was dark with half-dried blood, and her cheek and brow so broken and disfigured that the pretty outline of the rest of the face enhanced the horror of such ruin. The dropped mouth and uninjured cheek-bone displayed an artificial pinkness that stood out upon the chalk-white flesh like a second disfigurement.

An overturned chair still lay where it had pitched, and the mantel ornaments were huddled in a strange confusion in the grate. So far the room was as he had left it, but the distraught husband, the police-man, and the girl in the black negligee had gone. Instead, in the closed and mirror-covered folding doors, the scene was hideously duplicated. Then the dead body in the mirror shifted suddenly, and Novello sprang back with a cry; but it was only the landlady reentering. She advanced, a white sheet in her hands, and with a gesture curiously gentle laid it over the face and figure of the dead woman, paused a moment, and turned to' him with renewed briskness as he said huskily:

"Where are they? Where's Druce? Where's Miss Baring?"

"In there." She jerked her head backwards.

"Together?" said the little stage manager incredulously.

"Grogram won't let anyone budge till the sergeant comes."

"Can I help in any way?" Markham asked.

"You go in to that poor fellow, Mr. Markham. He'll be glad of you. Ah, he was drunk when he came to my doorstep, but he's sober now! As I said to Grogram, why wouldn't he keep his wife at home? But we all know Mrs. Druce had a will of her own. Will of iron. They've lodged with me before now, the Gordon Druces. And Mrs. Druce didn't at all like it that I let my rooms to Miss Martella. Quite set Mrs. Druce against Miss Martella, so I heard. Ah, I've seen her get her claws into more than one young woman! They took it meek because they had to. But she wouldn't try that game twice on Miss Martella. Ah, well, poor soul"—she looked down at the decent sheet and her voice hushed—"she's paid for all."

"But she didn't do it, Miss Mitcham," said Novello. "She couldn't have done it."

"God knows, Mr. Markham! If anybody had so much as breathed to me that Miss Martella—"

The landlady was lowering her voice to a confidential tone when the entry of the policeman checked her.

"I can't have you in here, mum. You know that. You go back to the prisoner, Miss Mitcham! That's where you can help me most. She needs a woman with her. 'Ave you brought the brandy, sir? Give 'er a tot then, will you? She's all anyhow at the moment—Must get her stiffened up before we take her along. I've sent for the inspector, but it's a matter of twenty minutes." He turned to Novello. "And I'd be obliged to you, sir, being as I understand, a friend of the husband—"

He shepherded them into the other room.

As little Markham told his tearful wife a couple of hours later, it wasn't his fault if he'd left her alone. Of course it wasn't his business, and of course he knew that Doucie was alone in the house and terrified; but hang it all, what could a man do? There was poor old Druce, all broken up, you know—

"Suppose you had been knocked on the head, Doucie, how'd I feel, d'you think? I'd want a pal, wouldn't I? To stand by me, with the woman who'd done my wife in sitting two yards away from me asking what was up. Yes, she did. I tell you, when I heard that I wondered that he didn't have a shot himself at leveling things up. But he just sat there stunned. It sobered him all right, I can tell you. I tell you I didn't like it. And yet I was sorry for the girl. She looked like a corpse herself, except that she never stopped asking questions. Just like a corpse sitting up and asking questions till the Mitcham woman shut her up."

Little Markham had an imagination, even if his one ambition, which was to play Hamlet if only in stock, would never be fulfilled; even if his squeaky voice was his only stage asset, and his salary four pounds a week. As he sat over his bacon and eggs he made his wife see quite clearly the sort of hour he had passed in that back bedroom two houses away, with the square window letting in the sunshine and the rattle of early carts.

He made her start as he had started, at the swaying looking-glass door, flashing the ill sight of death in and out of their view; made her turn in fresh terror at each moving shadow of an early passerby, shapeless and ghostly behind the frosted panes. He drew for her the policeman, hovering proprietorially between the chamber of the living and the chamber of the dead; and the landlady, in her astonishing dressing-gown, trotting to and fro between the cupboard and the table and the remote kitchen, occupied with unnecessary housewiferies. But what had mainly caught the little man's imagination was the collapse of his employer, the mighty Gordon Druce, who sat, his coarse face blubbered with tears and buried in his hands, while the girl talked to him.

"Yes, she did. Shameless, it was. White as a sheet and all that black hair hanging around her, and a great streak of blood on her hand. And she kept on putting it up to her head and smearing her forehead. Doucie—and what must she do but talk to him!"

"What did she say?"

"Oh—what a tragedy it was, and how sorry she was, and how it had all been an accident, and she was sorry to be so stupid, but what had actually happened? And Druce crying and cursing her, and she not taking in a word. And into the middle of it all comes the Mitcham woman with cups of tea, and by God, we drank 'em! All but Druce. He sings out, 'Give me some brandy, for God's sake!'

"And while I was getting out the flask the Baring girl says, 'There's some in the next room, shall I get it?' Grogram says, 'You'll not budge,' and she says, 'Perhaps you'll get it, then, I know there is some; I was offering it to Mrs. Druce just before—' And then she begins to stammer and cries out, 'Oh, what did happen? My head does hurt so.' And then the Mitcham woman tells her to sit down and drink it up. And before you could say knife, there we all were, meek as lambs, drinking our tea.

"Now that's the sort of scene you can't put over on the stage. No audience would take it. There we sat till the inspector turned up in a cab, and the doctor, and carted us all off to the station and took down the boss's statement and mine. Then they let me take him home. Martella Baring? Oh, they've arrested her. Well, what else could they do? I tell you she had the poker in her hand when we broke in. Least, it was lying beside her."

Mrs. Markham was practical. "But what about the show, Nello? Will Druce carry on?"

"I don't know. I don't know what'll happen. There's a twelve o'clock call for the company. I'm putting that up on my own responsibility. Murder or no murder, we've got to settle something. It's all very well for Druce, poor devil, but the rest of us have got to live."

"I can't get the Baring girl out of my mind. I suppose she did do it?"

"Who else? They'd had a row. The girl doesn't deny it. And we all know she'd a temper."

"So'd poor Magda for that matter."

"Dare say! But that don't give Martella Baring the right to do her in. Beastly it was, Doucie! You wouldn't think a woman had the nerve—blood and all."

Doucie shivered. "Nello—d'you know what the row was about?"

He said impatiently—for the excitement of the night and the loss of sleep were beginning to tell, and he was suddenly so tired that the knowledge that he must presently proceed to the theater, and be besieged by questions and direct the quaking business of the company, was a nightmare to him—"I tell you I don't know anything. The girl was too dazed to be questioned."

"No, but I mean to begin with. Do you know what put her back up against Magda?, It was something Magda said of her."

"What did she say?"

"She said Martella Baring might live a hundred years, but she'd never be able to put over Lady Macbeth. Baring was furious when I repeated it. Magda said she hadn't the temperament."

"Temperament? Coo!" said Novello, and stretched himself on the horsehair sofa to snatch a ten minutes' nap.

CHAPTER III Theater Call

Polonius: The actors are come hither, my lord! Hamlet: Buzz, buzz!—Hamlet

Gordon Druce, manager of the repertory company, and husband of the murdered actress Magda Warwick, had never in his life exchanged one word with Sir John Saumarez of the Sheridan Theater, Shaftesbury Avenue. Nevertheless, when Sir John's parts had been sucked dry by members of Sir John's own companies, he then regularly proceeded to make them his own.

Indeed, the genial Druce modeled himself upon the actor-manager, as far, that is to say, as à stout, noisy, plum-faced man can model himself on a man slim, languid, and perfectly tailored; and Sir John's pronunciation, gestures, and, it must be confessed, innumerable affectations, were law in the little company of whose existence Sir John had never heard. This it is to be a leader in the most imitative of all professions.

So much was Sir John's personality law that when Martella Baring, last of a weary line of applicants, confessed to Gordon Druce a passion for the stage, and six months' experience: he was checked in his instant gesture of dismissal, by her further confidence that Sir John Saumarez, because he knew her people, had been exceedingly kind, had granted her an interview, and had told her to go away and play stock in the provinces for at least two years; and that then he would see what he could see.

Little enough to go upon, but Sir John had notoriously a knack of making tomorrow's stars out of tonight's penny dips; and the girl was tall, handsome, eager, had a voice, and dressed very well. Gordon Druce was quite content to accept fifty down in apprenticeship fees, to pay her a salary of three pounds a week, and entrust to her his varied villainesses; she would, of course, provide her own clothes. And Sir John spotted winners, so why not Gordon Druce?

His investment did not at the first disappoint him.

Martella Baring had a sense of the stage as well as a passion for it; she attacked a dull scene with such vigorous enjoyment of the mere boards and scenery, situation and her own clothes, that she infected her audience with her own vitality. They liked her. They would give her villainies the continuous hisses that are better than applause, and call for her noisily when the curtain fell.

Such success did not endear her to the company, but it might have been forgiven her by all but the leading lady if she could have contrived to submit her own personality to the indefinable but strict theater disciplines. But she could not forget that she was Martella Baring, adventuring in a world that was Dickens, not real life. Her home had been real life; the stage was not real; it was a curious spectacle to her, and sometimes a slightly shocking one.

She was young and primly brought up. Mistaking the liberties of communal life for license, she snubbed where she should have laughed; and though she did her best to establish relationships with her fellow players, she could not help being, in her air, her carriage, her conversation, her arrangement of her dressing-room, her care of her clothes, and her choice of amusements, a walking criticism of the company. She adored the free and easy life; but she could not adapt herself to it, and she went about saying the wrong thing at the right time, and the right thing at the wrong time, till Handell Fane marveled at her wrong-headed courage. Indeed she made enemies with an artlessness and an unconsciousness that ought to have appeased her critics, who were all her elders; but your artist in pursuit of his art and in receipt of an inadequate salary seldom develops a sense of humor.

"One—two—three! Back—forward—throw!" She would wrestle out a struggle scene in the melodrama of the moment with a plump and plaintive Magda, and fall across the table according to stage directions, only to rise again crying: "No, it's wrong. You must hold my wrist higher up, or I can't get down."

She would be perfectly right; but as Magda told her husband, she wasn't going to be "must-ed" by a beginner. So Magda continued to be charming to Martella when they met, while she made life as difficult as she could for her in the thousand ways that a manager's wife can; and the less influential members of the company followed the lead of the manager's wife. Small affronts were followed by bigger ones, and infinitely petty misunderstandings were not helped by being imparted to every member of the company in turn.

The tension grew until Martella Baring, at last discovering that the affronts and misunderstandings were not fortuitous, that every woman's hand was against her, and as passionately indignant at the catastrophe of unpopularity as any child who has scratched its shins on the wicked briery bush in its path, threw up her part one tempestuous evening and walked out of the theater.

Her departure was good riddance to Magda Druce and a matter of indifference to others, until it became clear, not only that the life had gone out of the performance of Handell Fane, the leading man, but that the general understudy was quite incapable of sustaining parts that gave her predecessor no trouble whatever. Receipts dropped, not badly, but enough to disquiet the struggling head of the concern. To bring down an actress from London cost money and the season had not a fortnight to run.

Gordon Druce indited a stately letter informing his late "heavy lead" that her breach of contract rendered her liable to a claim for damages, and received in reply a polite note referring Mr. Druce to Miss Baring's solicitors, Martella—a fighter—having searched the telephone book for the name of an overwhelming firm.

Gordon Druce, who had not the faintest intention of spending money on anything so problematical as a damages suit, told his wife it was time that her quarrels ceased to interfere with business, and that he would leave it to her to get the girl back. Magda, after employing two-thirds of the company fruitlessly as intermediaries, wrote a civil note of apology, got a civil answer, and invited Miss Baring to supper to talk the matter over.

A reconciliation ensued, and the two ladies came down to rehearsal next morning arm in arm. Halcyon weather continuing, and a new play being put into rehearsal, Martella returned hospitality by inviting the Druces to supper. Gordon Druce's previous engagement with the local hotel-keeper could not be postponed, but his wife accepted the invitation and took her script along with her that she might run through the scene with Martella when supper was over.

This little history of interfeline warfare was, of course, known in detail to the company which assembled on the morning after the murder behind the lowered curtain of the Theater Royal, Peridu. The stage was already set for the next evening's performance; and the cardboard trees, the cottage with its painted window and its roses and hollyhocks, incredibly unreal in the Rembrandt light, made a fantastic background for the dowdy little group.

The members of the company were awaiting the stage manager; but the usual tedium of waiting was unfelt. The news that their manager's wife was dead, and tragically dead, was common property; so was the knowledge that Martella Baring and Gordon Druce were involved in the tragedy. The rest was guesswork. That excellent husband and father, the tired comedian Tom Drewitt, was sure that the manager himself had attacked his wife in a drunken fit. The middle-aged ladies who divided between them the minor female parts agreed with him, contributing recollections of some forty seasons to prove the invariably disastrous effects of liquor on the artistic temperament. While the unimportant understudy tried in vain to extract opinions on the tragedy from the principal actors, the supercilious Ion Marion and the shy, dark-skinned Handell Fane.

On the arrival of Miss Doucebell Dearing, however, there was a rapid rearrangement of the group. They crowded about her; for not only was Miss Dearing the stage manager's wife, but she lodged in Regency Terrace not three doors away. Who but Doucie should be in possession of the facts?

Doucie was not niggardly with her news, though her attitude to the tragedy of the night was somewhat influenced by the fact that when she had walked home the evening before with the murderess and her victim, and had begun to say good-by to them tentatively on Martella Baring's doorstep, the expected invitation to join in the supper party had not been given. Not, as Doucie said, that she minded in the least. But Martella Baring must have known that Novello had gone off with Gordon Druce, because Martella had invited Druce, who hadn't turned up. Well then, if she, Doucie, was alone for the evening, wouldn't it have been only natural to ask her in? But Martella had not invited the lingering Doucie, and it was clear enough now why she hadn't.

"It's as if I'd had a warning," said Doucie to the company, as she told her story of the night. "I said to myself, 'Well, that won't last: Magda eating out of Martella's hand.' If ever two women didn't hit it off, it's those two—and they didn't take me in with their billing and cooing, not for one moment. I said to Nello when he came in, 'Well,' I said, 'did Gordon come along with you to fetch Magda? There'll be fur flying at Number Ten by this time, I should think.'

"'No,' said Nello, 'I left him, and time too, drinking with Fane. Fane's a bachelor man. I come home to no woman without being in a condition to defend myself.' 'Well,' I said, 'that's more than Druce can say.'

"Nello's got his faults, but lifting the elbow is not one of them. So he left Druce and came home to me. Druce was pretty tiddly by then, he said, and Magda hadn't got back. 'What!' I said, 'wasn't she back before you left? Well, they are having a heart to heart. Fancy Magda!' I said, 'I always said she was a better actress off the stage than on. I can just see her sitting there holding Baring's hand and talking about the Ladies' Theatrical Guild. 'Never mind about them,' Nello says. 'Have you got those words yet?' Well, I hadn't, so we sat down to them till getting on for two."

"Didn't you hear anything?" asked the understudy. "They say there was a frightful scene—language—half the street heard them at it."

"No," Mrs. Markham confessed reluctantly. "I can't say I did. Not till the knocking. Novello looked out of the window, and then down he went at once, knowing what Druce is. I wouldn't marry a man that drank—"

"What's going to happen?" said the comedian anxiously. "D'you know, Mrs. Markham?"

"Couldn't say, I'm sure. Nello'll know. He hasn't had a wink of sleep, what with the police and all; and this morning he's got to see the undertakers. Still, he ought to be here by now. What time was the call for? Twelve? Ah, well, it's barely one."

The company, with two exceptions, agreed that so far there was no cause for complaint. The exceptions were the dark Handell Fane, who had withdrawn from the communal chatter to range the room aimlessly and restlessly, and fresh-colored, red-haired Ion Marion, who had pulled out a time-table and was running his finger down the columns. He surprised them now by breaking in.

"I shan't wait after one. A call's a call. Here I've been kept hanging about for over an hour already."

"We're all in the same boat, laddie," said the tired comedian.

"If Novello puts up a call for twelve, the least he can do is to keep it," said Ion Marion, and Handell Fane nodded agreement.

Doucie ruffled.

"My husband knows his job, Mr. Marion, thank you! He doesn't need advice when it's a matter of stage business. Not from a youngster who's not been on the stage two years. But a murder's outside of that. D'you realize all my husband's had to do this morning, Mr. Marion, with Druce on his hands, and the undertaker and the inquest and all? And you complain of him being late for call! When he does come he'll be ready for his work; and that's more than you can say of some people! Why, the sergeant said last night he ought to have been in the force! And I can tell you this, Mr. Marion, and you, Mr. Fane! If we get our salaries and fares back to London we'll owe it to my husband. That's worth waiting three-quarters of an-hour for, I should hope."

Ion Marion shrugged his shoulders, pouted his full lip, and muttered something about not arguing with women. While Fane stepped back from the angry little creature like a lean, mournful hound retreating before a yapping lap-dog, murmuring that he had meant nothing personal, that he had wanted, if he were not needed, to go and make inquiries. He was anxious to hear—Miss Baring—

"Ah, yes, I forgot, she's a friend of yours," Doucie was not mollified. "Well, you don't need to go inquiring, because I can tell you that much. She's at the police-station still; and there she'll stay if you ask me, Mr. Fane. Bail? Not much. Telling the sergeant she didn't know what could have happened, and the poker in her very hand or just beside: and blood all over her, Nello said—Why, whatever's the matter? You look as if you'd got the limes on to you."

Handell Fane had indeed turned a very curious color. His dark skin was mottled, his lips shook. Mrs. Markham abandoned her attitude of wifely indignation, and caught his arm, pushing him toward a chair.

"Whatever is it?" she repeated.

"The thought of blood always makes me sick," Fane answered.

"You sit down," Doucie ordered. And when he was in the chair, with closed eyes, trying to master himself, she stood by him patting his shoulder in motherly fashion, and saying as she caught Ion Marion's eye:

"It's the war; that's what it is."

Marion's twisted lip was ugly. "Blood? Mud was our trouble," said Ion Marion. "Blood washes off, but mud sticks. I'm going, Miss Dearing. You can tell your husband so. He has my address. He can write me if I'm wanted. But I'm not going to be mixed up—"

A sudden clamor of voices interrupted him, and advised them of Novello's entrance. Markham made no attempt to be impressive, no attempt to adopt the grave bearing suited to his responsibilities. He was just a weary little man, too much preoccupied with reality to waste energy on attitudes. He walked in, and sat down at the prompt table; and the company surrounded him, loudly inquiring.

"What's the latest, Nello?"

"Have they arrested Baring?"

"Where's Druce? Is he going to carry on?"

"Look here, Markham, I'm off. There's a one-thirty—and I only stayed on to oblige."

Markham did not attempt to answer individually. He let the company talk itself into a lull, then tapped on the table with the pencil he had been fingering, as a conductor raps with his baton to call his orchestra to order. The company, recognizing the same, authority in the little man with the creased clothes and reddish eyes, became silent in the course of a moment or two, and waited in an inquisitive half-circle.

"I've just come from Druce," Markham began. "He's not up to much yet, but this was something we had to get settled. There'll be no show tonight, of course; it wouldn't do. Anyhow, with two leads out of it, we couldn't carry on: so I suggested, and Druce agreed with me, that we'd better close down now."

Voices interrupted him:

"What about salaries?"

"What about fares?"

"I should have thought it 'ud be an advertisement—"

Markham silenced them with his pencil.

"About salaries, you don't need to worry: that'll be all right. Druce has got enough by him to settleup—and fares to London. As to moving on somewhere else and finishing out the tour, it isn't possible. First of all, as I said, it's not worth while getting in a couple of strangers just for the fortnight, even if we could lay hands on them by tomorrow; and in the second place, we haven't got a date in any other theater. Besides, I don't see Druce doing it. He's had this shock, and I may as well say myself I shouldn't feel much like it, after what has happened—playing over the same old scenes, and Magda dead, and Miss Baring in this trouble."

"Did you see her, Nello? She's been arrested, hasn't she? What's going to happen to her?"

Again Markham let the queries go by, and refused to be turned from his course of action.

"I've got the addresses of most of the company here. I'd better go through them in case anything more comes of this business, and we have to get into communication. I'll read them through now. Anyone that wants anything changed, say so."

He read out the names with the addresses attached to them, which, as it seemed, had boxed the compass for unfashionable points: London, N. W.—London, W. C.—London, S. E.—so all the addresses ended. The list appeared to be complete and correct. Markham put his notebook away and continued:

"You'll get your money this afternoon sometime. I'll see to it. I've got the check here to take to the bank. Better have something to eat now, and all come back at three o'clock. I could do with a bite myself."

The company accepted dismissal, made its comments, and dispersed with a promptness which may have owed something to the vision his words evoked of waiting chops, haddocks, and cups of tea. Only Handell Fane lingered. Markham, tired, hungry, and disinclined for further talk, disregarded his obvious anxiety and turned toward the door, Doucie twittering at his elbow. Fane hestitated, then deliberately stepped in front of them.

"Well," said Markham, halting. "What? Three o'clock I said. Didn't you hear? There's nothing to be done before then."

"What have they done with her?" Fane asked.

"Her? Who? Miss Baring? At the station still, I suppose."

"Poor thing!" said Doucie conventionally. "Come on, Nello, you know what it'll be—everything cold."

"Is she—how is she?" Fane persisted. "Did you see her?"

"I saw her last night," said Markham, touched by his concern and its evident cause. "She was rather dazed."

"Did she say anything?" Fane asked; and went on without waiting for an answer, "Is there anything she wants done—anything I could do?"

"I don't know about that," Markham answered. "I should think myself the best thing would be to let her people know."

Almost he had decided to let them know himself. He had her address, the only one in his little book that bore the direction—London, W. Fane broke in upon his thoughts with a cry.

"My God, Markham, they don't think she's done it? They can't think she's done it! Why have they arrested her?"

"They had to," said Markham awkwardly. "There was no one else, you see. But of course the inquest'll clear her. Must have been some sort of accident, of course!"

"Of course, echoed Doucie. "Don't keep him talking any more, Mr. Fane, he's fit to drop."

Fane stood back, his head drooping, as Ion Marion, carrying his heavy suitcase, ran down the stairs from the dressing-rooms, glancing down and putting to his lips the knuckle of his forefinger that had obviously newly received an unimportant cut.

"Well, so long, Markham!" said he bruskly. "Sorry and all that, old man! Beastly business. Wish I could help. But as I can't—Good-by, Miss Dearing! So long, Fane!" And, his knuckle once more to his lips, he was out of the stage door and gone.

"Well!" said Doucie expressively, as the swing door jerked into her face.

"Why?" said Markham, as he pulled it open once more and followed her out: while Fane, from the darkness of the passage stared after them as one dazed.

"Why?" said Doucie. "Do you know," said Doucie, "that he and Magda Druce were out together for the entire day the Sunday before last? Do you know," continued Doucie, with passionate impressiveness, "that last Thursday Gordon Druce had a row with both of them because he'd found them cuddling in the property room? They said they were rehearsing, of course," said Doucie generously, "and I dare say they were. Still, he needn't go off now without so much as saying, 'Miss Dearing, here's ten and sixpence, and I'd be obliged if you'd order me some flowers,' Poor soul!" said Doucie. "She wasn't my sort, and there's no doubt she got hold of them whether they liked it or not. But I do think," concluded Doucie, "he might have got me to see about a wreath. Heartless, I call it. Don't you? I tell you," said Doucie to her husband, as they sat down to their lunch of liver and bacon washed down with stout, "I'd rather travel with Fane, lackadaisical as he is, than that young Seethe-Conquering, any day of the week. He's got a heart, and head over ears too, poor fellow! Mark me, Novello, if Martella Baring turns out to have killed Magda, Handell Fane'll do himself in soon as look at you."

She sighed. In all this Doucebell Dearing's life only one man had ever suggested that he could not support existence without her. He had made romantic threats, but she had never discovered whether or no he had intended to carry them out. She had married him.

CHAPTER IV Enter Sir John

A my troth, I look'd upon him a Wednesday, half an hour together: ha's such a confirmed countenance. I saw him run after a gilded butterfly, and when he caught it, he let it go again—Coriolanus

It was an uncomfortable, rather successful afternoon party. One or two people had sung to an accompaniment of conversation, shifting chairs, and hidden teacups. But the singers were foreigners, used to these phenomena, and not disconcerted by them. The native warblers took themselves more seriously, and at each shrill whisper, at each tinkle, their wood-notes became noticeably more wild. These foreign persons, however, merely opened their mouths, smiled agreeably and sang with passion as though for their own amusement. Listeners were not obliged to be polite during their songs or to put on different expressions—cultured expressions.

Certainly there were times, the hostess thought, when one might, without seeming unpatriotic, be grateful for foreigners. She said as much to Sir John Saumarez, who stood beside her. He enjoyed parties, having long since learned how to make the best of them by declining all refreshments himself and refusing to supply them to others.

He was enabled to do this by the mere magic of being himself. Ladies did not expect cups of tea from his hands, and would have felt cheated had he wasted thus the time which might have been spent in talking to them. Parties therefore had no terrors for him, and he attended them frequently when matinées permitted. He stood near the hostess now and lent her an air while he surveyed the go and come of the guests. A stout lady draped in pearls approached.

"Maud," said the lady, "envy me. I know a celebrity."

"Lucky you!" the hostess responded, as was civil. "Who is it?"

"Somebody none of you know," the lady continued. "Somebody much more exciting than all your stage nobodies."

Sir John looked wistful, but the hostess did not introduce him. It would have been brutal. Instead she said:

"Do tell me! How tantalizing you are, Ada!"

"The latest murderess," the lady proclaimed, triumphant.

"Oh, my dear!" said the hostess. "How marvelous of you!"

But by this time she had been five minutes in the same place;

and though she was interested she knew her duty. She nodded sideways at the lady, and said, before she moved away: "Tell Sir John about it, won't you? He'll adore it."

"Yes, I will," the lady replied comfortably. "I'm dying to confide in someone. Sir John, who are you? Never mind, don't tell me. I should forget at once. Well, as I said, I know the murderess personally. Isn't that heavenly?"

"Quite heavenly," Sir John responded. "And who is she? And how did you come to know her?"

"Haven't you read the papers?" said the lady, astounded.

"I rarely read," answered Sir John.

"Neither do I," said the lady. "It always seems such a waste of time, don't you think?"

"I do," said Sir John.

"Well," the lady continued, "I'll tell you all about it, but first I must have a cup of tea or I shall parch."

"Tea," said Sir John vaguely.

"That tan-colored stuff they hand you in cups," said the lady. "Or don't you drink, either?"

"Very seldom," Sir John replied, "and never tea."

"How right you are," said the accommodating lady. "But still, about five one gets a craving—"

Sir John glanced at the lady's figure and saw his way.

"It's fattening," said he.

"Really?" said the lady, her face falling. "Even with lemon?"

"Certainly," Sir John confirmed. "More especially with lemon."

"Oh!" said the lady, and sighed. "Then I'd better tell you about the murder at once. If I can't drink, then I must talk to take my mind off it."

"Do," said Sir John, "tell me."

"I think you're a humbug, mind you!" said the lady glancing shrewdly at him. "But a nice one."

A foreigner began to sing.

"Shall we—" began Sir John, meaning, should they cease to converse, and listen.

The lady eyed the singer. "Only an Italian," said she; "and it's that very dull song of Orpheus's about his wife. Where was I when he interrupted us?"

"Lemons," suggested Sir John. "You don't take them in tea, because they're fattening."

"I must remember that," the lady said. "How little one knows! I suppose you're really some Sir John out of Harley Street?"

"No," he answered sadly, "out of Shaftesbury Avenue."

"That one! Heavens!" The lady meditated for an instant, then asked, "Didn't I begin this conversation by something very tactless about actors?"

"Did you?" said Sir John.

"Yes," the lady nodded; and added complacently, "How altogether awful! We needn't go into it, need we?"

"Tell me about the murder," said Sir John.

"Of course. I'd almost forgotten. And it's so rarely one comes to a party provided with a topic." The lady, though she remained standing, took on an air of comfortably settling down, and continued: "Well, I actually knew the girl's people in India. And I've seen the girl herself."

"Is it she who was murdered?"

"No, no, she's the one who did it—and with a poker too. Killed this other woman in a fit of temper. She had rather a sulky expression as a child, I remember."

"And whom did she kill? And why?"

"An actress in the same company. The usual quarrel, I suppose, over some man. Men are always causing trouble. They ought to be kept on a different planet."

"An actress you said?" Sir John asked. "Should I know her?"

"The murderess? Hardly. Martella Baring was her name. Unusual, isn't it? But then her mother was odd. She collected snuff-bottles."

"Martella Baring," Sir John repeated. "I've heard it, but where?"

The singer delivered himself of a very loud top note, and all the conversations round them swelled in accordance.

"Wretch!" the lady shouted. "Don't dare say you know her too!"

The note subsided and with it the conversations.

"I thought I was the only one," the lady lamented in her ordinary tones. "Don't take her from me!"

"Martella Baring," said Sir John for the second time. His memory was playing tricks with him. A name like that—one did not forget it. There had been an interview—a dark-haired girl—how long ago was that? Almost a year, surely! It must be the same. She had brought an introduction. Absently he accepted something from a tray that was held before him and continued to search in his mind. Yes, there had been an interview; and now the face came distinctly to his mind—a dark, defiant girl, with a child's smile that he had liked. Too raw, of course, for his theater. 'What did I do with her?' puzzled Sir John. 'Did I send her on tour? Did I tell her to go into a shop? What did I say?' A curious, intelligent, downright sort of girl—and now this! Very odd.

Absently he conveyed to his mouth the something he had accepted from a tray. It had a damp familiar taste which recalled him to the world of afternoon parties. He looked about for the lady. She was still there, regarding him with a kind of humorous envy.

"What's this?" Sir John asked.

"Tea!" said the lady emphatically. "And it was the last cup on the tray; and you took it; and you know my murderess. I could poison you."

She nodded affably and moved on.

Sir John found his hostess, said good-by, and decided that he would go on to a club. He needed the stimulus of masculine conversation. But which club? At the Exotic they were all far too clever; at the Minerva they were all far too nearly dead. He decided at last on the Wilderness, and drove there smoothly through rich London by-streets.

In the smoking-room Ruthven Traill greeted him.

"Hullo, John!" said Major Traill, "what's the matter with you? You're looking like your photographs."

"Heaven forbid!" answered Sir John, as was expected of him.

"Johnnie's tired out endorsing checks," said another friend.

"Wearing them, more likely," said Ruthven Traill, with a critical eye on Sir John's sponge-bag trousers.

Sir John laughed the pleasant laugh which he kept for this kind of baiting, and ordered a glass of sherry.

"Did you notice the tape as you came through?" the friend inquired.

"No," said Sir John. "Why should I?"

"Last race," said the friend laconically, strolling to the door. "You interested, Ruthven?"

"Penny Whistle for a place," Traill replied.

"Not a hope," said the friend—and departed.

"I always find your conversations so difficult to follow," Sir John complained.

"Not as difficult as horses," said Major Traill resentfully. "I've dropped eighteen pounds this week. Well, what have you been doing with yourself? Seeing life?"

"One plods on," said Sir John, sipping.

The friend reentered the smoking-room wearing a discontented look.

"Not through yet," he reported. "Nothing but a report of this inquest somewhere down in Wales. It's simply disgusting. Here's a piece of very important news delayed in order to give the public a lot of nasty details."

"That's the ornament to your profession," Major Traill reminded Sir John. "The temperamental lady who did in her rival. I only wonder it doesn't happen more often."

"Yes, a silly thing like, that," the friend went on unappeased, "and they hang up something really important that a lot of money depends on."

"She must be a Tartar, that girl," said Major Traill. "The poker, if you please! And asked the victim to supper first! However, you'll always find women, when they take to crime, far more thorough-going than men. The odd thing is this girl doesn't seem to be quite the class one would expect."

"It won't come your way at Scotland Yard, will, it?" asked the friend.

"No, they've got it in hand locally. We'll stand by, of course. But even a country chief constable couldn't foozle a thing like this." He turned to Sir John. "They say her people are quite decent—something or other in India. This girl wanted to go on the stage—wanted to earn her own living. I dare say that wasn't the only reason. There are more ways of earning a living than one. Why do girls leave home, Johnnie? So that they won't get left."

Sir John flicked a fragment of ash from his interesting trousers, and said coldly:

"You needn't go on, Traill, I think. As it happens, I know Miss Baring."

He walked out of the smoking-room, leaving consternation behind him—and to tell the truth, a little surprised at himself. He had obeyed an impulse, but that was nothing. That frequently happened. It was the direction taken by the impulse that astonished him. He had almost made a scene—he, who never made scenes save between eight-thirty and eleven—and he had publicly adopted as an acquaintance a woman accused of, murder whom he barely knew by sight. He was upset; it was half an hour before he could forgive himself;

CHAPTER V Black, White

Here I stand; judge, my masters.—Henry IV, Part I

Martella Baring looked curiously about her at the court, wherein were assembled her accusers, her defenders, her judge, and a host of strangers. It was an ill-lighted room with dingy paneling; not nearly as impressive as a court on the stage. The judge, eminent and witty though she knew him to be, was insignificant beside the stage judges who rose to her memory: the Doge of Venice, for example. His red robe was worn badly, his wig was shabby, and his little crimson face was merely cross as he peered over his pince-nez at the rustling gallery.

Her own counsel, Sowerby Sims, was equally disappointing in appearance. He was a thin birdlike man with a small head, on which his wig, yet smaller, rode askew. He did not smile at her to give her confidence. He took no notice of her whatever, but talked with his junior and once or twice laughed heartily. The prosecuting counsel impressed her only in so much as he resembled an earnest, aging retriever; what she could see of his hair curled in just the manner of a retriever's coat, and he had the same conscientious expression. Counsel and juniors all wore their gowns with undergraduate indifference.

She considered the jury, now being sworn. They had the faces that are observed in busses, and forgotten. Their names swiftly read, their voices inaudibly hurrying over the oath, meant nothing. They were not individuals, they were the Jury; her life or death would rest, ultimately, with them. But she could not realize this, and they appeared to her, in their self-consciousness, their every-day futility, as inadequate as those jurors before whom Alice gave evidence in the trial of the Knave of Hearts.

The gallery was more interesting. She was used to galleries and did not fear this one, which, however, was more like a dress-circle as far as clothing went. Martella, vaguely frightened by the lawyers, contemptuous of the jury, looked for comfort to this restless, yet eagerly attentive audience, and unconsciously selected, as was her habit, one out of the crowd of faces to play to.

It was the face of a man that she chose—half-familiar, yet, in this dull light, strange. It had a rare quality which she recognized: the promise of mobility, the power to let emotion come through. She had seen that face before; in London—India? While she wondered, the woman in the row before him leaned across to her neighbor, and he was hidden. Martella Baring, hearing her own name spoken, turned her attention to the clerk of the court.

"Members of the jury," he was saying, "Martella Baring is indicted for and stands charged on the coroner's inquiry with the wilful murder of Magda Druce, known as Magda Warwick. To this indictment and inquisition she has pleaded not guilty, and it is your duty to inquire whether she is guilty or not."

The jurors thus addressed, stared at the clerk of the court, then at the prisoner; and at last transferred their gaze to Mr. Tanqueray, K. C., as he rose to make the opening statement for the crown.

He gave the facts; the discovery of the murder, the weapon, the presence of the prisoner in the room with the dead body, the sounds of dispute previously heard by the woman of the house. He would show that the dead woman and the accused had not for some time previous to the night of the murder been on the best of terms; he would show that the accused was the last person to see the dead woman alive. Mr. Tanqueray ceased, consulted his papers, and called his first witness.

The police-surgeon, Dr. Trench, said that he had been called early in the morning of September 28 to Number Ten, Regency Terrace. There he found a woman lying dead. The cause of death was an injury to the head, which he described. The wound had evidently been inflicted by such an instrument as the poker produced in court. He had examined the poker at the time, and from the blood on it was sure that it was the weapon with which the crime had been committed. The woman whom he saw had been dead for half an hour. He had then gone to the police-station, where he had seen the accused. She appeared to be dazed. Her breath smelled of spirits. She complained that her head ached.

Examined by Mr. Sowerby Sims, he could not say definitely whether or not the accused was under the influence of drink when he saw her. Her speech was not affected; she pronounced her words properly; but she did not talk like a person in full possession of her faculties.

Mr. Novello Markham told the court how he had heard Mr. Druce, his employer, knocking at the door of Number Ten, Regency Terrace; and how he had gone down to him. While they waited to obtain admission he heard two screams in a woman's voice. He entered the house, and was the first to enter the room on the ground-floor where the dead woman was lying.

The accused was standing near. The poker, very bloody, was at her feet. There was blood on the accused's dressing-gown and one of her hands. He spoke to her. She put her hand to her head, and did not answer. He felt the dead woman's pulse. It was not beating, but he thought there might be life in her still, and asked the woman of the lodgings, Miss Mitcham, for brandy. She said the accused had some in a flask.

The accused herself said there was brandy in the flask; but when he took up the flask from the table it was empty. He returned to his lodgings and fetched some brandy of his own. When he touched Mrs. Druce again he knew she must be dead. Later he went with the constable, Mr. Druce, and the accused to the police-station.

He had known Miss Baring only during the time she had been with the company; about seven weeks. She was always polite to him and his wife, though the others found her difficult. He knew that there had been a difference between Mrs. Druce and Miss Baring. Mrs. Druce had told him, and he had seen it for himself. He had supposed that it was over when Miss Baring returned to the company after an absence of two days.

Cross-examined by Mr. Sims, the witness said that as a rule the company gave a new play every three days. The accused generally had long parts. She had been obliged to work harder than the rest of the company, who had played together before, and knew their parts already. The accused was always word-perfect, always to be relied on. She worked extremely hard. He had never seen any signs that she was lacking in self-control—quite the contrary.

Reexamined by Mr. Tanqueray, he admitted that Miss Baring had a temper. She would stand no nonsense from anyone. She was not popular with the company in general, though she had once or twice saved a scene from disaster. He described an incident when an actor had "dried up and lost his head." Miss Baring had spoken his lines, gagged, and invented business until he was able to go on. She always showed remarkable presence of mind.

Confound Tanqueray! thought Mr. Sims; I see what he's at. My witnesses to character aren't going to do very much good. Her self-control cuts both ways. Now for Druce.

The husband of the murdered woman, the next witness called, told how he had set out at half past two on the morning of the 28th to search for his wife, who had gone with his knowledge to have supper with the accused. He described how he had knocked, how he had been joined by Markham and the policeman, and how their colloquy had been interrupted by a scream.

Gordon Druce had obviously, during the weeks since the tragedy, been drowning his cares. His plum-colored face was mottled; his eye and hand were unsteady. He was dressed in a gray suit such as Sir John Saumarez had worn two seasons ago in the last act of "Diplomatic Pudding"; his manner observed the same model. The only begetter of both suit and manner, who was seated in the gallery, found himself disliking the man with a violence for which he could not account.

All the adroitness of his counsel, all the tragedy into which he had stumbled could not make of Druce a sympathetic figure. His bitterness against Martella Baring was ugly; natural enough in the circumstances, yet so expressed as to be unforgivable. When he came to tell of the scream which had startled him as he stood in the gray street, the court enjoyed a surprise and a sensation. Mr. Tanqueray asked:

"You have heard the accused scream before in the course of one of her parts?"

"Yes, at rehearsal, two days before."

"Did she do it well?"

"Exceedingly well. I distinctly remember praising her."

"Did you recognize her voice in this other scream that you heard as you stood on the steps?"

"Yes, I did. It was the same scream."

"The accused is, in your opinion, a competent actress?"

"Surprisingly so, considering her lack of experience."

"Did you ever know her to suffer from stage-fright?"

"Never. In all the years I have been directing theatrical enterprises I have never come across—never encountered—any young actress who was so self-possessed."

"Do you think that such a girl, finding herself in this tragic situation, would be likely to lose her head to the extent of screaming?"

"Not she; that would be the very last thing she would do."

Counsel asked one or two further questions, but did not labor the point. He had gained his effect: and Druce was not a witness to be proud of. He let him go.

But the counsel for the defense was not prepared to let him off so easily.

"You have admitted on oath, Mr. Druce," said Sowerby Sims, "that you had already consumed between the hours of eleven-thirty and two-thirty the entire contents of a bottle of whisky. In what condition were your faculties after that?"

"I am glad to say that one bottle of whisky makes no difference to my faculties."

"I dare say that is so. Do you think you were in a fit condition to judge whether a sound such as a scream were genuine or not?"

"I was definitely sober."

"You say so. This sound was totally unexpected?"

"Yes. By me."

"By you? Was it expected by anyone else?"

"I hardly think it came as a surprise to the prisoner."

"Do you mean to tell me that you could distinguish, at that hour, in those circumstances, after that amount of liquor, whether an unexpected scream heard through a closed door were genuine or not?"

"I'm sure of it. I had heard the prisoner give just such a scream two days before during rehearsal."

"You would carry that sound in your mind for days?"

"Not all the time, thank God!"

"Let me have your answer, please. Was that previous sound so present to your mind that, when you heard the other, you could compare the two with accuracy?"

"A good memory is part of my profession."

"Can you swear that the sound you heard was not the result of shock?"

"You couldn't shock that woman; she's got the devil's own nerve."

"Will you swear that this scream was in Martella Baring's voice?"

"Yes. I will."

"On your oath?"

"Yes, by all means."

Counsel let him go.

Miss Mitcham was called, the landlady of 10, Regency Terrace. She said that on the night of the 27th she was asked by Miss Baring to provide a supper for three. She did so. She did not buy any spirits. Miss Baring had some brandy which she kept in a flask. Miss Mitcham had seen this flask on the dressing-table just before the ladies came home. It was half full; as far as she could judge, there was nearly a tumblerful of brandy in it.

She went to bed when she heard Miss Baring and her guest come in, and was asleep before 12:30. Later she was awakened by voices below, quarreling. She could not hear what they said, she went by the tone. She was sure that they were women's voices. She would not swear that they were the voices of Mrs. Druce and Miss Baring, but they were shrill voices. The noise suddenly stopped, and there was no sound of voices at all after that. She went to sleep again, supposing that Mrs. Druce had gone home.

Some time later, she did not know how long, she was again awakened by the sound of knocking. It was the dead woman's husband Mr. Druce. She told him to go away, and then heard a scream. She came downstairs at once and let in the policeman and Mr. Druce and the other gentleman. She did not go into the ground-floor rooms to find out what was the matter. She thought it would be better to let a man see if there was anything wrong.

She confirmed Markham's description of the room, and the disappearance of the brandy. She could not say that Miss Baring was drunk. She was not herself, but she was not drunk. She never touched spirits, and had the brandy only in case of illness. She had never known Miss Baring to take anything, except a little stout with her lunch.

Ion Marion, the next witness, was one of those Englishmen with long faces, big noses, and full lips, who for all their fairness recall the portraits of the later Medici, and sometimes recall them in their careers. Fierce, intelligent, money-making, art-loving rather than artists, they are found in all professions, and never on the losing side.

He was questioned with regard to the professional jealousy which had existed between the dead woman and the accused. Mrs. Druce had said to him once, in the presence of Fane, that she was positively afraid of Martella Baring. He had understood her to mean, by this, that Miss Baring played the villainess on the stage with rather too much intensity. Mrs. Druce had complained several times that Miss Baring put too much energy into her acting; she had once shown him a bruise on her shoulder where she had fallen against a table in the course of a stage struggle.

He had not attached any importance to what Mrs. Druce said. Everybody in the company was aware that the two women disliked each other. Miss Baring never lost her nerve on the stage; on the other hand she was sometimes rather alarming. Did he mean violent? Well, her playing was sometimes exaggerated. Not violent? Yes, as far as acting went. Personally he preferred finesse to barnstorming.

Mr. Sowerby Sims, perceiving that the personality of this witness was not sympathetic to the jury, answered the cue.

"On what terms were you yourself with Mrs. Druce?"

"The best of terms."

"Just what do you mean by that?"

"Mrs. Druce and I were very good friends. She was extremely nice to me always."

"Were you on familiar terms with her?"

"Just what do you mean by that?"

"Intimate terms?"

"What's that got to do with all this? No, I was not."

"On sufficiently good terms for her to show you a bruise on her shoulder?"

"It was during a wait. She was in evening dress."

"I suggest that you were on intimate terms with Mrs. Druce."

"Your suggestion is a lie, and you are a liar."

The judge intervened. Mr. Sims asked another question or two, and sat down, thinking: Is there a line there? No, no. Stick to the main track. If we don't get them on that, we won't get them on other people's immoralities. Here's a sick man Poor devil!

It was Handell Fane to whom his thought referred. Fane did indeed look ill as he stood in the witness-box, though illness could not lessen his theatrical good looks. He was tall, olive-skinned, black-haired, with deep eyes under a good brow; a straight nose with flaring nostrils, flushed cheek-bones, and a full, well-cut mouth. He stared constantly, miserably, at Martella Baring. She smiled at him, a maternal smile; he answered it, wryly. So that's it, thought Sowerby Sims, watching; he's in hell. He'd give his ears to be standing there instead of her. Poor devil!

Mr. Fane confirmed Ion Marion's account of the two women's mutual dislike. He could not understand it. Miss Baring had been kindness itself to him, and to other members of the company. She had helped him in every possible way; if he ever got his nerve back it would be due to her. Counsel interrupted with a question about the dead woman's fear of the accused. Yes, he had heard Mrs. Druce say that she was afraid. He was with her and Marion at the time. It meant nothing; or if it meant anything at all, it was that Miss Baring was an infinitely better actress than anyone else in the company, and Mrs. Druce knew it.

Mr. Tanqueray did not keep Mr. Fane long. Neither did Mr. Sims. He was too enthusiastic—not a good witness. And he was so obviously in love with Martella Baring that anything he might say in her favor was useless. He was told to stand down; and his evidence concluded the case for the prosecution.

The case for the defense began. Mr. Sims knew very well that both jury and gallery were wondering what he was going to give them. His client had pleaded not guilty; but how Mr. Sims proposed to make that out neither gallery nor jury could guess. He had not tackled the evidence for the prosecution at all. He had allowed the most damning facts to be established without making anything more than the mere show of a fight. But he had a reputation. In the hope that he would sustain it, and show them sport yet, the gallery craned, the court was attentive when he called his first witness, a small, elderly, quiet-voiced, and exceedingly sane doctor—James String fellow, of Cavendish Square, described as a specialist in nervous diseases.

Counsel for the defense began smoothly enough.

"You have in the course of your profession encountered many disorders that have their roots below the surface of the mind?"

Doctor Stringfellow: "That is so."

"Among these disorders there is a mental process, is there not, known as dissociation?"

"Yes."

"Will you explain it to the jury as simply as you can?"

"I may put it in this way. We will suppose that an individual suffers an unpleasant experience. He tries to put it out of his mind, and calls in his subconscious mind to help him. He may succeed in keeping his experience out of his conscious thoughts, but it is not for that less active. This independent activity of the suppressed experience is generally termed dissociation."

"This activity may take many forms?"

"It is protean."

"Will you put that rather less allusively?"

"Yes. It may take many forms."

"Is one of these forms known as fugue?"

"That is so."

"Will you explain to the jury just what is meant by that term?"

"I can give you an example which has come within my own experience. A young man who had been sitting quietly reading suddenly found himself in an unfamiliar part of London—Greenwich, in fact—a place where he had not to his knowledge been before. When he sat down at his desk he had one shilling and some pence in his pocket. These coins were gone, with the exceptions of a halfpenny; presumably part had been spent on paying his fare. He was obliged to walk back hatless to his lodgings, a distance of some six or seven miles. From the moment he last remembers, when he sat down to read, and the moment when he came to himself in Greenwich, three hours had elapsed of which he had no recollection whatever. This is a very complete example of the state of dissociation to which the term is applied."

"So that while in this state a person may display behavior of a most complicated kind, lasting over considerable periods of time, of which in the normal state he is quite unaware?"

"That is so."

"On the return to the normal state, is there no memory of the actions which have been performed during the fugue?"

"None whatever. The experience of each phase is inaccessible to the other under ordinary conditions."

"This activity of the suppressed experience may occur in persons who appear otherwise normal?"

"That is so,"

"Is it possible that persons in such a state should perform actions which in their normal state would be intolerable to them?"

"Quite possible."

"For example, such a person might even perform an act of violence?"

"I should say that it was possible. I have not known of a case where it has occurred. However, it is possible."

"Supposing such an act to have been performed, no memory of it would remain when the person returned to consciousness?"

"None whatever. But the expression 'returned to consciousness' is hardly correct. The subject of a fugue cannot be said to be unconscious. A somnambulist is unconscious."

"Will you tell us the difference between somnambulism and fugue?"

"There is a close resemblance between the two; in fact there is no difference, except that one occurs in the sleeping state and the other in the waking. But the two terms must not be confused; they are not synonymous."

"Should you expect a person who had walked in sleep as a child to be subject later on to fugues?"

"Not necessarily, though in both cases the dissociation might be caused by the same repressed experience taking another form."

"You have heard the Peridu doctor's evidence on the state in which Miss Baring was found after the tragedy. You have heard police and other evidence as to her behavior. Is this consonant, as far as you can tell, with the behavior of a person emerging from a state of fugue?"

"It is possible; but I can give no definite opinion in such a case. I did not see her while she was in this alleged state. I cannot give an opinion based on hearsay."

"What I am asking is whether the account of her behavior agrees with that which might be expected of a person emerging from fugue?"

"As far as one can tell from the evidence, yes."

"The change from alternate consciousness to full consciousness comes suddenly?"

"Instantaneously in most cases."

"There would be a certain shock? A difficulty of adjusting the personality to unexpected surroundings?"

"Bewilderment, yes."

"Such bewilderment as Dr. Trench and Mr. Markham have said that they observed in Miss Baring?"

"It would be natural in a person emerging from a fugue."

"What would be the effect of alcohol if taken by a person in this state?"

"Very difficult to say. I have not had occasion to observe its effects on a person suffering from fugue."

"Supposing a person to be easily affected in the normal state, would you expect the same reaction to alcohol in the abnormal state?"

"It is probable that the reaction would be similar."

"Will you tell us the conditions which, in your opinion, contribute to bring about the state of dissociation?"

"I should say, roughly, previous mental strain; any excitement or pressing anxiety."

"Then mental strain of learning a great number of words by heart in a very short time? Would that be sufficient?"

"I should say so, in certain cases."

"Mental strain: the consumption of an unaccustomed amount of potent spirit, followed by excitement—a quarrel; would these combine to bring about such a state?"

"The previous mental strain alone might do so. The alcohol would cause physical excitement and loss of control. Fugue, however, as I said, is the result of a mental disturbance."

"Alcohol might be responsible for certain of the actions performed during the fugue?"

"We may assume, I think, that if a person in a normal state is liable to be excited by alcohol, that person will be excited in the same way when in an abnormal state. The difference lies in this—that while in the normal state the person would to some extent be aware of his own actions, in the abnormal state he would not be aware of them."

"And therefore not responsible for them?"

"I should say not."

Now, thought Mr. Sims, see what Tanqueray will make of that. He's a good witness, and it's an original defense. Water-tight, too. But I wish I knew if it were the truth.

Mr. Tanqueray threw his learned friend a glance of appreciation, and tucked back his gown with a gesture which warned the court that he was on his mettle. He began with some truculence, in what was known to the irreverent as his earlier manner.

"You say that a person entering into a state of fugue displays no outward symptom by which his state may be diagnosed?"

"No."

"Nor on his emergence from it?"

"No."

"You have in fact nothing but the sufferer's bare word for it that he has entered that state at all?"

"My profession and yours, sir, have a different outlook. We do not regard all men as potential liars."

The judge: "Do not make observations. Confine yourself to answering counsel's questions."

Counsel: "The behavior of the sufferer during this condition is outwardly normal. He alone is aware of the fact that he has regained full knowledge of himself. No outward sign marks the change. Would it not be very easy for a guilty person to take advantage of these facts?"

"You mean, to simulate such a condition? Yes, if he were aware that such a condition existed, which is not likely."

"Yet you say the state of fugue is common?"

"Not common; but well-known to members of my profession. I do not think that it is familiar to the laity."

"Is there any difference observable between a person in a state of drunkenness, and a person in a state of fugue?"

"Certainly; a great difference. Drunkenness displays physical symptoms; fugue does not."

"A person frequently emerges from the state of drunkenness

with a headache?"

"I believe so."

"Does a person wake with an aching head from fugue?"

"Not to my knowledge."

"There are many books published, are there not, dealing with psychological problems?"

"Yes; in my opinion, far too many."

"Is the state known as fugue described in these books?"

"In some of them."

"You would expect the library of a medical man to contain one or more of such books?"

"It would depend if he were interested in the subject."

"It would not be unusual, though, to find such books in the library of a medical man, no matter if he had specialized in that subject or not?"

"No, I suppose not."

"Such books would be intelligible to the laity?"

"I cannot answer that. It would depend on the book and on the reader."

The witness was allowed to leave the box.

If they can prove she read one of these confounded books, Mr. Sims thought, it will all go for nothing. But I don't see how they can. Thank God, continued Mr. Sims, with a fervor which would have surprised its object, for Lady Plumptre!

She was the next witness called, and she belonged to a familiar type, the thin, parrot-nosed soldier's wife, herself a dragoon; the truth-telling, snobbish, just, and unimaginative Englishwoman. Yes, her husband had been in the Indian Medical Service. Yes, she had known Martella from a child; had been at school with her mother, who died when Martella was born; had seen the child almost daily in India. When the child was sent home, had seen her when she and her husband were on leave. She had no children of her own. After the death of Martella's father, had suggested that the girl should come out to India to live with them when she left school.

Miss Baring contributed, of course, to the household expense. She had a small income of her own. This arrangement continued until Martella was twenty. Then she had wished to earn her own living; and she, Lady Plumptre, had put no obstacle in her way. She had not seen Martella recently; she had come home when her husband died, last year, and had since been living in St. Jean de Luz where living was cheaper; had joined some Anglo-Indian friends there—quite a little colony.

Counsel for the defense: "I suppose, Lady Plumptre, you know Miss Baring better than anyone else could? You have stood in the place of a mother to her?"

Lady Plumptre: "I have done my best, certainly."

"You have the knowledge of her that can only be attained by daily intercourse? What is your estimate of her character?"

"It is ridiculous to accuse her of a crime like this. Her father was a most distinguished man."

"Never mind about her father. Would you say that she was by nature kind, generous, and well-balanced?"

"I think that is true. A little wilful at times."

"But you would not describe her as uncontrolled in any way?"

"No, certainly not."

"Not violent in any way?"

"No."

"Not cruel?"

"No, she detested cruelty. The only time I saw her lose her temper was over a horse that had been ill-treated."

"From your personal knowledge of her, do you think it probable that she would ever strike another woman?"

"Certainly not. She knows how to behave herself."

"You can conceive of no provocation that would possibly shake her control to that extent?"

"No, quite absurd. She has been most carefully brought up in my house."

"Her self-control is unusual?"

"Yes, for a modern girl."

"Thank you, Lady Plumptre."

The prosecuting counsel was on his feet; there was a scent here which might be stale or might lead to a hunt. It was worth trying. He refrained from his usual tempestuous methods with this witness, who gave the impression that she could have dealt with such methods very adequately. Almost, he was bland.

Said Mr. Tanqueray:

"Will you tell us the reason why Miss Baring left the shelter of your roof after enjoying it for three years?"

"She wished to earn her own living; I raised no objection."

"What led to this resolution of hers?"

"Oh, stage-struck! She played once or twice in amateur theatricals at Simla. It turned her head."

"Had she no talent, in your opinion, then?"

"It wouldn't have made any difference, what I thought. Girls nowadays are totally unmanageable; they take no notice of what older people say who have a perfect right to criticize."

"Did you criticize this plan to earn her own living?"

"Her idea of the stage, most certainly. I thought it quite unsuitable. Her father would have been appalled at the thought of his daughter showing herself off in public, and so was I."

"Although you allowed her to take part in amateur theatricals?"

"Oh, but that was quite different!"

"Why was it different?"

"The viceroy was patron. Everybody used to act."

"Whether they could or not?"

"Oh, certainly!"

"You made your disapproval clear?"

"Quite clear."

"Was there any quarrel between you?"

"I don't think I understand what you mean."

"Heated words? Raised voices?"

"I am not in the habit of behaving like a fishwife; neither, to do her justice, is Martella."

"Very well. Now, Lady Plumptre, will you tell us a little more about this incident of the horse? You said that a horse was ill-treated and Miss Baring intervened. Will you be good enough to tell us just what occurred?"

"It was some years ago, in Simla. There was a cart with a very big load of grain whose horse didn't seem to be pulling well. Martella said, 'I believe there's something wrong with that horse.' I said, 'It's none of your business, my child. We shall be late for lunch as it is.' However she would not listen to me. She went up to the horse and lifted its collar: and there was a large sore. Then the argument began."

"What was the nature of this argument?"

"Well, it was extremely heated. She said the man was not fit to be in charge of any animal. He answered most insolently, and a crowd had begun to collect. I pulled the girl away by main force. It was unpardonable to make such a scene. I told her so afterwards."

"Can you remember no further details of the argument?"

"It was some years ago. Besides, it was all quite unimportant."

"You have been circumstantial enough hitherto. You have told us, for example, that the cart was laden with grain. Do you say that you can recall no further details of this scene?"

"It made no impression on me."

"Yet you have just informed the jury that this was the only occasion on which you saw this very self-controlled girl lose her temper. Do you ask the jury to believe that you have no recollection of any further details?"

"I don't know why you are insisting. As I said, the whole incident was quite unimportant."

"I put it to you, Lady Plumptre, that you are unwilling to give a full account of this scene because such an account would be damaging to Miss Baring?"

"Nothing of the sort. I don't wish to hinder the law in any way. If you ask me civilly I will answer."

The judge interrupted, leaning forward: "Attend to me, if you please. You are here in the position of witness, to answer questions, not to judge of the manner in which they are put. And you are not to decide for yourself whether facts are material or not."

"I'm sorry, my lord, but really—"

"Do not apologize to me. Answer counsel's question."

Mr. Tanqueray, vindicated, resumed his inquiries.

"If I mind my manners, Lady Plumptre, I shall expect you to improve your recollection. In the course of this scene with the driver of the cart, did Miss Baring become violent?"

"She was very angry. She used one or two rather strong expressions. Nothing very much, perhaps, as language goes nowadays. If only she'd stopped at that—"

"Did she have recourse to action?"

"She snatched his whip and cut at him with it I don't know whether she touched him or not."

"Now we have it. This incident, you say, occurred in India?"

"In Simla, yes."

"That is a wild spot, I understand. Are there no policemen in Simla?"

"Of course; natives. There was a native policeman quite close to me when this happened."

"Would not the most usual course have been to call in the policeman and let him settle the matter?"

"Exactly what I said to her at the time."

"But she was too much excited, I supppose?"

"Ridiculously so. The natives always do ill-treat their horses."

"Was she quite unlike herself?"

"She was always exceedingly obstinate."

"I am speaking now of the outburst itself. Did' it reveal to you a capacity for anger which you had not expected?"

"Naturally I was surprised."

"You had not before witnessed such lack of self-control in her?"

"Not to the same extent."

"Does not the recollection of this episode, now that you recall it more clearly, tend to alter somewhat the view which you expressed at the beginning of your examination, that the accused would be incapable in any circumstances of committing a crime of violence?"

"Certainly not, brought up as she has been."

"What has happened once, however, may happen again?"

"I should think it most unlikely."

Mr. Tanqueray held up a hand as she prepared to step down from the box. "One moment, please. Another question or two. Your husband, you said, was a doctor?"

"Yes. In the Indian Medical Service."

"Did he have a medical library?"

"Of course. Quantities of books. They were a perfect nuisance every time we moved."

"Do you recollect the titles of any of them? The subjects of which they treated?"

"It's not the least use asking me about books. I could not tell you the name of one. Martella was always reading, but I thought my husband spent far too much money on them, and they hardly fetched anything when I sold them after his death. So it's no use asking about books, for I can't tell you anything!"

Thank God, thought Mr. Sowerby Sims again, for Lady Plumptre! That almost makes up for the horse; but not quite. Not quite. Well, there's a night before us. Wearily he rose as the judge left the court. That day's sitting was ended.

CHAPTER VI White, Black

—For I will ease my heart
Albeit I make a hazard of my head.—King Henry IV, Part I

With confidence Mr. Sims called his next witness, Teresa Anne Walmsley. She would not let him down, he thought. If, like Lady Plumptre, she knew any incidental follies of the girl's youth, she would have the sense not to tell. He smiled on Teresa Anne Walmsley, known in religion as Mother Saint Hubert, as she entered the box, and would have been proud of her as a witness, but for the fact that she was a Roman Catholic—a fact which the jury, seeing her in that get-up, could hardly miss. Indeed, her white habit with the black veil, a dress ample yet severe, had a dignity that belonged, like the judge's robe and his own gown, to a more spacious and picturesque age.

The incident of which she had to tell had occurred when Martella was fifteen. She had been preparing for confirmation, "with her usual earnestness," said Mother Saint Hubert, smiling across at her. On the night before the ceremony she, with the four other girls who were to be confirmed, had been sent to bed a little earlier than usual. Mother Saint Hubert, who was not the superior at the time, had been directed to call them in the morning, and to help with their dressing. The white dress, veil, and wreath were laid at the foot of each child's bed. When she came into their dormitory next morning at seven, four were already awake; only Martella lay still in a heavy sleep. She was fully dressed; her hair had been carefully brushed, and she wore her veil and wreath. Mother Saint Hubert, in her first surprise, had scolded Martella; but the girl's astonishment and alarm were so evident that she had realized the truth.

"And that was, in your opinion?"

"The child had been excited for days; she was on the eve of a great event. I came to the conclusion that she had dressed in her sleep."

"As the result of the previous nervous strain?"

"Yes. I have known something of the kind happen before with girls who are sensitive and imaginative."

"Had she any recollection of having dressed herself?"

"None at all. She was very much distressed and frightened."

"How long did this condition of distress and alarm last?"

"Not long. She was always a very brave child. When I explained to her what I thought had happened, she grew calm at once. She begged that her confirmation should not be put off on account of this."

"And it was not?"

"No. We thought it better to let the excitement have an outlet; take its natural course. She slept normally that night, and did not walk in her sleep again while she was with us."

Mr. Tanqueray, at the end of his learned friend's examination, rose to question the witness. His tone was not civil. "You have lived in a convent, how long?"

"I have been professed for twenty-three years."

"Make that clear to the jury. How long have you lived in a convent?"

"Nearly all my life. I was educated in a convent school, and became a postulant at twenty."

"Do you think that after spending nearly all your life in a convent, shut away from the world, you are capable of judging whether actions are normal or not?"

"I can answer only that wisdom comes by opportunity of leisure."

"That is an epigram?"

"It is a quotation from the book of Ecclesiasticus."

She stepped down, victorious, and Mr. Sowerby Sims rose to call his next witness. The gallery rustled and whispered; pencils traveled fast at the reporter's table; and there was a little stir in court, as in a theater when the lights go down and the curtain is to rise on some legendary player. Mr. Sims' next witness was the prisoner at the bar.

She crossed to the witness-box, self-possessed, but with eyes a little puzzled, that opened wide to take in the court from this new angle. A watcher in the gallery admired her every pose. Breeding! thought this watcher. It tells; guilty or innocent, it tells. And as he caught her look for an instant, he gave her a little nod, that was to mean admiration and a salute for her courage. She saw it, perhaps; but already Mr. Sims was at his questions.

"Now, Miss Baring, where were you on the night of September 27?"

"What time of the night?"

"From seven, let us say, until ten."

"At the theater. I told you I had arranged to play the part."

"What was your motive in returning to Mr. Druce's company?"

"Oh, well, when they came and asked me civilly I gave in. Lord knows, I didn't want to put them in a hole. As I said to Mr. Druce, 'You be decent to me and I'll be decent to you.' I didn't want to quarrel."

"You were once more, therefore, on friendly terms with him?"

"Oh, yes!"

"And with his wife?"

"She was charming to me. It was a great relief. I hate all this business of cutting and not knowing people in the same company. It's so childish."

"You had no further cause for complaint against Mrs. Druce beyond what the witnesses have told us?"

"No, she went out of her way to be nice. I really think she did mean it."

"So it had been merely a professional difference between you?"

"Well, we never did get on. Still we had no personal quarrel—not of my making."

"These professional squabbles do not amount to anything very much?"

"They seem to be inevitable. I've never been in a company where there wasn't something of the kind."

"Well, this professional difference had come to an end. What was your next move?"

"I didn't do anything. We just carried on."

"Did you take no steps to cement the reconciliation?"

"Oh, you mean asking them to supper? I'm so sorry. I didn't see what you were driving at. Yes, of course I asked them to supper. I thought it was only polite."

"You asked Mr. Druce as well as his wife?"

"Of course. Not that I thought he'd come."

"Did he say he would come?"

"Oh yes, he said he'd come. But you know what managers are. They'll say anything to keep from being badgered."

"And did he, in effect, come?"

"No, I told you he didn't. That's the whole point."

"How did you prepare for this supper?"

"Oh, Miss Mitcham saw to it. I gave her ten shillings and told her to get as much of a spread as she could."

"Did she buy any spirits?"

"No, I forgot to tell her to."

"Did you have any spirits in your possession?"

"Yes. I was coming to that. You see, I knew that if Mr. Druce came they'd be wanted."

"You don't take spirits yourself?"

"No, I can't stand the taste. Stout, now—"

"Did you have stout that evening?"

"Oh no, never at night. It's indigestible."

"A moment ago, Miss Baring, I asked you a question which you, no doubt inadvertently, omitted to answer. Were there any spirits in your possession on this particular night?"

"Oh, I'm sorry, I thought I said so. I had some brandy in a flask. I got it out first thing. I thought Mrs. Druce would like some."

"Why, since you never take it, was this brandy in your possession?"

"Well, other people like it, you know. And then, in case of illness—"

"Did you offer it to Mrs. Druce?"

"Yes; but she wouldn't have it. She said later, perhaps, when we'd gone through our bits."

"Bits?"

"We were running over some of our words together. We'd arranged to. That was half why I'd asked her to supper."

"The words of a new part?"

"Yes, for the next play. We did a new play every three days."

"Was this part a long one?"

"About the longest I've ever tackled."

"As long, for example, as Lady Macbeth?"

"Oh, much longer—and tricky, you know. Lots of little short answers. It's almost impossible to learn it on cues. You must have the other person."

"How long were you given to learn this long and tricky part?"

"The usual three days."

"Have you a good memory for words?"

"You have to have a good memory to play stock. But of course, it does mean sticking at it night and day."

"How do you set about learning your parts as a rule?"

"Well, I have to have a night to sleep over it. If I once say the whole part over before I go to sleep, I'm sure to know it in the morning. It's as if your mind went on working. I'd rather work for two hours at night than twelve hours by day and play in the evening."

"You had been working at this part all that day?"

"I'd been working at some part or other all day ever since I'd joined the company."

"In addition to playing at night?"

"Of course."

"You were accustomed to go over your parts when you returned from the theater at night?"

"Until four in the morning sometimes."

"Very well. Now to return to the evening when you asked Mrs. Druce to supper—you had been to the theater as usual?"

"Yes."

"Did you come home immediately after the play?"

"No, we had a run through. We often did. A scratch rehearsal."

"At what time did this end?"

"Oh, a little after eleven. I couldn't be sure to the minute."

"And after that you went home?"

"Yes."

"And Mrs. Druce accompanied you?"

"Mrs. Druce and Miss Dearing. As a matter of fact I wanted to ask Miss Dearing in too; only I knew her husband would be meeting her at home, and I hadn't enough for four."

"Did you have supper at once on arriving at your lodgings?"

"Yes. We took off our things, of course."

"And when supper was over what did you do?"

"Well, we began to go over our words together. We had one or two scenes together in the play."

"Was it necessary for any of these scenes to raise your voices?"

"Yes; the usual heroine and villainess scenes, you know."

"How long did you work at your parts together?"

"I really couldn't tell you. I never look at the clock. I only know I was frightfully sleepy and hoped Mrs. Druce would go. Instead of that she put down her script and settled down to discuss everybody's character in the company."

"Were you prepared to listen to her views?"

"Well, I don't know—of course she could be awfully funny. I don't want to say anything about her now she's dead. But she made people seem mean."

"Now will you tell us in your own words what happened after

you had ceased to work at your parts?"

"Well, I brewed some cocoa and offered it to her. As matter of fact I offered her the brandy again. But she wouldn't have it. Then she went on talking about the company—just saying little things—rather catty about most of them—nothing important—just how they looked, how they acted—you know the sort of thing. I'm afraid I was rather stiff, because I knew she'd repeat what she'd said next day and say I'd said it. She always did that, though honestly I don't think she realized.

"Then she began to discuss certain people. And I said I didn't care to discuss them and got up. And she got up too and leaned against the mantelpiece, and said something rather sneering about my acting and my prospects. And I flared. I told her that on the whole my prospects were not too bad, and I gave her my reasons. She said that if I knew what she knew, I wouldn't be so sure of help from that quarter—the quarter I did expect it from.

"I said that anyway it was no affair of hers. She said that she'd show me if it was her affair or not; and I said that I wasn't going to stand interference or insolence. Then she gave me the strangest look—as if she were half frightened and half angry—and she said, 'You how dare you?' And I don't remember any more. I just don't remember."

The cross-examination could get no more out of her than this. She was childish, flippant, dignified occasionally when it was least expected of her; and quite frequently rude. There was a breeze when Mr. Tanqueray asked for details of her last dispute with Magda Druce. Did it concern a person?

"I won't tell you. It's nothing to do with the case."

"The cause of your quarrel with the dead woman has nothing to do with the case?"

"I told you, I didn't quarrel with her."

"The cause of your 'flare-up'?"

"No. It hasn't anything to do with all this."

"You did not quarrel?"

"I've told you till I'm tired—no."

"But you were not on as good terms at two o'clock as you had been at twelve?"

"No, I suppose not. But it takes two to make a quarrel, and I simply wouldn't."

"You refused to discuss the matter?"

"Yes, I did."

"Why did you refuse to discuss it?"

"You're trying to ask me the same question round another corner. I won't tell you. It's no use going on."

The judge intervened.

"I must warn you, prisoner at the bar, that this obstinacy may very gravely affect the jury's view of your case. You come voluntarily into the witness-box to give the court all the help you can, by answering the questions which counsel has a right to put to you. If you refuse to speak, your action in coming into the witness-box ceases to have any value."

Martella Baring answered, with the politeness of a niece to a trying uncle:

"Thank you, my lord. But you must see that I can't answer some of his questions. Will it do if I give you my word of honor?"

"If you do not choose to answer, I cannot make you. I have warned you. Go on, Mr. Tanqueray."

On went the duel—thrust, parry, and riposte—thrust, retreat. Mr. Sowerby Sims meditated, tying and retying knots in a piece of pink tape. Rice had been wrong, he thought, to insist on putting her in the box. If they'd kept the girl out of it there was a bare chance on the doctor's evidence, and the nun's. But Rice had counted on her appearance and manner to help. Manner! She was wrecking her chances with every gesture, every lift of her fine head, and with every too ready answer. Mr. Sims did not see much hope when, at the end of the cross-examination, he rose to make his final speech for the defense. There was only one line for him to take. He put details aside and concentrated on that.

The jury could see for themselves, he told them, what manner of woman the accused was—a gently bred, self-controlled, courageous woman, who, after a childhood spent in luxury, had gone into the world to make her own living. She chose her profession, earned a footing in it, worked hard and was kind.

She had a sense of balance: she saw the little jealousies and quarrels in their true light, laughed at them and let them go by. She protested when protest was called for, but not until she had good grounds for complaint. In a trying situation she had behaved with dignity; and finally, when she found that her withdrawal from the company would leave it in difficulties, she had yielded with a good grace.

This woman, the jury was asked by the prosecution to believe, was guilty of the most dreadful crime known to the law, the only crime to which was still attached the penalty of capital punishment. This well-balanced, educated woman, with discipline bred in her, a soldier's daughter, this woman, said the prosecution, had with a sinister motive, asked to supper the wife of her employer; had got drunk; and in the course of a drunken dispute had brutally murdered her guest with a poker.

He invited the jury to consider how that squared with the known character of the accused, with the frankness and courage which they had had the opportunity of observing for themselves while she was giving her evidence. How, counsel asked them, as reasoning men and women, could they reconcile these two opposing aspects of a single personality?

Well, it could be done—but not as his learned friend suggested. It could be done if they were to accept the evidence of two witnesses whose integrity no one could doubt—Dr. Stringfellow and the superior of the convent which had harbored Martella Baring as a child. They had the doctor's word for it that severe mental strain may bring about in certain persons a condition in which the patient is neither conscious of his actions nor responsible for them.

They had heard the accused's account of the work which her parts involved; an account corroborated by Mr. Markham. Here was the mental strain, constant and extending over six weeks; enough to send off its balance a mind so delicately balanced as to be liable to fugue. There were persons so liable, and he thought, from the evidence, that it could not be denied that the accused was one of these persons.

Through some hidden flaw in the mind, whose cause was unknown even to herself, she became deprived of consciousness and readily entered this state wherein the body still functioned but was no longer subject to the control of the will. The directing intelligence, for a time deposed, might return to its throne only to find desolation for which it could not account, by which it was puzzled, and of which it might be bitterly ashamed.

Mr. Sowerby Sims did his best; but he did not argue; he did not dare to argue. And when in a fine frenzy he brought his speech to a close and sat down again to tap with his fingers on the table before him, he knew that Tanqueray would make no more than two mouthfuls of his case.

His foreboding was justified, although the closing speech for the crown was not long. Apparently, said Mr. Tanqueray, it was not denied by the defense that the accused did actually kill Mrs. Druce; only responsibility was denied. This murder was committed, say the defense, in a state of unconsciousness known as fugue, to which the accused is liable. They bring a doctor's evidence to the effect that such a condition is known to the medical profession; they bring the evidence of a lady who describes one hysterical incident of the accused's childhood, a case of somnambulism; but now, note this—their own witness has said that somnambulism and fugue are not identical; and a person subject to the one is not necessarily subject to the other.

He would pass on the evidence of Lady Plumptre, another witness for the defense. Her evidence, owing to an unfortunate slip, had an effect which the defense could not have anticipated. It did in fact exactly cancel out the evidence of the two other witnesses; for it was not asserted that the assault which Lady Plumptre described was committed in a state of fugue; the defense did not dare to assert that. No, this was a lapse of control if the jury liked; but not a lapse of consciousness.

The accused, during her attack on the driver of the cart, was perfectly aware of her actions. She showed then that she was capable of violence, of violence which shocked the lady who had known her all her life. He asked them as reasoning men and women—and it passed his understanding how his friend who had so described them could then have offered them such an astonishing interpretation of the facts—as reasoning men and women, could they say that this other fatal outburst of violence had not for cause a similar loss of control? Could they say that they believed in this very convenient loss of consciousness? Could they reject the possibility of a conscious act of violence, only because the accused was an educated, kindly, and normally self-controlled woman?

Deliberately, without passion, Mr. Tanqueray put aside the picture that the defense had drawn of a woman tossed helplessly in some storm of the mind, and set another in its place. There had been a dispute. The accused refused to reveal its nature or its cause in detail. The accused was found in the room where the body lay, with the blood-stained poker by her side; the flask of brandy, containing, according to Miss Mitcham, the best part of a tumblerful of spirit, was empty.

Mrs. Druce did not take it; for that they had the accused's own statement, if they chose to believe it. And the accused greeted the police surgeon, an hour afterwards, with the complaint that her head ached; her breath smelled of spirits. Doctor Stringfellow said that drunkenness will cause headache; they might take his distinguished word for it. He said also that a person emerging from fugue showed no such symptoms; they might take his distinguished word for that, too.

In considering the subsequent conduct of the accused, they were to remember that she was an actress, and a very accomplished one; that she was cool in stage emergencies; and that in this tragic emergency it was not applause that was in question, but her very life. He would pay the jury the compliment of assuming that they could dispense with rhetoric from him. He had given them the facts as they had been established in court. It was for' my lord to review these facts, and for them to judge.

CHAPTER VII Trial by Jury

They'll fill a pit as well as better; tush, man, mortal men, mortal men.—King Henry IV, Part I

Colonel Plendary, the mild competent foreman, surveyed his charges.

"Well, ladies and gentlemen," said the foreman, "we've been told to consider our verdict, and I think we can best do it sitting down. Ladies, will you sit together? As you please."

There was a shifting of chairs, a shuffling of papers. Pencils were sharpened, and everyone assumed an expression of concentration, while inwardly wondering just what was to happen next. How did twelve people, fortuitously assembled, ever arrive at any conclusion? They looked, not in vain, to the foreman for aid.

"With your permission, ladies and gentlemen," he began, "I propose that we should not waste time going over all the arguments we've heard during the past two days. I take it we've all listened, and we've all made notes. It's not the arguments or the evidence we've got to consider now, but the conclusion we've to draw from them. I therefore propose that each member of the jury should give the decision he's come to privately, and explain, if he can, how he's arrived at it."

The jurors looked at each other. Each one of the twelve knew the verdict he would have given as an individual, but did not care to make public the mental processes whereby the verdict had been reached. The habit of the majority was to leap to conclusions and cling to them. Logic had no place in their minds; they were used to following their instincts, their convenience, the judgments and circumstances to which they had been accustomed. The foreman's request secretly appalled all save two of his hearers, but they acceded to it, and made appreciative signs when he called for a show of hands.

"I'll read out the names," said the foreman, bending over his list. "Ladies first. Mrs. Walker-Wheeler."

"Yes?" said the lady addressed timidly. "Were you speaking to me?"

"What conclusion have you come to, madam?"

The neat lady, with blue eyes and a pearl and turquoise brooch, rose to her feet.

"Guilty," said the neat lady, and sat down, smoothing the skin on the back of her plump hand.

"Do you wish to amplify that?" the foreman asked. "To give us your reasons?"

"Oh no," said the lady. "I just think so, that's all. I've thought so all along."

The foreman made a mark against her name and read out the next on his list. "Miss Lampeter."

This was a different matter. Miss Lampeter, who wore a monocle and very well-cut clothes, was feared by all the men; Mrs. Walker-Wheeler too would have feared her, but for the saving fact that Miss Lampeter was unmarried.

"Not guilty," said Miss Lampeter, in the accents of Oxford. "I shall give my reasons in sequence. One should justify, it seems to me, any opinion one gives in this very important matter."

She selected one from the sheaf of neatly scribed pages before her and read:

"First. The evidence of Doctor Stringfellow appears to me conclusive. Anyone who has followed the trend of modern psychological investigation must be aware—"

The eleven jurors listened in silence to Miss Lampeter's dogma. They reflected that all this education for women was a mistake; that if Miss Lampeter thought they were fools she was wrong; and that she was wrong in trying to teach her grandmother, vicariously, to suck eggs.

"—on these grounds, and after due consideration, I repeat that Martella Baring must be considered the victim of circumstances; and the verdict must be 'Not guilty.' " She sat down, pulling up her skirt at the knees as she did so. The foreman coughed and called the next name.

"Mr. Preevy."

This was a morose person who had made no notes, but looked constantly at his watch and drew designs on his nails in pencil during the less interesting evidence. He now said, tilting back his chair:

"There's only one way to look at it. Either women are responsible, or they're not. If they are, hang 'em for murder the same as men. If they're not, don't try 'em at all. Just give your wife a good talking to next time you catch her at it."

The other jurors looked at the morose one with disapproval.

"I must remind you, Mr. Preevy," said the foreman, "though it shouldn't be necessary, that a woman's life depends on our discussion."

The morose juror was understood to reply that false sentiment made him sick. The foreman waited; but at last, realizing that this was as near to an apology as the other was likely to give, asked him for his verdict.

"Oh, guilty," said the morose juror. "She did it, of course. Doesn't deny it. If you're going to hang people for murder, she'll have to hang. But the whole system's wrong."

"She's had a fair trial," said the juror on his right. "There's nowhere else outside England they give murderers such a fair trial."

"Fair!" Mr. Preevy scoffed. "About as fair as mud. Somebody gets killed, and what's your remedy? Kill somebody else. That won't make up for it."

"Why don't you vote not guilty, then?" the juror asked.

"Because the woman is guilty," said Mr. Preevy. "I'm not going to vote lies."

"I hear your answer, sir," said the foreman. "Next, if you please; Mr. Harris."

"You ought to go and live in Russia," said the juror named, rising, but keeping an eye fixed on Mr. Preevy. "That'd be the place for you. See what sort of justice you'd get there."

"You can't get away from fools," Mr. Preevy retorted, "wherever you go."

"Gentlemen!" said the foreman. "Mr. Harris, your verdict?"

"Guilty," answered the juror, "but I think she ought to be recommended for mercy."

"We'll consider that separately, in due course," said the foreman. "Is there anything you'd like to add?"

"No," said the juror, "only it seems to me all that talk about fugues was a bit thick. I don't believe in doctors, anyhow. Why, they can't cure the simplest thing! They can't cure a cold in the head; you've got to let it take its course. I wouldn't take a doctor's word for anything."

He sat down.

"That's a very sweeping statement, surely," said Miss Lampeter, training her monocle on him. "May-one ask the reason for your prejudice?"

"Let us keep to the main point if we can," the foreman interposed. "Mr. Mallard."

"It's not prejudice, it's the truth," Mr. Harris continued, disregarding. "They can't cure the most everyday things. They can't cure a corn. And then they come here and talk to us as if they were gospel."

"That's right," another juror agreed, "about all they can do is invent a disease and then cure what you haven't got."

"Can we smoke?" a young man inquired suddenly from the far end of the table.

"As far as I'm concerned," the foreman answered, "that is, if the ladies don't object."

"There you are again," said Mr. Preevy. "Why should the opinion of a minority be asked, simply because it's a different sex?"

"It's a mere formula, of course," said Miss Lampeter, lighting a thin black cigar, "but rather charming. Women haven't yet completely exchanged their privileges for their rights."

"I think," said Mrs. Walker-Wheeler, "that it seems rather unfeeling."

The jurors, remembering that she had voted guilty, stared at her.

"It's all so very dreadful," she continued, and I don't think we ought to do anything that would make us feel—that would not show nice feeling."

Miss Lampeter gave the womanly woman her grave consideration, as a child at the zoo gravely considers the quagga, or any other astonishing beast. There was a short pause.

"Shall we proceed?" the foreman asked, leaving the other question to settle itself. "Mr. Mallard, I believe I called on you."

"I didn't get a chance to answer you, colonel," Mr. Mallard said, "but now I'll take the opportunity. I don't like the notion of condemning a woman to death."

"Tchah!" ejaculated Mr. Preevy.

"Well, of course," said the foreman, "it need not imply that. We may recommend her to mercy, as Mr. Harris has reminded us."

"I don't like the notion," the juror persisted, shifting his feet. "What's your opinion, colonel? You've got a grasp of these things."

"I mustn't give my opinion if it's going to prejudice yours," said the foreman.

"That's how these lawyers go on," said the juror. "Mustn't give an opinion, mustn't ask this question, mustn't ask that question. Too many rules and regulations. I dare say it's fair enough," said the juror, "but it beats me how they ever get at the truth."

"Still," said the foreman, "it's not a very complicated case, except for the medical evidence."

"Yes," the juror went on, "and that's another thing. What's all this about walking in your sleep in the daytime? How can a person walk in his sleep if he's awake?"

"Well, it's not quite that," the foreman explained. "It just means that the person doesn't know what he's doing. I myself am sometimes absent-minded. I put on odd socks, and things like that."

"So'm I," said the juror. "Often I've gone downstairs to fetch something and come up again without it. But that's not murder. Fact is, I don't know what to think."

"Better give the prisoner the benefit of the doubt, in that case," said the foreman, "if you're not sure."

"She did it," the juror agreed, "I'm sure enough about that. What

I don't know about is what these doctors say."

"You don't want to take any notice of doctors," Mr. Harris intervened. "They don't know what they're talking about."

"No," said the juror, "that's right, and she as good as says she did it."

"What she says is of very little value," said Miss Lampeter; "she was in an abnormal state."

"And it looks like she did it," the juror continued, pursuing his thoughts, "so it wouldn't do to let her off. If I say guilty, colonel, that doesn't mean she'll get hanged, does it?"

"Not if there's a recommendation," the foreman replied. "That comes later."

"Guilty, then," said the juror, and sat down.

The foreman made a note and called the next name. "Mr. Smith."

"I agree with Mr. Preevy that the whole business is hateful," said the young man who had asked about smoking. "It's too much responsibility to put on our shoulders. Either we've got to let her go free, and that's not fair to the rest of the world if she's guilty; or we've got to hang her, and that's barbarous."

"If we recommend her to mercy—" the foreman began.

"Mercy!" the young man almost screamed. "That's what you call it? Twenty years cut out of a life; the best years. And to spend them in hell. Have you ever been inside a prison? It takes a civilized community to think out a punishment like that. It's worse than barbarous; its devilish."

"I think you exaggerate," said the foreman steadily. "It's no use confusing the issue in this way. Evil-doers have to be punished somehow. You can't run the world on sentiment."

"No, but that's what we try to do," the young man answered. "Save the unfit, spawn more babies, and then get up glorious wars to be rid of them. The world's a reeking pit of sentiment."

"Your verdict, Mr. Smith?" said the foreman in his orderly-room voice.

The young man checked, hesitated, smiled a wry smile.

"Guilty," said he, and lighted his cigarette again with shaking fingers.

"Mr. Arthur?" inquired the foreman.

The small tidy man with two fountain pens in his waistcoat pocket answered without rising: "Guilty. I don't see what else we can say, on the evidence."

"You, Mr. Ludovici?" the foreman asked.

"It is what I say, let her go," responded Mr. Ludovici in rapid Italianate English.

"Not guilty," the foreman inquired, his pencil held ready.

"Guilty, yes," said Mr. Ludovici with an indulgent smile, "only not for hang."

"You mean, you want to recommend her to mercy?" asked the foreman.

"No, no, no, no," said Mr. Ludovici. "Let her go. Not guilty. A woman, what is that? It is not like a man. She means no harm. Yes."

"But if you think she did it, you must give a verdict of guilty," said the foreman. "That's how it goes in English law."

"I am English," said Mr. Ludovici. "Two years. I know what is law. It is what I say, she did right."

"You mean, you don't think she did it?"

"Yes, I think. I think she did right to kill this other. Woman should not be patient. She should not put up. That is no good; such a woman, I would not give sixpence. But this one she take the poker, fight, strike—that is right, what I say."

The foreman gazed helplessly at him, and at the other jurors. They gave him no assistance.

"I take it," said the foreman at last, "that what you mean me to understand is, 'Not Guilty'?"

"That's right," said Mr. Ludovici smiling.

"Five against, and two for," Miss Lampeter reckoned, "and it's ten minutes to six now."

"Do you suppose," inquired Mrs. Walker-Wheeler of her neighbor, "that we shall be kept very late? My husband will be expecting me—"

"Well, if we can come to an agreement," said the neighbor. "Personally, I share your opinion. I only hope these others won't keep us here till all hours arguing."

The foreman summoned him, and he broke off to say:

"Guilty."

"I don't want to seem heartless," went on the lady, "but after all, even with a case like this, ordinary people have to live, haven't they? And we're such a long way out; Highgate."

"Highgate, are you?" said the neighbor. "So are we. Coventry Road."

"Oh, of course I know Coventry Road," said the lady with animation. "Such very nice convenient houses. We nearly took one."

"Guilty, you said, Mr. Waddell? I didn't quite catch—?

"Yes, sir—guilty. I agree with Mr. Arthur. There's no other verdict possible on the evidence, and the personality of the girl."

"You've hit the nail on the head," said Mr. Arthur. "That's a woman you couldn't take by surprise. She's an actress born. Druce—poor chap, I don't care for the look of him; but it struck me very much what he said about the scream."

"And that time on the stage when the man lost his nerve," said Mr. Waddell, "and she kept her head. Don't forget that."

"Yes," Mr. Arthur agreed. "If you want my opinion, gentlemen, it's this. They had a quarrel about some man. (I rather wonder there wasn't more of an attempt made to get the name out of her. He might have been able to throw some light). Well, they have their quarrel, this girl loses her temper, hits out at the other woman, and kills her. Then she says to herself, 'If I want to save my neck, I've got to act!' And, by God, act she does!"

"She might have given herself a knock into the bargain, and said someone else got in and did it."

"She was too clever for that. She knew how easy it would have been to disprove. Not a soul was in or out of that house but her, and Mrs. Druce, and everybody knew it. So she pretends to have a fit, pretends to discover the body, pretends to scream—"

"What about the sleep-walking?" asked Mr. Mallard. "What the nun said?"

"You can't trust these Roman Catholics," said Mr. Arthur, "they all hang together. Besides, there's nothing in their religion against telling lies."

"Oh, come," said the foreman, "that's rather strong."

"Well, there's nothing in that," said Mr. Waddell. "We all know what girls are at that age; hysterical. She's more likely to have read about this fugue business, and remembered it. Her uncle was a medical man. He'd have that book, most likely—or if not that one, another."

"Lady Plumptre said she was always reading," commented Mrs. Walker-Wheeler. "I wonder at her allowing it. Medical books for young girls—"

"Let us get on," said the foreman. "Mr. Nether-coat, may I hear your opinion?"

"Guilty, I suppose," answered Mr. Nethercoat, "I don't see how we can bring in anything else. I've been trying to look at it all round; and you can't get away from the fact that she did it, and doesn't deny it. If she was drunk at the time—well, that's no excuse. I can't see what they were getting at with this fugue idea. It doesn't sound a likely thing to me. I never heard of anybody going like that, and my sister's a nurse in a hospital."

"It's guilty, then?" asked the foreman.

"Yes," Mr. Nethercoat agreed. "Though I don't say she planned to do it. I don't know if that counts in the verdict. It should, to my mind. Anyone loses their temper at times."

"We'll talk about that when it's time to consider the recommendation," said the foreman. "Now, the last name; Mr. Zeal."

Mr. Zeal, a thin man with an enormous forehead, rose and gathered their attention with the eye of a lecturer.

"I agree with the majority," said Mr. Zeal precisely. "I'm sorry for the girl, personally, but that mustn't be allowed to stand in the way. I disagree, however, with the last speaker. In my opinion the story of the fugue is genuine; and that being the case it is liable to recur, possibly with the same result."

"What?" said Miss Lampeter. "Yes, of course. That's a point I hadn't considered."

"You must consider it, my dear lady," Mr. Zeal insisted. "It's of cardinal importance. One of these gentlemen, Mr. Smith I think, said that the world was run on sentiment; to some extent that is so, and it is to be deplored."

"Hear, hear," said Mr. Preevy.

"Trace any social evil to its source," continued Mr. Zeal, his hobby-horse gathering pace, "you will find that the initial causes are weakness and greed. Now, sentiment is weakness. Sentiment refuses to nip any evil in the bud because there may be involved a certain amount of temporary suffering. Now, with this poor girl you have to consider not this one tragedy only, but others that may follow it. There may be other crimes lying latent in her, which are brought to the surface during these periods of fugue to which she is liable."

"You mean," asked Miss Lampeter, "there may be a split personality in her; one of the persons is cruel and violent, and the other just an ordinary woman?"

"Undoubtedly," said Mr. Zeal. "It is obvious that it must be so. It would be a very stupid story, this story of hers, if it were not true. If we set this cruel personality free, we must be prepared to shoulder the responsibility; which I should not care to do, for one."

"If we let her go," Miss Lampeter pondered, "and anything happened—"

"That blood would be on our heads," said Mr. Zeal.

The other jurors listened. The argument did not interest them; they thought it far-fetched; what interested them was its effect on Miss Lampeter, whose once rigid views now seemed to incline toward those of the majority. They would be home, thought one or two, at a reasonable hour after all. They listened; wondered, and began to respect Mr. Zeal. Miss Lampeter's monocle dropped, and so for a moment did her manner.

"I say, all of you," she exclaimed to the silent jurors, "it's pretty awful!"

They stirred uncomfortably, crossed their legs, rustled papers. It was pretty awful, they thought, but there was no need to dwell on it. The foreman reading their wish, decided to get the ordeal over.

"Do you wish to modify your verdict?" he asked Miss Lampeter, who sat staring down at her clasped hands. She did not answer at first. She shook her head, not in negation, but as if to free herself from a net of intolerable thought. The foreman waited.

"I suppose so," said Miss Lampeter at last. "I suppose I ought. Sentiment—it's all wrong, I know. It harms the future. That's what we have to think of and not of the poor girl."

She wrung her hands together; then, meeting the foreman's eye, nodded. He altered the mark against her name.

"What about yourself, colonel?" asked Mr. Mallard.

"I'm afraid—" said the foreman slowly.

"Naturally you don't like convicting a soldier's, daughter," said Mr. Waddell, "but we've all got to face facts."

"I don't allow the fact that her father was a soldier to weigh with me," the foreman answered, "at least, I hope not. I am trying, as you all are, to judge of the rights and wrongs of this case without reference to my personal feelings."

He rose, squared his shoulders, and faced the eleven jurors. The gravity that had settled on them was reflected in his own troubled eyes.

"I share your opinion, ladies and gentlemen," said the foreman. "That means that with one exception we are agreed that the accused woman is guilty of murder. The exception is Mr. Ludovici. He admits her guilt, but as far as I understand him, is willing to let her go free. I don't quite follow his idea, I admit; but I don't think that he can maintain his attitude in the face of our decision."

He looked at the dissenting juror, who felt the tension surrounding him and answered:

"She did it, yes, I think. If it is not to have trouble by her—"

"I don't want to bring pressure to bear in any way," said the foreman.

"No, no," said Mr. Ludovici. "If you all agree, I agree. What you say, I do."

"It's not such a light matter as that," the foreman began; Mr. Ludovici interrupted.

"This is England. It is different here. Laws here—they are strong. What is a woman? Nothing. But the laws—yes. I came here to live because of the laws. They are to protect. They must punish."

He made a gesture two thousand years old, that was his by right of direct descent; a turning out and down of the thumb toward the ground. The foreman bowed slightly, and addressed the others.

"We've reached our verdict, then. It is unanimous. I don't believe, ladies and gentlemen, there's one of us who doesn't feel a load of responsibility at this moment. I ask you, for your own sakes, not to make your final decision without considering the question from every side, every possible angle. Time is of no importance. Don't think there's any hurry. We can take a week, if we like, to make up our minds; and it would be worth it a hundred times if there were any uncertainty."

The eleven jurors did not answer, or move. In silence uncounted seconds went by.

"I take it," said the foreman at last, "that your decision is final. It remains now only for us to decide whether there shall be a recommendation to mercy. We may do that, I think, by a show of hands. Those in favor?"

Hands were lifted, counted; the foreman noted them. Silence persisted, and lay like a weight upon the room.

"I may tell the clerk of the court, then," said the foreman, "that we are ready?"

They gave assent; and still in that heavy silence he rang for the messenger.

CHAPTER VIII Sir John Creates

And one man in his time plays many parts.—As You Like It

Sir John Saumarez, that well-known actor-manager, dismissed his car at the park gates., He walked; he thought; he frowned. Occasionally he roused himself to admire the massed chrysanthemums of a London autumn; and presently, turning into Knightsbridge, he purchased at an expensive flower shop half a dozen of those very large blooms that, to the irreverent, resemble nothing so much as the fleecy heads of French poodles. With these he proceeded to the pleasant house in Sloane Square where dwelt the one relative with whom Sir John Saumarez could, as he put it to himself, be himself.

For the Jonathan Simmonds of his cradle days, was not, had never been, truly himself; and his Aunt Delia, though she refused to exchange Simmonds for Saumarez, had always appreciated his point of view. His parents had died long since, and his other relatives lived in convenient limbos—Stockport, Clacton, and Burton-upon-Trent; but Delia Simmonds, elderly, elegant, independent, with a house in Pont Street and an earl's daughter for a secretary, provided the home atmosphere of which, bachelor as he was, Sir John Saumarez could not—he said it frankly to his interviewers—have too much.

And indeed the pair understood each other as much as they liked each other; and it was as natural to Sir John to take his tea and his worries to his Aunt Delia, as it is natural to some men to take their worries to somebody else's Aunt Delia.

And Sir John Saumarez was worried. Delia Simmonds knew it when he came in, and flinging down the evening paper on a sofa, crossly presented her with the chrysanthemums.

"Unnatural abortions," said Sir John gloomily, as she exclaimed over the marvel of their size, form, and color. She knew him; she was not perturbed; she gave him his opening:

"Where have you come from?"

"The Baring trial."

"Oh, were you there again? I couldn't go today. I had a bridge party. Well?"

"Convicted."

"Of course. It was to be expected. Recommended to mercy, though?"

"Oh, no."

"Wasn't she? Didn't they? I'm surprised."

He fidgeted. "She had a manner, you know, in the witness-box."

"Brazen?"

"Not exactly. But she made the jury feel that she wouldn't thank them if they acquitted her, and would think them fools if they convicted her. Magnificent, but not conciliatory."

"Poor soul!"

"Yes, but she argued with the judge," said Sir John with irritation. "When he told her not to interrupt, that she would be allowed to say what she had to say later on, she told him it was all very well for him, but if he were in her shoes he wouldn't bother about precedence; that he'd just answer a thing as soon as it was said, especially when it wasn't true; and that he ought to try and see things from her point of view. She was rather regal about it."

"My dear John, she must be mad."

"Not a bit! Quite courteous and confoundedly sane. After all, the etiquette of a court can't seem very important when you've a rope round your neck—as she pointed out."

"If it weren't a tragedy, it would be laughable."

"Yes, but you didn't feel like laughing," said Sir John, interested. "That was odd about the woman—her magnetism. She might have made a great actress—you felt it. You felt that she was a born fighter and that she had a right to use any weapon she could. And she did. It was quite a courageous effort. If she'd been palpably innocent it would have gone down; but as she was palpably guilty it was an unfortunate sort of courage."

"Poor wretch!" said Miss Simmonds. And then: "Well, my dear, I think I've spent my afternoon better than you did. I won twenty pounds: and from Salome Deringham. I like to see Salome lose—so good for her to unshekel."

"It's the duke I'm sorry for," said Sir John absently; and without a change of tone, continued: "D'you know what she said at the end?"

"Salome? She said a good deal. She gets nasal over the score."

"Salome? I'm speaking of that unfortunate child Martella Baring."

"Oh, are you?" said Miss Simmonds, with a sudden sharp look at her nephew.

"When they asked her if she'd anything to say, all she said was—'But it's ridiculous! It's just ridiculous. I can't take it in!' Just like that."

His practiced voice had rung out high, indignant, moving. It moved Sir John even more than Miss Simmonds. A pause ensued which the lady did not break; she perceived that her nephew was encouraging an emotion, and awaited consequences with respectful interest. For she knew well enough that her nephew, though placid in his daily walk and a pillar of respectability, had inherited her own father's capacity for making large fortunes in a state of, as it were, testy abstraction from the routine of respectability.

But where, in her father the cause of these aberrations appeared to be a mere irritation with Clapham, in the grandson they were invariably heralded by emotional stress. Sir John, in the grip of his emotions, could be an eccentric genius who returned to her drawing-room after incredible and well-advertised irresponsibilities with an enormously enhanced bank balance, and a countenance that besought her to give him tea and say no more about it.

So she waited. "Did you follow the case?" said her nephew at last.

She nodded.

"Nothing struck you?"

"Only that it was rather dreadfully obvious."

"What was obvious?" said Sir John sharply.

"The motive. Oh, very understandable. Here's an excitable, vulgar woman letting herself go, and an excitable well-bred woman holding herself back. I dare say the wretched girl's account of it was true enough; the quarrel really took her by surprise; and when she did lose control she really didn't know what she was doing, or what happened. Other people's rages are infectious. When you've always controlled yourself you'd let go worse when you did let go. Rage—it would get hold of you, as influenza gets hold of very healthy people," said Miss Simmonds.

"Then you think," said her nephew slowly, "that willingly or unwillingly Martella Baring killed Magda Druce?"

"But she admitted that, my dear John. The actual killing was never in question."

"It wasn't in question. Exactly."

Sir John rose. Unconsciously and with most exquisite accuracy reproducing yet gilding the manner of Mr. Tanqueray addressing the jury on behalf of the crown. He brought down his fist upon the table; and a teacup fell, lay where it fell, and was presently crushed beneath Sir John's heel as he stormed the room. It did not matter. He did not observe it. Miss Simmonds observed it; but knew that it was not her best china and that it must not matter.

"And will you tell me why it wasn't in question? Will you tell me—" He broke off. His manner changed: "It's too late," said Sir John jadedly, returning to the sofa. "After all, a mere jester—a poor player who struts and frets his hour—why should they listen to him? To a mere John Saumarez? Even though, mark you this, Delia, even though a woman's life, a young and a beautiful woman's life hangs on the player's trick of seeing what the man of affairs doesn't see. But there it is.

"I feel it sometimes," said Sir John quietly. "They look on us—how shall I put it?—as mere manikins of the emotions. Mere manikins," repeated Sir John with relish, "not men who think and feel and are ready if need be to do more than think and feel, but act. 'Why, yes, act,' they say to us, 'act—but upon the stage. In real life leave action to your betters.' Well, we leave it," said Sir John: "and a woman goes to the gallows."

"What have you got up your sleeve now, Johnnie?" said Miss Simmonds cozily.

He pulled in his chair, his delightful face alight with excitement. "The brandy, Delia. The nip of brandy. What happened to the brandy that Martella offered Magda Druce, and that Magda Druce didn't drink?"

"She drank it herself."

"So they implied. But she wouldn't have it. Said she was sure she hadn't."

"Naturally."

"But why—naturally?"

"Well—"

"I say, why naturally? Why should she deny it? It wouldn't have made any difference to her case to admit it. She was not responsible for her actions at the time; that was the plea. And she'd confessed, or as good as confessed, to a murder. Why boggle at a drink of brandy? There was another explanation, too, that she might have given."

"I suppose she didn't like to have it thought that—"

"Will you attend to me, Delia? Observe the obstinate folly of the creature. 'Did you drink it?' 'No!' 'Did Mrs. Druce drink it?' 'No!'

How easy to have said, 'Yes, Magda Druce drank it!' That would have been credible. Magda Druce, we know, was not the sort of woman to go through an evening without some kind of stimulus. Credible, therefore, to say, 'Magda Druce drank the brandy, grew excited, attacked me. I defended myself!' But this ridiculous girl admits the murder, admits the dispute, and denies any possible explanation of the brandy."

"It's odd," said Miss Simmonds, "but I don't see that it's important."

"Nobody saw that it was important. They assumed that she was guilty; she assumed it herself; they assumed that she had forgotten the incident; and so they never considered the other possibility."

"What possibility?"

"That she had forgotten the incident because the incident never happened. In fact, that she was telling the truth."

"Well?"

"Well, suppose she was telling the truth—suppose she never drank that brandy—suppose, Mrs. Druce did not drink it?"

"Well?"

"Well, then who did? Because, Delia, whoever did was the murderer."

"What? When she confessed—"

"She confessed to the struggle; but she thinks she didn't drink the brandy. Can't you see how important it is?"

"It's important because she didn't know it was important. Is that what you mean?"

"That's it. Both sides assumed that she killed, because she didn't deny it. The killing wasn't in question. The question was, Is killing murder? Prosecution says, 'She was drunk when she killed.' Defense says, 'She may have been drunk when she killed. What does it matter? Anyhow she wasn't responsible.' When she says she can't remember drinking it at all, but supposes she did if they say so, nobody takes the slightest notice. Interesting, isn't it?"

"Interesting? It's thrilling. But where does it lead? What are you going to do about it?"

"Do? Well, for the moment, continue upon the assumption that she was telling the truth."

Miss Simmonds gaped at him. "Telling the truth? You mean the truth throughout?"

"Throughout."

"Then—then"—Delia's shrewd face grew suddenly grave and pitiful—"why, then, the poor girl! The poor girl! It's horrible."

"Pretty horrible! All that vehemence, that indignation, that disregard for the forms, that—bad taste, one might call it—did call it—"

"Yes, it helped to convict her. It prejudiced the jury so patently."

"Well, all that palpable theatrical display—"

"Wasn't display at all?"

"Not at all. That was innocence, Delia. All that came of a good conscience."

"And inexperience."

"And a fine healthy resentment of injustice."

"I see—the incident of the horse over again."

"The incident of the horse over again."

"The poor girl!" said Miss Simmonds. "The poor fool innocence of it." She shivered. "It's that that touches one."

"Yes. It was that which convinced me. No one who was guilty could afford to behave like that. A blush is guilt; but there's the blush of innocence. We forget that. You remember the friar's speech?

'I have marked
A thousand blushing apparitions to start
Into her face!' "

Sir John rolled out the phrase with an enthusiasm that worried Miss Simmonds; for he had an intermittent hankering to play Hamlet which she always and severely discouraged.

"But, Johnnie—"

He held out a hand for silence.

"'And in her eye there hath appeared a fire
To burn the errors that these princes hold
Against her maiden truth. Call me a fool—' "

finished Sir John triumphantly, "if that girl isn't telling the exact truth about the business as she remembers it; and nobody had the sense to see it."

"Except you."

"Except the poor player. Even so." He smiled at her. "We players, Delia, we have our faults, but—we do observe. It's our bread and butter just as it was William's. 'And in her eye there hath appeared a fire!' William knew, bless him!" said Sir John indulgently.

Delia Simmonds dug her sharp little chin into her fist. "But she confessed," she said, unconvinced.

"Forgive me, my dear, that's just what she didn't do. She said there'd been a row and a struggle, and that the other woman flung herself at her, and that the next thing she knew was seeing Magda Druce lying dead on the sofa, and so she supposed she'd done it. Sowerby Sims nearly threw up the case when she said that, and no wonder! It gave the case away. But suppose, nevertheless, it was true."

Two spots of color had come into Delia's cheeks. "What are you going to do about it, Johnnie?"

"Ruthven Traill does dramatic criticism in his spare time," said Sir John gently. "That review of 'Griselda' in the Daily Pillar-Box was his. Ruthven, dear fellow, affects to teach us our business. He suggested, if you remember," said Sir John, coldly, and quoting with extreme accuracy, "that 'if Sir John Saumarez would occasionally go out into the highways and hedges of real life for a model, instead of depending entirely on his shaving-glass, he would cease to be the extremest example of Narcissism since Louis XIV.'

"As you know, I never look at reviews. Frankly, it's not worth my while; but I happened to be at my dentist's one morning, and—er—turning over the morning papers came upon it. Now Ruthven's a dear fellow; and as you know, Delia, I look upon that sort of thing as the—er—necessary corollary of a certain—ah—position. I can afford to smile.

"At the same time," said Sir John, viciously flicking a cigarette ash from his gray trousers, "it would amuse me to go out into the highways as he advises, and, possibly, teach Ruthven Traill as much about his own business as he seems to know about mine."

"And what a stunt it would be, too," said Delia.

"My dear aunt!"

When Sir John called Miss Simmonds 'his dear aunt' she-knew that she had erred, and erred badly.

"I beg your pardon, Johnnie," said Delia Simmonds solemnly.

He forgave her. More, he generously saw her point.

"I am afraid that there would necessarily be in the long run, a certain publicity attached," said Sir John regretfully. "I don't see how, if I succeeded in proving her innocence, I could prevent that."

"No," said Miss Simmonds.

"Well, we won't meet troubles half-way," said Sir John finely. "And, you know, all this may lead to nothing. She's had a fair enough trial. I may be wasting my time. But if—Delia, if I were right—" His eyes gleamed.

"Where are you going to begin?"

"Interview Markham. Run down to Peridu. Generally—ah—nose around," said Sir John.

"You haven't got long."

"That," said Sir John, with his crumpled smile, "is the stimulus. I am among the few actors of my acquaintance, Delia, who enjoy the flying matinee."

"You're a heartless creature, Johnnie," said Delia Simmonds, kissing him affectionately as he rose to go.

"Nothing of the kind," said Sir John indignantly.

"You don't let me finish. Quite heartless. Look how you behaved to Myrtle Percy, although she adored you."

"Business is business. She never knew her words, she was a nuisance behind the scenes, and she played to her own-friends," said Sir John grimly.

"Still, it did for her, leaving half-way through the run. She'll never get another management to trust her."

"That's what I intended," said Sir John. "If an actress or an actor, I don't care how well he acts, doesn't respect his boards—"

"Oh, I agree with you! Still, professionally, you killed her."

"I did."

"It was heartless, and you know it. You are heartless, Johnnie, and I've always said so. And yet"—Miss Simmonds observed her nephew sideways, like a thrush observing a snail—"here you are, preparing to spend time and trouble on a woman who's nothing whatever to you."

"Public spirit," said Sir John.

"Public grandmother! I can't make it out. It isn't as if you were in love with her," said Miss Simmonds airily.

"No," said Sir John. "It isn't as if I were in love with her."

The phrase remained in his mind as he walked thoughtfully down the steps and signaled his taxi. It accompanied him into the taxi; it drove home with him, entered his lift, his luxurious flat, ate his dinner with him, went to bed with him; and at each recurrence of that phrase, the fine dark face, the angry brow, strong mouth, and candid eyes tortured his memory....

"'Fie, fie, unknit that unkind threatening brow!' " began Sir John several times during a restless night; and thought that it was time he gave the public some more Shakespeare. Petruchio now—a fine part, doubled with Sly. One needed the right Katharine. Most Katharines were too old. A dark Katharine, with fire, young. Katharine didn't need experience, only coaching by an expert.

'Fie, fie, unknit—'

Martella Baring, if she had come back to him at the end of her two years' training, might have been useful. Instead, the silly creature hangs a rope round her neck, and herself pulls it tight. He shuddered at the thought of that rope a month hence, tightening round the long white neck. A month—he had less than a month. He would see her lawyers tomorrow about an appeal, so soon at least as he had interviewed little Markham. What a day, and he supposed to be having a holiday!

"It isn't as if I were in love with her," said Sir John to his shaving-glass, next morning, angrily, and instantly cut himself rather badly under the left ear. And damned his razor, his Aunt Delia, and all dark ladies.

CHAPTER IX Ways, Means

Come, my coach!—Hamlet

Fog poured in at the dirt-filmed window of the lodgings in Ladbroke Grove. The sparse plane-tree opposite was no more than thickening of the yellow gloom: and the light perched in space above the lamp-post to the right of number twelve had as little power over the morning misery of November as the meager fire within over the cold and misty front parlor.

The breakfast table was as meager as the fire, and Doucie Dearing in a stained kimono that had been so effective in the revival of—the Geisha, was it, or the Mikado?—at Lesser Polterton-on-Sea five years ago, with her pretty face unpowdered and her golden hair unwaved and dark at the roots, ran her little finger round the empty jar of anchovy paste and sighed.

"Going round the agents today?" said Doucie to Novello, who had left the table and, hunched in the ancient horsehair armchair, was hanging over the fire holding his chilled fingers toward the mound of coal-dust and the pale blue smoke. He answered without turning:

"May as well. Coming?"

"May as well."

Neither moved.

"There won't be so many a mornin' like this," said Novello at last, hopefully. "Might get to see someone. You never know."

"That's what everyone will say to themselves," said Doucie. "I'm not coming, Novello. What's the good? I'm sick of traipsing round from office to office, just to hear 'em say, 'Nothing for you today, dear!' Better stay where we are. We may as well have the good of a room while we've got it. We shan't have it long as far as I can see."

"Oh, stop it, Doucie!"

She stopped—too dreary to be quarrelsome. There was another pause that little pinched Novello Markham broke at last, cheerfully.

"When Druce sends me back that thirty bob—"

"Why you ever let him have it in the first place, that's what I'd like to know."

"He's bound to send it soon. When he does we'll have our cards put in The Stage again. Twice that's led to something."

"Did you write and remind Druce, like I told you?"

He nodded.

"Any answer?"

"Well, I'd have told you, Doucie, wouldn't I?" said Novello mildly; but his mildness infuriated Doucie, though it did not infuriate her with him.

"You know perfectly well," said Doucie passionately, "that we shall never hear from Gordon Druce again. Your nature's against you, Novello. It's what I've always said. You'd give the flesh off your bones, you would. D'you think I don't know perfectly well, and everybody doesn't know perfectly well, who' it was kept the company together for Gordon Druce and managed his money? And what thanks did you get? D'you think I've forgotten the life Magda Druce led you because you wouldn't look at her, the yellow cat?"

"Death pays for all," said Novello mildly.

"And then you go and lend Druce thirty bob—for orchids! I bet she'll relish that, lying under our roof and rent, so to say. No, you'll never hear from Gordon Druce again. And where the next job's to come from I do not know. Always told you you stuck to the same company too long. If only you'd run about a bit when you were younger, and got in with managements like Cohen's or Saumarez's, we shouldn't be sitting here without work, with all the Christmas tours fixed up and not knowing where the next kipper was to come from."

He sighed, but he did not answer her; and she stood looking down at his small shabby person with the deceptively fierce face atop, and shook her head over him. She thought: With his eyebrows he ought to have got anywhere, let alone his mouth. He's got a mouth like grim death, and yet—and yet—I don't know what's happened to Novello.

She did not understand that to run Gordon Druce's company efficiently as he had done it, had been occupation enough for a meager little Napoleon with a kind heart. She did not quite understand the success though she saw plainly the failure; yet she did not, for an instant, though she scolded, cease to believe in her Novello's star. But she felt that he needed a mixture of reproof and encouragement, and she tried, as a helpmeet should, to give it.

"I'm not blaming you, Nello," said Doucie sorrowfully. "But you've got no verve. That's what you ought to have more of—verve!"

The word brought back to little Markham's mind his wedding day, and the bottle with some such word on its gilt shoulders. "Veuve" somebody—a good brand—the best. He remembered being grateful to it at the time. Now he answered regretfully:

"Yes, I could do with a glass, I can tell you. But I'm afraid for the moment it won't run to fizz."

Doucie shook his shoulder, impatient for such vagueness and the slight upon her French accent.

"Well, why don't you do something?" cried Doucie. "Why don't you go and see 'em?"

"See who?"

"Who? Any of 'em."

"Why not Saumarez?" said Novello, achieving a joke.

"Well, why not Saumarez? Write for an interview. You know he never refuses outright. He just says come, and then all you see is Foulkes. But you stand up to Foulkes. Insist on seeing him," said Doucie grandly.

"It would be tactfuller to wait till he sends for me, wouldn't it?" said Novello ironically. "Doesn't do to make oneself cheap. But if he actually asks me to come and see him, well, we might think about it, mightn't we, Doucie? Well, what is it, Mrs. Didsome?"

"You know what it is well enough, Mr. Markham!" returned the landlady without amenity. "And I should be glad if you would attend to it if it's no inconvenience."

She folded her hands on her stomach and gazed over Novello's head. Doucie took up the challenge, and fenced for time.

"Oh, your bill, you mean?" said Doucie, with something of the manner in which she had once played the Silver Pheasant in "Under Two Flags." "Let me see—how much is it?"

"One pound, seventeen, it is," said the landlady; "and there's two three ha'penny stamps on to that, and the pot of anchovy wot I sent Annie out for—one pound eighteen and a penny it is," said the landlady with some emphasis—and stood immovable.

"I don't believe I've got that much by me," said Doucie, "and I don't like to ask you to take a check."

"No, that I quite see," the landlady interrupted; "and I may as well tell you, Mrs. Markham, these rooms is engaged from the day after tomorrow; so I'd be glad if you'd settle up now so I can start the week easy."

"My husband has been expecting a remittance," said Doucie. "It ought to have come this morning."

"Ho!" said the landlady incredulously. "Indeed! Then I dare say this'll be it."

She drew a letter from her bulging pocket—a square rich letter—handed it to Markham and folding her hands, waited for the further excuses, which after twenty years of letting rooms could hold for her no surprises.

"Yes," said Doucie, gallantly fencing still, "a remittance from the manager of our last tour. My husband saw him through a lot of trouble and lent him a good bit of money one way and another: and then, of course, he didn't like to press for it back: so I dare say that's what it is—"

"Doucie!" cried Novello into that taut situation—and his voice had a note of unnatural calm that spoke reminiscently in his own ear of his life's great moments—funerals, his first trousers, a legacy, and a declaration of love—"Doucie! It's what they call telepathy, Doucie—that's what it is!"

"What is?" cried Doucie; and the landlady, her animosities forgotten, craned into the scene.

"What you said—about me—about Sir John. He wants me."

"What?"

"He wants me," said Novello Markham blissfully,

"He wants you?" Her pretty mouth began to draw down a little at the corners, like the mouth of a child on the edge of tears; for great joy is not unlike great grief in its effects: and here was great joy come to the Markhams. "He wants you?" began Doucie, her mouth quivering, her eyes beginning to fill.

Novello, white with excitement, patted her shoulder, trying to be wise and dispassionate. "It's all right, dear. Don't think about it too much. It won't be anything, you know. It—it couldn't be anything. It couldn't be—of course it couldn't be anything—"

The quiver in his voice steadied his wife.

"Why shouldn't it?" demanded Doucie, her voice clearing. "Why you do always run yourself down so, Novello, I don't know. Not much compliment to me. What's he say? Here, let me look!" And she snatched the letter from her husband's hand.

It was a real letter. There was the famous imprint crowning the pale blue paper, the silhouette of Sheridan addressing the House of Commons, the mask of comedy trodden under foot—and the imprint was in red.

"It's personal," breathed Doucie, who had once had an appointment at the Sheridan. "If it was Foulkes wanted you the print would be blue. The red is Sir John's private letters."

"Oh yes, it's private; he's signed it himself," said Novello carelessly. "Be glad to see me at twelve o'clock!" continued Novello, glancing at the black marble timepiece with the malachite Cupid.

"Twelve o'clock? That's early, I should say," the landlady interposed. "Now when I had Lorence K. Lorence here, he wouldn't so much as look at his breakfast till twelve, and then only a cup o' tea. He used to have two lemons brought up with it always, and my girl thought they was for the tea; but one day she came in sudden and she see him rubbing one over his face, swearing where it got into where 'e'd cut 'imself shaving. 'Well,' she said to him, 'whatever do you want to be doing that for?' 'That's to keep the skin white,' he says to her. Yes, I thought, when she told me, leaving off whisky 'ud do it sooner and come cheaper, too."

Doucie did not heed. She was on her knees at the chest of drawers, rummaging like a terrier among her husband's stage clothes. She swung round on her heels at last, displaying a bright blue navy suit, limply hammocked across her two arms.

"Could you let me have the loan of a rub of benzine, Mrs. Didsome?"

Mrs. Didsome fingered the undoubted traces of wet white with grave interest.

"Petrol, I'd advise," said Mrs. Didsome; "though there's some likes methylated."

"Whatever you've got'll do," said Doucie eagerly.

"Well, I 'aven't got neither of 'em as it happens. I was only passing the remark."

Novello interposed. "I won't wear that suit at all," said he. "It's too light by day. I'll wear my brown."

"You will not wear your brown. There's places," said Doucie significantly, "where it's rubbed."

"And that reminds me," said the landlady, "talking of shine, how about 'is shoes? They'll want doing."

"Oh Lord!" Doucie wailed. "And it's nearly eleven now."

"I tell you wot," said the landlady, swelling like a pythoness inspired, "Didsome shall do 'em, and be glad to. Give 'em 'ere!" She put her head into the passage and screamed, "Didsome!"

A subterrannean rumble answered her.

"Didsome!" the landlady screamed once more; and again was answered from below. But the voice had drawn nearer, shifting like the voice of the ghost in "Hamlet," and appeared from its tone to be obeying its own injunction to swear.

"Come up 'ere!" the landlady continued. "I got a job for you."

The novelty of this could not be resisted. It drew the voice up the basement stairs, where it materialized to the waist of a personage with a drooping mustache and large pale ears.

"'Ere," said the landlady, tossing the shoes at this vision, "and look sharp!"

The vision received the shoes, and without inquiry or comment sank below ground. The landlady reentered the Markhams' room and began to dispose of their difficulties one by one with the wide sweep, combined with the attention to detail, of the born tactician.

"You'll get into your trousers," she informed Novello. "Never mind about the seat; you won't be turning round much after you get there. And I'll hot up an iron and press your tie. Then you'll want a nice clean 'andkerchief; and 'ow are your socks? 'Ole in the toe? That'll never show. You see to 'im, Mrs. Markham, and give me the things."

They worked for the next half-hour—Doucie, the landlady, even the landlady's husband in his dark retreat, combined their endeavors to turn little Markham into the likeness of a prosperous, competent man of business, without a care or a debt in the world. By eleven-thirty it was done: and little Markham, walking delicately to save the polish on his shoes, went down the street with the bearing of a man who has an appointment with a brilliant future at twelve o'clock precisely.

Doucie turned back to the little fog-laden sitting-room, and sat down to wait for his return. The excitement had died out of her and left her dumpish. Mrs. Didsome observed it.

"Now, I'll tell you wot I'll do," said the landlady affably, "I'll toss you up a snack early; for I should say you need it. You didn't 'ardly touch your breakfast. Well, wot shall it be? Wot do you say to a nice Welsh rarebit? Plenty of cheese in the 'ouse. That's one thing I will not run out of—cheese! And I'll send out Mr. Didsome for a pint of porter. It's no trouble, dearie, he'd go anyway. And porter's wot you need. You're as white as the curtains and I don't wonder at it. I remember when Didsome got 'is job—on the corporation dust-carts it was. 'Ad to wear one o' these great wide 'ats. 'E looked a scream. 'E come 'ome to me and 'e says, 'I got a job.' I come over quite faintlike, wot with the surprise and all. You sit quiet, dearie, and I'll see to your lunch."

But Doucie could not sit quiet. The two soft crimson patches where tears had dried burned till they actually hurt her cheeks. Her heart grew calm, only to reexcite itself, till she felt as if she were living in a lift. She watched the slow hand of the clock—for the minute hand stayed perpetually at three minutes past the hour—and then looked away from it, as a cat turns elaborately from a moribund mouse only to round on it sharply. Had it moved? It seemed to Doucie that it never had moved.

The lunch came—she ate it. She wandered about the room, tried to read Home Chat, took off her stocking to darn a ladder, put it on again; and then, said Doucie, telling the story afterwards, "Something seemed to say to me—'Dress I' I don't know why," Said Doucie, "but I just felt—fog or no fog, it's the morning for my crêpe georgette!"

So Doucie, governing her restlessness, had got out the crêpe georgette, and put it on; and had no sooner put in on, than she took it off again, because the outspoken electric blue of the crêpe georgette enhanced the metallic glitter of Doucie's hair, and made more noticeable the sudden ceasing of the glitter half an inch from the parting.

Doucie had a quiet, happy, busy half-hour with a bottle of peroxide, dealt next with her complexion, sketched in a new mouth, and polished her nails till, as Mrs. Didsome put it, "Monkey brand wasn't in it for reflection." Then scented, gilded, powdered, and perfectly happy, she put on the electric blue georgette once more, and was hesitating between a blue paste or a real Tecla necklace, when the front door-bell rang loudly.

Mrs. Didsome, laying lunch, ran to open it; and Doucie waited breathlessly to welcome Ulysses returned.

But no Novello appeared. There was instead a male murmur and an exclamation in the voice of Mrs. Didsome. Sighing, Doucie turned away from what could be no affair of hers—turned toward the window. She had not time to be astonished at what she saw—the gleaming car incredibly drawn up outside—for the landlady came swiftly along the passage, sketched a knock, and entered panting.

For an instant Doucie was frightened. She imagined an accident—Novello hurt—an ambulance bringing him home. But the landlady's demeanor reassured her. Mrs. Didsome's bearing, at the moment, was modeled on that of the butler who had paid her attentions thirty years before. Her arms hung by her sides; she bowed forward a little from the waist; but her expression was undisciplined. She beamed; her eyes rested on Doucie with pride. In the very accents of the butler she announced:

"Sir John Saumarez would be obliged if you could make it convenient to call on him at the Sheridan Theater! 'E 'as sent 'is car."

Then in her own voice:

"What 'at'll you wear, dear?"

CHAPTER X Antechamber

Now this overdone, or come tardy off, tho' it make the unskilful laugh, cannot but make the judicious grieve.—Hamlet

Meanwhile little Novello Markham had arrived at the stately portals of the Sheridan, had entered that famous hall, where, from forget-me-not blue satin walls, an alleged Romney gloomed at an authentic Frith, while at the head of the main staircase Sir John, a little larger than life and a good deal younger, smiled a welcome. Little Novello, however, did not climb the staircase; but, skirting a bronze basrelief of Sheridan himself toying with certain Muses, and guided by the same instinct that directs a homing pigeon, discovered, not far from the box-office, an inconspicuous door, set in the wall like a panel.

He slipped through it unhindered, climbed a staircase whose

spotless walls recorded in a series of photographs Sir John Saumarez's successes and successes of esteem for the last fifteen years, and arrived panting at a second door marked "Office" and "Private." He entered, presented his card to a medaled veteran, was shown into a little room, half boudoir, half card-index; waited. Waited.

Waited.

He waited until he had rehearsed every possible form of opening speech so often that he really knew the more promising ones by heart, before the door reopened; but, reckoned by theatrical time, he was attended to with flattering promptitude. The medaled hero had a smile for him as he ushered him into the sanctum of the godling Foulkes, and Herbert nearly rose as he greeted him, offered him a cigarette, and asked him to wait. He waited. Waited..

Waited.

Waiting was more amusing in the office of Herbert Foulkes than in the boudoir, and Herbert Foulkes conducted a pleasant and continuous conversation with him and three telephones.

The conversation was interrupted at last, however, by the ringing of a fourth telephone, and to Novello Markham's imagination, it had a stronger note than the other three.

That will be Sir John, thought Novello.

"Yes, sir? Yes, he's here, sir! Just this moment arrived. Certainly, sir! I'll send him up to you at once."

Herbert Foulkes put down the receiver.

"That was Sir John," said Herbert Foulkes intimately to Novello. "He wants you to go up to his flat. I'll show you where the lift is."

He preceded the agitated Novello down the corridor, and showed the gold and blue barred lift gates. He waited with him till the liftman, downward-swooping, answered their summons, and the blue-lined car had sunk level with the corridor floor; then, amazingly, he held out his hand.

Novello took it.

"Good luck!" said Herbert Foulkes tenderly; and as Novello told Doucie later, let go and made a face at him. What he described thus irreverently was Mr. Foulkes's version of Sir John's effulgent smile, which, after the manner of classics, had suffered considerably in translation.

CHAPTER XI A Joint Engagement

Like to a double cherry, seeming parted,
But yet a union in partition.—Midsummer Night's Dream

The study to which a man servant admitted Novello was an apartment so perfect, so like the study of any stage ambassador, that Novello at once felt at ease, as though it were, indeed, one of those three-walled rooms in which so much of his working life had been spent. And Sir John, standing by his own fire, was the same faultless Sir John of the photographs, familiar as his setting—and as unreal. Little Markham discovered, to his surprise, that he had got his stage-fright over; and he had a fleeting sense of relief that he had refused to put on the blue suit. For Sir John was in blue—a creation to which Novello's mere coat and trousers were as rush-lights to the moon.

Sir John did not advance to meet him; but his expression was considerate and welcoming. They shook hands.

"Sit down, won't you?" said Sir John indicating a chair.

Novello obeyed. Sir John continued to stand, looking down on his guest, taking in details with a lazy glance or two. Novello would have been surprised to learn how accurately, though as yet superficially, he had been assessed.

"I've seen you before, Mr. Markham," Sir John began charmingly, "though you were not aware of it. You mustn't think I'm trying to flatter if I say that I was a good deal impressed."

In a haze Novello wondered … which part? … where? …

Sir John hesitated. His air, if Novello had been in a condition to observe and detect it, was very much that of a small boy who has rigged up a telephone with string and two golden syrup tins between his bedroom and the tool-shed. He would like to display the achievement to the second housemaid, who found him the tins; but—is she to be trusted? Has she the intelligence to appreciate the work of art? After all, she did supply him with the tins! Well, risk it.

"It seems to me, Mr. Markham," said Sir John, thoughtfully, "that we artists have a double function. We use life to create art, and we use art to—how shall I put it?—criticize life. You agree?"

"Certainly—most certainly," said little Markham fervently.

"I knew you would. But, Mr. Markham, between artists, do we always fulfil our double function? Are we not so much occupied in using life to create art, that we forget our other function? Do we not sometimes forget to apply the technique of our art to the problems of daily life?"

Markham coughed. His immediate problem was the payment of Mrs. Didsome's bill, and he did not see how the technique of his art was going to help him pay it.

"Apply the technique of the stage to the problem of daily life," repeated Sir John.

Markham coughed again, and Sir John checked himself and smiled dazzlingly.

"I foresee your objection," said Sir John swiftly. "You are going to say, 'What opportunities can the round of daily life afford?' I tell you, Mr. Markham, the opportunities recur and recur again. You've seen me, I dare say, in the problem play, that is, as I think—er—the critic of the Pillar-Box termed it, the highbrow shocker. But when such a highbrow shocker occurs in real life, does the public call in the actor? No. Perhaps it is as well. For it takes the exceptional actor as well as the exceptional man, to seize the opportunity of fulfilling his double function, to apply the technique of his art to a problem of real life. I know you will agree with me."

Markham agreed—and accepted a cigarette from the tortoise-shell box. But though he agreed, he did not comment. Better keep quiet, he thought, till I see what he's getting at. He's getting at something, for all his talk. For Sir John's protective pomposities were well known. Markham's shrewd little face was intent. He watched for Sir John's meaning to emerge as a huntsman watches for a fox to break covert. His silence, the silence of a man who will not talk unless he has something to say, pleased the arbiter of his destiny.

"Mr. Markham," said Sir John shrewdly, "I read your thoughts."

Markham started.

"You are saying to yourself, Mr. Markham, this manis—talking through his hat. Eh? Of course you are. You wouldn't be the practical man I take you for otherwise. Let me explain myself. I have something to say to you; and I don't quite know how to begin. And so," said Sir John, with an airy wave of the hand, "I ramble; I discant; I, as it were, present you with the conclusions of a theorist instead of the premises which the practical man demands; while you, of course, are wondering to yourself, as a practical man, why on earth I have brought you here."

He paused, too much absorbed for the moment in his own problem to notice how the knuckles of Markham's right hand grew white grasping the arm of his chair. He continued his deliberate statement.

"The fact is, I was anxious to gratify a whim of my own. I am an inquiring man, Mr. Markham: I ask continual questions—of the universe—the Fates—and my fellow-men. You too, I imagine, do not let life pass you by without inquiry. Inquiry—that brings me at last to my object. Mr. Markham—I listened to you in court. You gave your evidence, if I may say so, as an artist, and as a man, in a way that impressed me. I feel that you will not at once accuse me of idle curiosity if I come to you with an unusual request. May I ask you now to give me something more than a repetition of your evidence? Mr. Markham, I want from you the inner history, if you can recall it, of the Peridu murder."

Little Markham had to swallow once before he could answer. In spite of his disclaimer to Doucie, he had hoped; and the phrase "I have seen you before" had set him on a pinnacle. He understood now, and accepted the situation gallantly; but there was an instant before he could recover control, and Sir John saw it.

Sir John knew that look though he did his best to keep out of its way, and deputed to Foulkes the task of refusing work to the applicants who besieged him. It struck like a whip through his pomposities, to touch his artist heart. It stirred unbearably the pity he genuinely felt for those who could not share his success. In self-defense, knowing that if he did not, it would haunt him in solitary moments, at dinner table, in the tumult of a first night, he answered the look in words impulsive yet measured.

"But first you'll forgive me if I refer for an instant to the question of business. I understand that you are at present undecided as to your future arrangements. I had hoped that we could induce you to act as stage manager for the first tour of 'Griselda's Garter,' which I am sending out at Christmas. Foulkes spoke to you of this, I expect? No? Ah, no doubt he expected me to broach it myself. I repeat, Mr. Markham, you impressed me in the witness-box as a man of business and a man of feeling—an ideal combination, Mr. Markham, in our profession."

Little Markham swallowed again. Sir John continued, carefully looking away:

"I had thought of some arrangement upon a yearly basis. However, it will be best to discuss that with Foulkes. I hope you'll be able to come to us; your provincial experience should be of value."

Now, he thought, he might allow himself to meet Markham's eyes. The smoke of the cigarette had invaded them, it seemed, but that could not disguise the amazement, the instant hero-worship, that showed there. The little man cleared his throat and answered, not without dignity:

"Thank you, sir! I'm free at present. I've had a lot of experience that might come in handy, as you say."

"That's settled then; we will regard you, from today as"—he

smiled—"a Sheridanian!" said Sir John, and smiled again, and was proceeding. But something in that face once more arrested him. "Well? What is it, Mr. Markham?"

Little Markham flushed.

"Sir John—I—it's my wife—Sir John, we've always been joint, as you may say, Sir John. Would it be asking too much—if a part—any part—Sir John—"

Sir John was amused. "Mrs. Markham acts!"

"Acts? Sir John—it's not for myself—but if Doucie—my wife—could only get her chance—"

Sir John's smile was a benediction upon marital attachment. Novello was aware of its indulgence, and strove to assert his Doucie's independence of the need for indulgence.

"Sir John, you may say I'm prejudiced—Sir John, I've been stage manager for ten years now, and I give you my word, even a good wife may not always be the right thing in a company—if you know what I'm getting at, Sir John. But my Doucie—my wife, I mean—she's been my right hand professionally. There is no one she can't play at twenty-four hours notice, or less—from a Marie Tempest part to a Marie Lloyd part. She has her off days, I don't deny it. Only this summer I had to speak to her. She'd had a quick change over from a Maisie Gay to an Irene, and it told on her—there's no denying, it told on her. And after a week, I said to her straight out: 'My dear, this can't go on! We shall have to go into Shakespeare if you can't pull yourself together.' Well, she didn't say much, not more than was reasonable; but she thought it over, and for the rest of the tour—I give you my word, Sir John, she was Tallulah—pure Tallulah."

Sir John nodded, encouragingly.

"She was with you at Peridu?"

"Oh yes, sir, a joint engagement. She under-studied poor Magda Druce. The comic chambermaid was her own part, but she doubled one or two nights when Miss Baring was off, to oblige."

"To oblige Miss Baring?"

"To oblige the management, Sir John; we couldn't trust the understudy, though I don't say she wouldn't have done it for Miss Baring. Between you and me, Sir John, my Doucie was the only woman in the company who hadn't her knife into Miss Baring all the time. But they dressed together and they got on well; though my Doucie had to hold the scales impartial as you might say, being S. M.'s wife. But she liked Martella, Doucie did."

"Ah, well, I've no doubt, Mr. Markham, that it would be possible to arrange an—ah—joint engagement. 'Griselda's' a big cast. Is Mrs. Markham in town?"

"She's at home now, sir, waiting to—" He flushed up and broke off, only to begin again. "It's a big thing to us, Sir John, the engagement; I'd like to say—"

Sir John waved aside the little man's emotion.

"It would perhaps be better if Mrs. Markham joined us. Is she on the telephone?"

"Well, Sir John, not exactly on. But there's a tobacconist round the corner who will always oblige with a message."

Sir John, the artist in action, laughed. He adored the rôle of fairy godfather.

"I don't think we'll trouble the tobacconist. Oh, is that you, Foulkes? Have you Mr. Markham's address? Ladbroke Grove, ah! Send down one of the cars at once to Ladbroke Grove, and give my compliments—What? Yes. That's it. At once if she can make it convenient."

"She will, sir," murmured Novello, fervently.

"He's to wait. He's not to come back without her. That's all, thank you."

And Sir John, whose thoughts were already at his next sentence but three, wasted a smile upon the receiver before he recollected himself and hung it up.

He turned once again to Novello, who, perceiving that the scène à faire was upon him, bright-eyed with past emotion and present tension, presented, in his passionate attentiveness, as Sir John instantly realized, the perfect foil.

Privately registering a decision that if the little man could only keep it up he would not waste him on a tour, Sir John spoke, opening the scene with his well-known crisp yet bland tensity. He had once been impersonated by that young devil Claus Kitten, at a Green Room Rag as a piece of buttered toast; and the nickname stuck. Sir John had not appreciated the compliment, but it was, nevertheless, a wry compliment. For his light touch in moments of emotion made him very dear to his audiences, who liked to feel all things neatly, and he went down with his audiences in the same effortless manner as the buttered toast of the company at their afternoon teas.

"I was at the Peridu trial," said Sir John, "as I think I explained to you. I was interested; I followed it with care. At the end—I wonder if this will surprise you—I came to the conclusion that the decision of the jury was altogether wrong."

Little Markham regarded him dumfounded.

"It was assumed that she was guilty," Sir John continued, "because she did not deny it. It was assumed that no other person could possibly have committed the murder. It was difficult I grant you—her character, her answers, the folly of her defiance in the witness-box—Was she playing a part? As a man of the world, I answer, perhaps; but as an artist—and here I bring to bear my knowledge of the human mind, my imagination—I think not. I apply, in fact, the technique of my art to this problem of life that presents itself."

"Good God!" said Little Markham. This was what Sir John had been driving at. Sir John had watched, had followed, and had seen what he in the thick of it had forgotten or misrepresented to himself, the real Martella. In that cloudy atmosphere of the court involuntarily he had looked, not for innocence, but for guilt; had twisted her answers and glances toward guilt. The thought of another murderer had never occurred to him, as it had occurred neither to prosecution nor to defense.

"But I saw her with my own eyes," he protested feebly.

"And what did you see? A woman standing by the dead body—an empty flask of brandy that neither she nor the dead woman had touched. Was there no other person in the house that night? Who knows? It was never in question. She was dazed, the doctor thought and you thought. What was the cause of that? Drink? She never touched it. Her head hurt her, she told you. What was the cause? Drink? I give you the same answer. A person emerging from a fugue has no pain in the head. Martella Baring was neither drunk nor in a fit. What then? Think it over, Mr. Markham!

"Another point: why did she fetch the poker from the room in which she was not sitting? Odd, wasn't it? And the pain in the head, if it were not caused by drunkenness, might have been caused—how? Think it over; think it over, Mr. Markham. Mean while, as we have a little time to wait," said Sir John, "do you care for a cocktail at this hour? I dare say your doctor tells you, as mine does, that alcohol in the morning is immoral; but I prefer to go for my advice to the Psalmist—is it the Psalmist?—'Wine maketh glad the heart of man!' Still, there's no need to be too oriental, no cloying cherries; a very dry Martini, don't you think so?"

Markham agreed, a trifle absently; for he was, in all simplicity, obeying orders. He was thinking it over. A bell was sounded and answered. The cocktails appeared upon a lacquer tray.

"Success to our researches," said Sir John, lifting his glass.

Little Markham nodded and drank recklessly. He had not breakfasted; but the liquor could make no difference to him. He was drunk already, more completely than ever whisky had made him. Spiritually little Markham was under the table. He said, as he set his glass down:

"Sir John—I am grateful—" A hand attempted to wave his words aside, but he was no longer speaking of his own concern. "I am grateful," he repeated, "for this chance to do something for

Miss Baring."

"Ah!" said Sir John, looking at him with approval. "So you do share my opinion?"

"I didn't, Sir John! I was no wiser than the rest of 'em. But you're changing my mind for me. God knows why she admitted it—but she wasn't the sort to kill—off her head or on it."

"No, but if she didn't kill Magda Druce—who did? Someone killed her."

"That's right, sir, but who?"

"Ah—who?"

Sir John began to pace his room, gracefully steering a course among the furniture, from the mantel-piece to the window, from the window to the desk, from the desk to the mantelpiece again.

"We have only two points to go on," said Sir John at last. "She did not do it; and she confesses to having done it. Somehow we have got to reconcile those two statements. And the first thing of all is to admit within our calculations a third person—a person unknown."

"That's one more than the lawyers allowed," said Markham.

"Quite so. The lawyers took it for granted that no third person entered that room until you appeared with Druce and the policeman. But we are not lawyers; we can afford to neglect facts and give rein to our imagination."

For a moment neither spoke. Then Markham asked: "It didn't strike you she might be shielding somebody?"

"I thought of that," Sir John answered, "but it will not do, I'm afraid. There appears to be nobody with sufficient claim on her—"

He broke off. Markham answered his look.

"So I thought," said Sir John. "No, that theory is tempting. It squares with that obstinacy of hers. That question, you remember, of the person she discussed with Mrs. Druce during their supper—I should very much like to know who that was. But we must dismiss the idea that she is shielding someone. No sane woman carries quixotry to the point of hanging, unless for the sake of someone very dear. And," concluded Sir John, with satisfaction, "there is, so far as we know, no such person in her life as yet."

"If it wasn't for her saying she did it," said Markham almost irritably, "there'd have been a chance. They were ground-floor rooms; anyone, a tramp could have got in at the back. But when she admitted it they didn't look any further."

"But where, in that case," said Sir John, "would be the motive? Invariably there is a motive."

"No, sir, pardon me—not always. I read the Sunday papers a lot," Novello excused himself, "and it looks to me as if two out of five murders were done in a panic, because the fellow lost his head."

"The view taken by the prosecution, in fact," said Sir John.

"Not quite, sir," Markham contradicted. "Suppose now a fellow gets in at the back—a tramp or such like—sees the window open and thinks it a chance to steal—suppose Mrs. Druce sees him—she might have seen his reflection in the glass of the folding-doors. She calls out and starts to wake the house, and he knocks her on the head and bolts."

"Yes," said Sir John slowly, "but what about Miss Baring? She'd have seen him too."

Novello Markham hesitated before he answered.

"If you ask me, sir, Miss Baring mightn't have noticed. She—you see, she wasn't used to spirits, and that flask was empty. She'd been working hard, and she might have taken more than she ought, not being used to spirits."

Sir John did not comment. Markham went on:

"God knows I don't want to say anything against Miss Baring. It's not against her, looked at properly. It's to her credit that she never took anything and couldn't stand it when she did. I tell you, sir, when I saw her there leaning on the mantelpiece, that was the first thought crossed my mind—"

"That she was drunk?" said Sir John, bluntly.

"There's some go like that," said Novello, out of his ten years' experience of touring companies. "Go white and dazed. They'll stand drinks to strangers out of the money they've saved up to buy boots with, and wake next morning and say they've been robbed, and you can't make them believe the truth about it."

"For the sake of argument," said Sir John, "we will suppose that it was so. But why should your imaginary intruder enter a room where he was liable to be heard or seen at any moment through the folding doors?"

"People do a lot of silly things when they're desperate," said Markham, "and anyhow, they were talking, the two women. You know what that means—wouldn't notice Gabriel's trumpet."

"But why should he attack Mrs. Druce?" Sir John asked, and continued before Markham could answer: "Don't think I'm trying to discourage you by raising objections. I'm interested; I raise objections for the sheer pleasure of having them answered. You are very plausible, Mr. Markham. Continue! Why should the unknown attack Mrs. Druce?"

"She might have seen him. Miss Baring said she thought she remembered a look of horror on Magda's face. She may have seen him then, coming at her."

"Surely Miss Baring would have some recollection of the actual struggle?"

"She might not; you can't tell. He might have knocked her down first. If she got a blow on the head she wouldn't remember just what went before. I fell off a bicycle once," said Novello, with feeling. "Or she might have seen it and thought she was doing it herself, if she was in that state."

"Miss Baring doesn't appear to me the sort of person—" Sir John was beginning, when little Markham, forgetting reverence, gratitude, all save the point of issue, cut him short:

"We've got to leave Miss Baring out of this—cut her right out. She didn't do the murder; she didn't see the murder; or if she did, she don't remember it and can't be any use to us.

"There's only two people left in, like there was to start with. But it's not the same two—there's Magda Druce, poor woman—"

"And X," said Sir John. "The person unknown."

CHAPTER XII Ask the Policeman

Give me your hand; come, we must needs dine together.—Timon of Athens.

In the silence that followed, while Sir John strolled to the window, Markham, deserted by his confidence, had leisure to view his own behavior with misgivings. He had contradicted the great man; he had taken the words out of the great man's mouth; he had brushed the great man's comments aside as lightly as flies. In fact, led on by enthusiasm, he had presumed.

With apprehension he waited while Sir John from his high window surveyed clouds, chimneys, and below them the hurrying people, small as mice. Minutes went by, and still Sir John's impeccable back presented itself. Markham sat still, cursing his improvised theory of the crime, that appeared, for all Sir John's urbanity, to contain one premise that he could not stomach. Certainly, Markham admitted to himself, it was not very nice to think of a lady getting drunk. He wouldn't like it at all if some man were to say it of Doucie. Doucie must be on her way by now, he thought; and perhaps, with his silly arguing, he had done in their chances.

The clock, after a silvery prelude, struck one. On the stroke Sir John turned.

"You'll have luncheon with me, won't you? And Mrs. Markham too when she comes. There are more points to consider. I am inclined to think that Peridu itself has not been sufficiently explored for evidence."

"They had her confession; they didn't need evidence. Why

should they look for it?"

"Exactly. But we don't accept her confession, and so it becomes our duty to search for evidence. That follows, I think, and I am rather wondering—"

But the door was opened before he could proceed, to disclose the small form of Mrs. Markham in her blue crêpe georgette. She wore a black hat: her gloves' luster paid tribute to the borrowed rub of benzine. She had; on tour, entered the drawing-rooms of many a stage countess; she knew just the manner that was necessary, and brought it into play from the first moment. Novello, proudly watching, admired her; and secretly asked himself how the devil she had managed to get into her best clothes in so short a time. He could not know that as soon as he had departed, a warning voice which she had obeyed, had said to her—dress!

"So good of you," Sir John was saying, "to let me bring you here at such short notice."

"Oh, I was quite glad to come," Doucie answered, "glad of the breath of fresh air. What a charming flat you have, Sir John! So handy, with Piccadilly and everything so near!"

Even while he looked and admired, Markham was troubled. He understood his Doucie; but Sir John—Sir John might not guess the actress that lay hidden beneath the veneer of the woman of the world.

"My wife's had as much experience as myself," said he. "Been going ever since the war, playing everything but Shakespeare. She's a very quick study; gets put upon sometimes on that account. Don't you, Doucie? And as for costume—"

"Quite," Sir John interrupted gently. "But all this is business. And we may leave business aside till after luncheon. I think, if you don't mind, we'll have it at once, and not wait any longer. I confess I sometimes find it difficult to wait till a reasonable hour for my luncheon."

"Oh, so do I," said Doucie, a touch of pathos in her voice which surprised her husband. He could not know of the snack—that premature meal, the nice rarebit, the porter for which Mr. Didsome had been sent out, and for which he would in any case have gone.

"Then perhaps you would ring, Mr. Markham," Sir John suggested, and smiled at the couple. This happiness, he thought, how easy to bring about, how satisfying, how romantic an achievement! At the back of his mind the business man, whom the romantic despised, considered Doucie, found her a useful little woman for the Number Two Company, took in the probable cost of her clothes, and range of her emotions, and assessed her very justly at the definite amount of money per week that she, as an actress, would be worth to Sir John. The bell was answered.

"Luncheon!" said Sir John. "At once. Mr. and Mrs. Markham will join me."

The slave of the bell retired.

"Mr. Markham," said Sir John to Doucie, "has been giving me his views on a certain matter in which we are both interested. He is going to be good enough to lend me his collaboration.

Doucie, as a member of the profession, was aware of Sir John's soubriquet. She therefore discounted in her mind the obvious meaning of this statement, and translated it. It meant, she thought, that he had offered Nello something in the Number Three. And yet—and yet—Sir John did not ask intending members of the Number Three to lunch.

"Of course," said Doucie, "I've always said my husband could do anything, given the chance. He's never got the proper credit for what he did. I don't say it because he's my husband; but I've seen a lot of S. M.'s; and really—never saw one that could come up to him—never in a hurry, never loses his temper—"

"I'm not speaking now of his professional collaboration," said Sir John, "though that too has been discussed. It is his views on the Peridu murder that have so interested me. He believes that if the crime were to be approached from another angle, we should reach a different result."

"And get Martella off, you mean?" Doucie asked, surprised out of her grand manner.

"I hope so. Mr. Markham shares my conviction that she was not guilty. I wonder if you agree?"

In a flash Doucie guessed at the cause of Sir John's interest, knew what she must say, and said it:

"Agree? I never thought it for one moment! Haven't I always said, Nello, that nobody who knew her could ever think it for a moment? Why, that girl's kindness, and the way she never said a catty thing, and the way she'd lend you anything you wanted—You couldn't wish to have a nicer girl in any company; and clever too, and never too proud to take a hint. Many's the time she's asked my advice, for all she was playing heavies—yes, and taken it too. It's all very well for these lawyers, arguing round and round till you can't hear yourself think; but I dressed with Martella Baring for six weeks, and there's not much you don't know about a girl after that. Oh, Sir John, are you going to take it up yourself? Have you found anything out? Nello'd be ever so glad to help, and so would I! Poor thing!"

Sir John did not interrupt her. He found pleasure in listening to praise of Martella Baring, pleasure which, as he told himself, was the result of hearing his own judgment of her confirmed. The business man's insinuation that he would not have valued Mrs. Markham's confirmation of his judgment on any other point was instantly snubbed down, and the romantic bowed Mrs. Markham into the dining-room with dignity unimpaired.

It was an excellent lunch, though Doucie could not appreciate it at its true worth on account of the snack and the bewildering variety of forks. Novello, keeping an eye on Sir John, worked out the problem of the forks as he did, and enjoyed his food. At first there was little talk. The guests waited for their host to lead them, and the host was preoccupied. He could not see the immediate step to be taken. At the end of the second course he became aware of the silence and took his guests into his confidence.

"It is perhaps hardly a subject for conversation at a meal," he began, "but after all our time is short. You'll forgive me, I know, if I recur to this matter of the trial." And then: "Tell me all about the company—the men of the company—I dismiss the women. The only woman physically capable of—ah—poker-work, was Miss Baring herself, they tell me. But what of the men?"

"Well, there's me," said Markham innocently. Sir John laughed. "Ferocious as is your general aspect, my dear Markham, you have, I fancy, an alibi."

"That's true,' said little Markham, relieved.

"But what of the rest? What of your comedian, for instance, who did not give evidence?"

"Tom Drewitt? No, sir! His wife had a baby a month ago. He hadn't time for goings-on. A good husband, Drewitt! No, sir, if you're looking for romance, so to speak, it would be among the youngsters—Fane, now, or Ion Marion."

"Fane, now!" Sir John was thoughtful. "I was interested by him. Liked him better than Marion."

"Everybody liked Fane, sir. You couldn't not. A bit soft, but that was the war. They say he was a good actor before the war. Started in a circus as a kid and had worked his way up to Number One tours and occasional London. Small part and understudied lead. 'Hamlet' and 'The Third Floor Back'—that sort of part. Lost his nerve in the last offensive. Funked London when he got back. Though I have heard, sir," finished Novello doubtfully, "that you yourself had sent for him."

"Possible—quite possible," said Sir John airily. "Foulkes keeps an eye for me on the younger generation; but we'll find out." And stretching out an arm to the silken doll on the occasional table behind him, he threw off the toy and took up the receiver beneath.

"That you, Foulkes? Did we ever send for a Mr. Fane? Handell Fane. Yes, that Fane. Oh! Oh, we did, did we? What for? Revival of Paolo? Indeed. I wasn't told. Ah!" He turned to the Markhams, the receiver at his ear. "Yes, you're quite right, Mr. Markham. But Mr. Fane, it appears, was not free. Eh, what's that, Foulkes? You thought it a little surprising? Oh no, not at all. Why? Foulkes, I'm shocked. Avoid egotism, Foulkes! We are not the only management that revives classics. There is the Old Vic. Hush, Foulkes! No doubt Mr. Fane had his reasons for lurking, like Edgar—Edgar, Foulkes! You don't know him? Never mind. No, he's not playing in the West End now. It's all right, Foulkes!"

He put down the receiver and said more soberly: "Well, Markham, he was sent for, but he couldn't arrange to come to us. Can you continue the history of this eccentric?"

Little Markham had a sense of justice.

"Why, sir, he didn't come because he knew he wasn't ready for a big job. He'd rather postpone his chance than lose it, I guess. You see, he'd lost his nerve, Sir John. He came to us to cure himself, with plenty of first nights and quick studies."

"Ah! An artist then. He knew himself. That's rare," said Sir John with quick appreciation. "I like him for that. The golden rule, Markham: Know thyself. So easy, and yet how few of us—how few. Continue!"

"Well, sir, Mrs. Druce had played with him before the war. She made Druce take him; said he'd been a draw before and would be again. And so he was, except when he got stage-fright. But there it was. He'd go through a play without batting an eyelid for five nights, and then Magda looks at him for a second too long, or Miss Baring puts in one of her damned new readings, begging your pardon, Sir John, and Lot's wife isn't in it with Fane. Didn't even gag. Just stood and let the world go by!"

"Remember the secret panel scene, Nello!" Doucie prompted.

"Yes, there's a case in point. You remember the panel scene in Buckingham? Your scene, Sir John. Well, at the first night Martella had to haul Fane out of the secret room and say his lines for him and bundle him back at the end—he was that paralyzed. She kept her head as usual, and they never spotted anything in front. But I tell you, sir, it was ticklish.

"And afterward Fane bumps into the prompt corner looking like a chewed rag. 'My nerve's gone,' he says. 'I tell you it's gone for good. What am I going to do?' 'Oh, get out,' I said. 'Go and cry somewhere else! If I were Miss Baring I'd skin you alive. I've got the light cues to see to. You've made me miss one already with your tomfoolery. Get out!' I didn't see him again that night. God knows where he got to."

"I'll tell you where he got to, Sir John," said Doucie. "He went to Martella's dressing-room."

"Steady, Doucie," said Novello uneasily.

"Oh, nothing anyone need mind," said Doucie, woman of the world. "And we heard every word they said."

"We?" said Sir John frowning.

"Magda and me. We heard all Fane said anyhow. You know how that high voice of his carried, Nello. And Martella wasn't being horrid to him. She was just laughing, nicely, you know. I heard her say. 'Goodness, that's nothing, Mr. Fane! Let's do some rehearsing every day till you feel really sure of yourself.' And next day they began running over their scenes in odd corners. And I will say she steadied him. He never fluffed when she was on the stage after that. He saved his fluffs for Magda."

"For Mrs. Druce? He was uncomfortable with Mrs. Druce?"

"Yes, and Magda didn't like it—upset as she was already about Marion going. She'd have sold her soul to keep him. But there it was—Marion was out for himself. Nello said he'd never stay."

"No," said Markham, "not even on the salary he screwed out of the Druces."

"How much?"

"Ten, Sir John," said Novello with wide eyes. "It's a fact—and he only halving leads with Fane."

"It wasn't fair," broke in Doucie passionately, "with me and Nello at nine. Oh, it wasn't fair, Sir John! And Fane only got sixteen; and he'd played London and had twice Marion's experience. It wasn't fair."

Sir John nodded. He perfectly understood a bitterness he had himself once known.

"I did say something to Druce myself once," said Novello mildly. "But Druce said it was his wife's affair. She'd booked Marion and Fane, you know, while Druce was under the weather." And he lifted his elbow significantly.

"Did she?" Sir John lifted an eyebrow. "Both men?"

"Well, the fact was, Sir John, she had to have someone in tow. But as my wife said to me, she wouldn't tow Marion for long. He knew what he was doing. I'd bet on his being in London before Fane, for all Fane's start. I've met his sort before."

"Fane's the better actor when he doesn't dither," said Doucie professionally.

"Ah, it isn't acting that gets you anywhere," said Novello compassionately to his Doucie. "Many a time I've told her, sir, if it was only acting wanted, she wouldn't be tagging round with me in the provinces. But London doesn't only want acting," said Novello wistfully. "It wants push and go and—damn you, I don't want your money! I'm doing this to pass the time! Push and looks and je ne say quor," said Novello, his bright eyes devouring his leader. Then, completing the survey, "But principally je ne say quor," finished Novello with a sigh.

Sir John sipped his liqueur. "Ion Marion—Handell Fane, Anyone else?"

Novello reflected. "Tom Drewitt—James Jameson—but the Drewitts can vouch for him—the ladies—Druce himself—the supers—that's all, Sir John, inside the theater. But outside"—he threw up his arms—"the world's wide, Sir John. It might have been anybody. Tramps—and with tramps you've a motive—robbery! But otherwise, where's the motive?"

"Just so, where's the motive?" Sir John finished his liqueur with a sigh. "I don't know where to begin, Markham, do you?"

"Oh yes, sir," said Markham modestly, "I should say I knew where to begin."

The two stared at the serious little man.

"But if Sir John doesn't know, Nello—" began Ducie admonishingly.

But Sir John choked her with a smile and a lift of the hand. "We'll hear it, please, Mrs. Markham. At present I'm completely in the dark. If your husband can light a candle I'm the first to be grateful. Go on, Markham, where would you begin?"

"Why, sir, at Peridu! You see, sir, we've got to work on this idea that it was a third person killed Magda Druce. It might have been someone from outside or someone who was in the house already. But we know that there was only Miss Mitcham in the house besides Magda and Miss Baring. That leaves someone from outside who got in and did the murder. If he got in, he must have got out again. If he got out again, he must have made off somewhere, and if he had far to go through the streets, the chances are somebody noticed him. That's what I'd like to do—go to Peridu and ask questions. Find out if there's anyone in the whole town heard or saw a man walking through the streets at three that morning."

Sir John lighted a cigar, not answering.

"Of course," said little Markham, "as I said before, it's clumsy, but you've got to make some sort of beginning."

"Well," said Doucie, "there's that man to start with, that you thought you saw going round by the bakery."

"The policeman?" Her husband shook his head. "That was nothing."

"But it wasn't," Doucie insisted, "it wasn't the policeman that came along afterwards—Grogram."

"Tell me, please!" Sir John begged.

"You say, Nello," said Doucie. It was his story, and though she longed to tell it, for in her opinion Novello always spoiled a story, she held back.

"It's only this, sir," said Novello. "When I heard the knocking that night I got up and went to the window. I saw Druce, and I thought, he'll have the police soon if he goes on making that row. Then I saw a policeman coming round by the left, by the corner of the bakery. I said to Doucie here, 'Just as I thought! Here's the constable!' Doucie came to the window and looked out. 'Where's your constable?' she said. Well, I'd taken my eye off him to speak to her, and sure enough there was nobody in sight. Then she said to me, 'Oh, yes, I see now, there he is!' But when I looked there was another policeman coming round a different corner."

"What had become of the first one?" Sir John asked.

"I couldn't say, sir. He must have turned clean round and gone back."

"You're sure it wasn't the same man?" Sir John asked.

"No, sir! Couldn't have been. The corners are a hundred yards apart in this kind of square, and I only took my eye off him for two seconds."

Sir John sat silent once more, turning his empty glass in his hands, while they waited. At last he asked a question: "Are you free this afternoon?"

"Yes, Sir John."

"Can you give me a day or two of your time?"

"Yes, Sir John."

"Then, if I may suggest it," said Sir John, "my car shall take you home at once—no, no, Mr. Mark ham, finish your sweet; it's not so urgent as that—and wait while you put a few things into a suitcase." He caught Doucie's eye, imploring. "And Mrs. Markham too, if she will be so good."

"Oh, Sir John," Doucie murmured, incredulous, ecstatic. "Do you mean—"

"Yes," said Sir John. "We're going to Peridu!"

CHAPTER XIII Three Poor Players

APOTHECARY: Who calls so loud?

ROMEO: Come hither, man! I see that thou art poor.—Romeo and Juliet

Dusk was darkening a pink sky as the canary-colored Bentley drew into the Peridu station-yard. Sir John and his companions stepped out and hastily-effaced themselves within the station itself, while the car, with equal swiftness, but with no more actual sign of hurry than the swift and golden moon shows as she rolls over the horizon, rolled out of sight.

For the three travelers had elaborated a plan of campaign which required an instant elimination of the Bentley. Peridu was to be lured into talk; Peridu would not talk to the Bentley. Behold then three poor travelers, strolling players, strolling into Peridu down Station Road, and playing if not the rogue at least the vagabond, with as much energy as if the king and queen were watching. Sir John. Saumarez turned his collar up, ruffled his shining-hair, and set his hat at the wrong angle—which made, as Doucie gigglingly observed, quite a difference—and for the rest relied upon his art.

Doucie and Novello had no need to rely upon their art. In spite of the brown suit and the electric-blue georgette, they looked what they were—two poor players. As such Peridu recognized them, welcomed them for old sake's sake and their famed connection with Peridu's most thrilling event since King William refused to drink the waters there—twice—and the mayor fell down in a fit on his return from the Great Exhibition. On the Markhams' introduction Peridu was gracious to the third poor player also.

Doucie and Novello booked a room at their former lodgings; but the sister of Grogram the policeman, who officially did not let lodgings but "obliged" bachelors of good repute rather often with beds and breakfasts, was more than ready to accommodate Sir John. Grogram's sister—she had apparently no name of her own—placed a first-floor bedsitting-room at Sir John's disposal.

There he left the suitcase which Novello had carried for him from the station-yard; and though, as the policeman's sister told him, her gentlemen, bearing in mind her six children and her brother's house and her widowhood, never expected her to provide meals—breakfast was another matter. Grogram? Oh, Grogram was out. It was his late night. Did the gentleman want to see Grogram?

Well, they'd know at the police-station, if the gentleman couldn't wait till the morning.

The gentleman thought that they might just as well look up Grogram at the police-station. The landlady, intrigued by this unusual desire for her brother's company, and still more by the quality of the suitcase, prepared to relent yet further, and suggested knocking up a supper for the gentleman "for once" and "to oblige!"

But Sir John refused. He was sincerely terrified, not so much by the chamber in which he was to pass the night as by its several furnishments. The flockbed with its tester, brown rep curtains lined with turquoise blue, and turquoise blue sateen valence; the lace mats upon the mahogany double washhand-stand; the stuffed one-eyed otter upon the chest of drawers; the family of owls anchored upon antlers of an unknown beast above the door; the enlarged photographs of the man Grogram in his youth; the greenish Brussels carpet, its worn patches reinforced by mats of gingerous fleece; the rag quilt on either side of the bed, and the patchwork counterpane upon it, weighted as a king's pall—Sir John looked upon these things till, like Sheba, there was no more spirit in him.

"Is—is it aired?" asked Sir John wildly, perceiving an opportunity for retreat.

"Aired?" said the policeman's sister. "I should say it was aired. I had a joint 'ere in the spring," said the landlady reassuringly, "at least they came to me as joint. 'E used to set 'er shingle for 'er," said the landlady. "Every night, 'e used to—water-waves—hours they took over it! Did it with hot water and one of them shopping nets. Aired? You needn't worry. They 'ad a row in the end though, and she left sudden, and 'ow 'e did take on! Didn't seem to fancy anything but pineapple afterwards—tinned pineapple and weak tea, day in, day out! So I went back to singles after they cleared out. There was Mr. Percibell," said the landlord's sister thoughtfully, "and Mr. Mewsey, and that young Fane what give witness in the case,—yes, 'e was the last. But I've 'ad some of the kiddies in and out of it till yesterday. It's aired all right."

Sir John, revived by the word Fane, and the oblique reference to the object of his visit, made no further attempt at withdrawal. But receiving from the landlady a door-key of incredible size and solidity, and promising in return not to wake the children on his way upstairs, washed his hands, disarranged yet further his appearance and hastened forth for a walk-about, as he fondly imagined, with the Markhams.

He was undeceived. Walk-about was a phrase entirely incorrect as a description of the rest of the afternoon and evening. For Sir John's tentative suggestion for a cocktail and early dinner first at the Red Lion, before investigations began, though welcomed glowingly by Miss Dearing, was instantly struck aside and trampled on by that fighting bantam cock Novello, upon whom, now that his own crowing ground was reached, the direction of the expedition appeared inevitably to devolve.

For the grateful little man had flung himself into the business with an ardor that stupefied Sir John, accustomed as he was to good service. But service is one thing, and hero-worship another. It became dreadfully plain that Novello Markham perceived in the dull details of the expedition—the booking of lodgings, the parleyings with landladies, the inspection of exhibits, the pursuit of clues, the interviews with managers, policemen, stage-hands, inspectors, and the proprietor of the Red Lion—opportunities for Sir John to apply the technique of his art to the problems of life, to exercise that acumen, that awareness of the significance of trifles, that instant grasp of the situation, that power of reducing opposed personalities to a state of submissive servitude, which Novello so obviously took for granted that his patron possessed. Sir John had but to come, to see and conquer—but it was Novello's business to provide the opportunities.

He provided them till Sir John's feet were red-hot in his shoes, and his bannerlike smile but a faded tatter of itself. Late afternoon wore into evening and evening into night, arid still Markham would not let him dine.

"Miss Mitcham first, sir, I fancy," began Novello briskly, while Sir John transferred the large door key from one pocket to another, in the vain hope of adjusting its weight. "We'll pick up what we can there, and then go on to Marion's lodgings. They're a goodish way, but the trams run part of it. The show will be on by the time we're back, and we'll drop in for it. After that we might step along to the station for a chat with the inspector. He knows me. And perhaps across to the Red Lion and get a sandwich while we talk to the proprietor. And after that," said Novello doubtfully, "well, if Grogram's on his beat, it'll be about all we can do tonight, unless of course we get a clue to someone else whom we ought to see. But you'll get clues out of 'em right enough, sir. We can leave all that to you," finished Novello admiringly.

"There's tomorrow," began Sir John faintly.

"I know, sir, I know. You've got to be up bright and early and back in town tomorrow, sir. I realized that. It's awful the way time's creeping on. You can't afford to waste a minute, sir, if we're to get her clear. You needn't tell me that. Well, you shan't complain of waste of time, sir, if I can help it," said Novello earnestly, "not if we're up all night."

Thus cheering his leader with comfortable words, he piloted the little party to Regency Terrace. The first visit was to Markham's own lodgings to let Sir John look from the window and see for himself the lie of the street from above.

"That's where the first policeman stood, Sir John; and that's where Grogram, the second policeman, come running. You see, don't you, sir, it couldn't have been the same man. The distances are too great. Though why the first didn't come along when he heard the row still beats me. Well, we'll find that out at the station. Now, sir, Miss Mitcham's!"

They left the disappointed Doucie to crane after them from the window and continued their foray.

But if Sir John had begun to call himself a fool for mixing himself up in a profession that was not his, in order to fail where experts had not succeeded, his mood changed once more as Novello rat-tatted at the door upon which Gordon Druce had once hammered drunkenly and desperately. His sense of the gravity of the business deepened once more; his knowledge, too, of that queer latent capacity in him to succeed fantastically where others failed.

Also the situation was becoming once more familiar, and his sense of the stage awoke. He was so accustomed to having his entrance worked up for him that he had found the business of assisting at' such working-up, though a novelty, an intolerably tedious one; but once the scene was ready set for him, Sir John could enter—and did. Miss Mitcham recognized the fact at once. She might not know his name or his fame; she might never have seen him act; nevertheless, she knew a personage when she met one, however disordered his attire.

She reacted impeccably, withering the small maid who had admitted them with eye, and tongue. "Good evening, sir! Alice—why didn't you show the gentlemen straight into the sitting-room? That'll do now—don't argue with me. This way, sir! Certainly, sir! Of course, sir! Any question you wish to ask. The room itself? In here, sir! Anything I can do. Yes, sir, I knew Miss Martella well, poor lamb! With her grandmother for many years, sir, 'ousemaid first, then parlormaid. The 'ole business is perposterous, if I may say so, sir. You might as well convict Princess Mary. Excuse me, sir, but I can't 'ardly bear to speak of it."

But though she was anxious enough to help him, Sir John got little from her, save reiterated asservations of Martella's innocence.

"Could anyone have got into the house from the back? Look for yourself, sir!" She drew him into the inner room and showed him the window. It looked directly onto the stage door of the theater itself, with its built-out, flat-roofed porch, and double row of dingy dressing-room windows above. The window was nearly level with the porch roof, lifted high as a tall man's waist above the pavement.

"Easy enough to get in," Continued Miss Mitcham, "but it's a drop down again inside, sir!" And indeed, the window was set high in the wall as if the floor within was sunk below the level of the street. "I really don't see anyhow how anyone could have got in with the aspidistra filling up the window, not without upsetting the aspidistra, that is. Look at the size of it!"

"It's a fine plant," said Sir John. "Still, if he knew the room?"

"Well, sir, but who did? My callers don't come into this room; and I don't have many. I keep myself to myself, and did from a girl."

"Did Miss Baring have many visitors?"

"Only out of the company, sir. Mrs. Markham now and again, and Mr. Fane and Mr. Marion to tea: and little Mr. What's-his-name—the funny man with the squeaky voice."

"Tom Drewitt," said Markham.

"Drewitt, that's him. He came once."

Sir John turned. He had been walking about the room as he talked, shifting the folding doors to see if an intruder's head would be visible behind the aspidistra leaves, if he could get across the room without being reflected in one or other of the mirrors.

"A squeaky voice? Ah, that reminds me. In your evidence, Miss Mitcham, you spoke of hearing voices, angry voices?"

"Yes, sir, and so I did."

"Women's voices?"

"Yes, sir!"

"And one was Miss Baring's?"

"I wouldn't swear to that, sir. I didn't."

"No, I remember. But you swore at the time that they were women's voices?"

"Oh, yes, sir! You can't mistake a woman's voice."

"I've known a contralto—" Markham began.

"Oh, but they were high," said the landlady, "quite high."

"Just so." Sir John nodded, and returned to his folding doors, and after a moment passed behind them; while Novello, in accordance with their previous agreement engaged their hostess's attention.

This was easy to do. He had only to ask questions and listen with interest while she described the virtues of Martella's grandfather and grandmother, and the glories of their house and grounds. Indeed she got as far as the garden and was involved in the description of the greenhouse in which the aspidistra's infancy had been passed, when a feminine voice from the passage broke in upon them:

"Miss Mitcham! Miss Mitcham! Oh, God, Miss Mitcham, where

are you? The kitchen chimney's afire, Miss Mitcham!"

Miss Mitcham paled. "That Alice—" she began, and swept doorwards.

"One moment, Miss Mitcham," said Sir John gently, reappearing at the same instant.

"Excuse me, sir, but I can't stop now. That Alice of mine has set the chimney alight. Didn't you hear her calling?"

"That was me, Miss Mitcham," said Sir John. "Or is it 'I'? Do you know, Markham? I never know."

"Lord, sir," began Novello, as slowly and with delight he took in the situation. "That's one to us."

But Miss Mitcham was annoyed and would have said so if she had been given time. Sir John, however, was before her.

"I am ashamed to say, Miss Mitcham, that I played a trick upon you, for which I know you will forgive me. The high voice, Miss Mitcham, that you heard that night needn't have been a woman's—you've just admitted it."

Miss Mitcham was ruffled. "I haven't admitted anything, sir. No need to, I've nothing to conceal. And I must say, playing a trick like that on me in my own 'ouse, I don't like it. I don't 'old with tricks. I'd like to know what you mean by it, sir! Not at all funny, I call it. Chimney on fire, indeed! Brought me out all of a tremble. I'll thank you to keep your tricks to yourself another time, sir! And you, too, Mr. Markham, setting there grinning!"

Sir John's smile left his face, and he said sternly: "Miss Mitcham, do you realize that your evidence, as it stands, will hang Miss Baring, and that it is false evidence?"

"What's that, sir?" The woman's pleasant face whitened, and the anger died out of it. "Hang Miss Martella? Me? Why, dear lamb, I'd cut off my hands for her! But I had to tell the truth, didn't I? I swore to tell the truth. You mean to say my evidence—" Miss Mitcham's face began to pucker. And Sir John, having subdued, hastened to console.

"I'm not blaming you, Miss Mitcham. You told what you thought was the truth. We all know it. We all respected your distress. But it's a fact, nevertheless, that if you had not been so sure the voices you heard were women's voices the whole course of the case might have altered. You were sure you heard women. I had to prove to you that a man speaking in a high voice might, sleepy as you were, have deceived your ear. I have proved it. Be thankful that I have. It will help to save her life, Miss Mitcham, this trick that I've played upon you. And now, Markham—Yes, you shall hear later, Miss Mitcham; but I can't wait now. It's a question of time just now. Forgive me if I startled you. Good evening!"

He flashed his smile upon her as he swept Markham into the passage. "The theater, Markham, eh?"

"Well, sir, we did say Marion's lodgings," began Novello, much impressed, but still sticking to his program.

"Ion Marion had a deep voice. Two members of the company excluding yourself had high ones. Possibly, of course, the voice doesn't belong to the company at all. Nevertheless—the theater next, Markham," said Sir John, stepping out.

Novello looked up at his leader admiringly as he trotted beside him. Sir John was in charge.

But at the theater the two men received a shock. Neither manager nor stage-hands, though quite ready to talk, had anything whatever to say. Even the garrulous stage doorkeeper, proud of remembering every actor or actress to whom he had ever handed down letters from his rack, did not altogether deserve the ten shillings that passed at the close of the interview from Sir John's hand to his.

No, said he, there had been the usual letters for a few days for the company to be redirected; but no inquiries from unpaid landladies, no telegrams, nothing unusual. Mrs. Markham, as Mr. Markham knew, had written to inquire if her stage ring had been found; and it had, and he had forwarded it. As for the luggage of that murdering woman, that had been taken to the police-station or somewhere; he didn't know. And the dresser had packed poor Mrs. Druce's stage clothes with Mr. Druce's.

No, nothing had been forgotten in the dressing-rooms either. There was the usual mess of course, papers, grease paints, envelops and so forth, left behind. It was natural there should be after a six weeks' stay. A basin had been broken, a fixed basin under one of the windows in a first-floor dressing-room now he came to think of it. "But whether the Druce company did that or the next crowd, sir, I couldn't really tell you. Oh, yes, and one of the gents in the same room left his cigarette-case lying. I couldn't send it on—no address being left. So perhaps you, sir—" The stage doorkeeper fumbled in his lockers.

"I'll see to it," said Markham, mechanically holding out his hand; for he was accustomed to such small commissions. And the doorkeeper put into it an ivory case.

Thus unsatisfactorily the conclave ended; and the police-station, though it welcomed them, was not much more helpful. The local inspector liked his own voice and views, and the weary Sir John had to listen to a great deal that he had heard before, as well as much that he did not wish to hear, before little Markham could succeed in extracting the whereabouts of all the town policemen on the night of the crime. Their whereabouts, however, did not explain the presence of the policeman whom Markham was beginning to believe he had dreamed, not seen.

The extreme depression of the two investigators as they walked away at last was not lightened by realizing that it was long past closing time, and that the hotel would not welcome demanders of a meal, but not a bed, at half past eleven at night.

Timidly Novello suggested "a snack with me and Doucie, Sir John, before I see you home." Gloomily Sir John acquiesced. Yet the meal which, in spite of Doucie's efforts, was not a riotous one, had its moment. Filled but not satisfied by new bread, bloaters, raspberry jam and cheese, refreshed if not stimulated by a warm purplish beverage, Sir John came at last to the stage when he could be cheerful.

"May I smoke?" Sir John's eyebrow lifted winningly as he felt for his cigarette-case. Novello, hospitably anticipating, brought out his own in a hurry.

"Have one of mine, Sir John?"

"That's not your case, Nello!" cried Doucie.

Novello, realizing that he had brought out by mistake the chryselephantine trifle entrusted to him, threw it hastily down and began another search as he said: "It's Marion's. Got to forward it."

"Pretty," said Doucie, picking up the case.

"Look, Nello," said Doucie, snapping open the case, "it's got an inscription: 'M to Him.' I bet you Magda gave him that," said Doucie, her eyes gleaming. "Ah, that's how her money went! That cost something," said Doucie, examining the detail of the inlay. Why, that would pawn for ever so much—even now, with that brown mark, all over it! Pity," said Doucie, displaying the interior of the case. "Wonder what he spilled on it?"

"That," said Sir John, holding out his hand for the case, examining it, snapping it together, putting it down again, and lighting his cigarette before he spoke, "that, my dear Mrs. Markham, is a smear of blood."

"What?" cried little Markham, picking up the case in his turn.

Doucie snatched it from him. "It'll wash off," began Doucie. Then she caught her husband's eye. "Oh!" said Doucie in another voice. "Blood?"

"No, I don't think we'll wash it off, Mrs. Markham," said Sir John agreeably. "If I were you, Mrs. Markham, I'd get a nice clean handkerchief and wrap up that case very carefully indeed and give it to your husband to keep. And I think, Markham," finished Sir John, "that, all things considered, we will go back to town tomorrow as soon as we can get the car. We haven't done all we might, Markham, and I would like to locate your policeman, before we shake the dust of Peridu from our shoes; but one cannot have everything, and I think we have a clue or two to go on with. Yes—I wish we could have located your policeman," said Sir John rising to go. He added with a sigh: "And I wish you had allowed me to sleep at the Red Lion, Markham, instead of airing once more that impossible couch."

"Allowed, Sir John?" began little Novello nervously, as Doucie made a gesture of horror. "But, Sir John, you yourself—"

"Don't contradict me, Markham!" implored his employer. "Not now. I couldn't bear it. Think of the stuffed otter, Markham, and lead me gently to my doom. Good night, Mrs. Markham!"

"Au revoir, Sir John!" said Doucie with her best smile. And then, to round it: "A riderverci!"

She bowed the two men out, and fetching a clean handkerchief, employed herself till her husband's-return in wrapping up gingerly the gorgeous ivory case.

CHAPTER XIV The Policeman's Helmet

Peace, children, peace,
Incapable and shallow innocents—Richard III

Like Joseph, whom, in his organizing ability, his sense of the dramatic, and his taste in clothes, Sir John resembled, Sir John dreamed a dream.

He dreamed he was lying on a bag of damp tennis-balls, and that whenever he turned on that uneasy couch several balls rolled from under him and had to be found and restored to the main heap before his own slumbers and his friends' game could continue. He chased those tennis-balls through pricking shrubberies of barberry, retrieved them from beneath dead bodies and out of policemen's helmets, and ran up iron ladders into his own flies after them, because they had been tossed there by the elusive Handell Fane.

Handell Fane on the stage below was playing the French ambassador to Ion Marion's Henry V., and throwing tennis-balls about the stage—bounce, bump, bump, bounce! To locate more clearly the bouncing tennis-balls, Sir John opened his eyes; for it would be incorrect to say that he awoke. His state had been too tormented to be in any sense asleep; but he became aware that he had shifted from one state of consciousness to another.

"'Fugue', I suppose they'd have called it," said Sir John aloud, with extraordinary bitterness.

"I beg your pardon, sir," said a penetrating voice. "I didn't catch—Quiet, can't you, Johnnie!"

Sir John turned on what was left of the tennis-balls, which he now perceived were a mere dream version of the innumerable lumps in his flock mattress, and beheld the sister of the policeman Grogram at his bedside. One hand carried a large cup of tea, in a saucer filled with more of the mahogany-colored liquid, which lapped, agitated, against two rapidly decaying lumps of sugar, while with the other hand she steadied against her shoulder a hearty infant, who smiled at Sir John with an air of confidence that Sir John recognized as familiar though he could not tell where he had seen it before.

"Take it, sir, or 'e'll 'ave it over," said the landlady, hurriedly extending the cup and saucer. "Quiet, Johnnie, can't you! Edith, take Johnnie's 'and."

Mechanically accepting the beverage, the bewildered knight raised himself on his elbow and looked wildly outwards and down, and then perceived that his hostess was addressing, not himself, as for a fantastic moment he had imagined, but a sturdy male child imperfectly habited and still more imperfectly groomed. The boy clung to her skirts, while a younger girl, clasping a writhing kitten, strove with him for what was evidently regarded as a front seat.

An older girl, immediately behind the group, was weighed down by a large laden tray of black tin and a cold in the head, while the procession was completed by the figures of yet another boy and girl of that indeterminate age which the unmarried guess at six, seven, eight or nine. These last two alone did not crowd admiringly about the bedside, but with the air of habitues wandered round the room, taking stock of Sir John's luggage and fingering his clothes.

Sir John drew a deep breath, but he was not allowed to speak.

"Want to see my kittay?" demanded the small girl, and thrust forward the squirming sausage of fur.

"Quiet, Edith! Will you 'ave the tray on the bed, sir, or shall I pull over the chair?"

"Oh—oh, please don't trouble," said Sir John helplessly. "If you would put it down somewhere—anywhere—" said Sir John wildly, "I'll see to it myself. I—I'll dress first—I'll get up at once."

"Oh, don't say that, sir!" returned the landlady, while the eldest daughter approached the unprotected Sir John from the other side of the bed. "I know what you theater gents like! 'A cup o' tea and a kipper before I get up and I'm a new man, ma!' as my last lodger used to say. Put down the gentleman's shoe, Edith!"

"Boat for my kittay!" returned the infant.

"Drop it, I tell you! Gladys, take the cat away from 'er, do!"

She watched magisterially while Gladys, laying the tin tray

heavily across the lodger's legs, obeyed, then continued to speak regardless of the wail that immediately rose from the doubly defrauded Edith.

"Quiet, Edith! The children will follow me about," said the landlady confidentially. "It's 'ma, this!' and 'ma, that!' When would you like your 'ot water? When you like. Don't mind me! Live and let live, I say, though I never do make the beds before one as a rule. My gentlemen aren't often early."

"I'd like it as soon as possible," said Sir John, gingerly raising himself to a sitting position, for the tray, at each movement, gave a semi-musical wallop which shook but did not overturn its contents.

"You shall 'ave it," said the landlady agreeably, "as soon as I've got my brother's breakfast. 'E's just come 'ome. What is it, Edith?"

"Want my kittay!"

"Well, you can't 'ave your kitty, see! Albert, leave that suitcase alone, d'you 'ear me? The trouble they are to me," continued the landlady, "what with lodgers who 'ate children, and lodgers who encourage them to 'ang about," said the landlady eyeing Sir John accusingly, "you never know where you are, when it's 'olidays or 'ooping-cough. It's 'ma, ma, ma!' Upstairs and down."

Here the boy Johnnie gave unmistakable indications that it was not holidays that had at the moment kept the family at home; and Sir John, flinching, assumed his dress-rehearsal voice.

"If you would kindly put the tray on the table and let me have the hot water at once," said Sir John, "I will get up."

"Just as you like, of course," said the landlady, resigned, "though you'd better eat your breakfast where you are. I would. Run downstairs and put a couple of saucepans on, Gladys. And leave that bag alone, Albert, d'you 'ear me!"—in sudden wrath. "Time and again I've told you not to meddle with the lodgers' luggage. I'll 'ave your uncle take you to the lockup if you can't stop touching. Remember what come of it last time! Will always be touching," said the landlady confidentially, strolling however to the door as she spoke. "Some lodgers don't like it. There was one we 'ad in the summer—Fane 'is name was—time of the Druce case. You 'eard about the Druce case, I dare say?" The land-lady paused wistfully, the door-knob in her hand.

Sir John, suddenly feeling that the night, the bed, the breakfast, even the surrounding infancies were supremely worth enduring, called his craft to his aid, and nodded indifferently.

"My brother," said the landlady, "was the one as found the body. Called in, 'e was, by the 'usband. Done 'im a lot o' good, the Druce case did."

"Prettay kittay!" interrupted the enterprising Edith, who, having long since recovered possession of the animal, now appeared on the farther side of Sir John's couch, having crawled beneath it. "Like to stroke my kittay?"

The technique of art applied to the problems of life, said Sir John to himself; remembered Martella's tragic face and the last article in the Pillar-Box, and shifting on the tennis-balls, put out a friendly hand and tickled the kitten's ear. Edith, enraptured, hurled herself bodily on the bed, while the landlady from the doorway, commented approvingly.

"Well, fancy now! Look at that! There isn't many she takes to. Got some of your own, I'll lay. Ah, it's easy to tell. Now my last lodger, 'im I was telling you of, 'e wouldn't 'ave 'er near 'im, bless 'er little heart: as for Albert—really the way 'e went on that morning about Albert! I said to 'im at last—'Well,' I said, 'the child meant no 'arm.' "

"What had Albert done?" inquired Sir John, restraining the interest in his voice, while he surrendered to Edith what was left of the lumps of sugar.

"Done? Why, the child come in with me, as 'e did just now, and sees Mr. Fane's bag lying in a corner: and of course 'e's bound to open it. 'Oh Ma!' 'e says, the gentleman's got uncle's 'elmet.' And so 'e 'ad. I saw it myself. One of them stage policeman's costumes. And reely I couldn't see what 'arm it did the 'elmet, the child seeing it. It wasn't as if 'e'd put it on or anything. But the way Mr. Fane took on, you'd have thought it was wedding-cake!

"You never 'eard anything like it. But then theatricals they do go off the deep end easy. The late hours, I dare say. 'Well, reely, Mr. Fane,' I said, 'you needn't be'ave like Uncle Rex in his off-time, if the child 'as touched what 'e oughtn't.' And then 'e calmed down—said 'e was nervous of getting 'is stage-clothes spoiled, being the management's property. 'Well, what did you bring them away from the theater for then,' I said. Oh, he says he'd brought 'em 'ome to sponge and press. 'Well,' I says, 'you needn't be'ave as if Raw-head and Bloody-bones was after you, if you 'ave brought 'em 'ome to sponge and press! Shouting and cursing and frightening the child! Give the clothes to me and I'll press 'em for you,' I says, 'if that's 'all.' But no, he wouldn't 'ear of it. But 'e give Albert a shilling, and that was the end of that. There wasn't no 'arm in 'im, you might say," said the landlady. "But there it was: 'e couldn't bear anyone touching 'is things. And I will say that for 'im," said the land lady meditatively. "I've known others. Edith, come off the gentleman's bed!"

Sir John, his mind agog with thoughts which longed to translate themselves into action, surveyed with impatience the processional exit of the policeman's sister and her family. When the door banged behind the final child, he sprang from the bed so recently and so reluctantly abandoned by Edith, shaved himself, dressed himself, and sped forth to find Markham and communicate his news. They would, he thought, return instantly to London; they would invade the office of Trenny Rice; they would give Trenny Rice to think.

Sir John was preoccupied as he strode toward the Markham's lodgings; but even so, he could not help observing the unwonted quiet of the streets. They were bare, save for dogs; they echoed; and from some steeple came the clang of a bell.

"Confound it!" thought Sir John. "It's Sunday, of course. Nothing to be done! Rice always goes out of town. Another day wasted! But I'll write; he'll get it first thing tomorrow."

And he proceeded at a more moderate pace, wistfully considering the breakfast he had forsaken, the scent of warm fish, the pleasant, sharp odor of bacon; he longed for these almost with passion.

"Odd!" mused Sir John. "One is not, as a rule, emotional about breakfast. Not in London. But here things have other values. Emotions here may be stated in terms of kippers, and a child's dirty, prying fingers may open the gates of a prison."

Pleased with his neat phrasing, warm with his walk, and hungry after his unquiet night, Sir John ascended briskly the steps of the Markhams' lodgings, about which the smell of frying sausages hung like a garland; knocked, and went in.

CHAPTER XV The Legal Mind

Master, master! News, old news; and such as you never heard of!
—The Taming of the Shrew

Sir John stepped out of his car at the door of a small and perfect Georgian house, which stood in a cul-de-sac somewhere in the City of London. It might have been the house of a duke had it been situated farther west; but the tide of fashion, ebbing, had left it high and dry. Now, in the paneled rooms where once gentlemen in laced coats bent to ladies, clerks bent over desks, and black tin boxes rose in tiers to the molded ceilings.

It was, in fact, the office of Sir John's solicitor Mr. Trenny Rice, senior partner in that enormous firm Danby, Mareschal and Cuff. The firm dated back some hundred years, and its present partners were descended in the direct line, though their names differed from the original resounding three. Mr. Trenny Rice was the nephew of the last Mr. Cuff, Horatio Cuff, who had, at some time in the nineties, been President of the Law Society, and had collected furniture as a hobby. Some of his spoils were to be observed still in the room of Mr. Trenny Rice, and Sir John, entering, was tempted by them for the twentieth time to yield one day to the line of costume.

"Well, Sir John," the lawyer greeted him, "how have you fared?"

"Your room is exquisite," Sir John rejoined. "Why do I live in a gaunt modern building? My ceilings are too high, my fireplaces lack proportion. I don't know how I have the temerity to surround myself with Heppelwhite. Some day it will take vengeance. You permit your clients to smoke?"

"I encourage them to smoke," said the lawyer. "I have some cigars here."

Sir John waved them from him. "At eleven in the morning? No, no. The hour demands a cigarette. But I would accept a match."

He accepted the match, lit his cigarette with care, and sat back in reverie. Mr. Rice asked no questions. He, too, sat back, with the tail of a humorous eye on the clock. He would give Sir John three minutes, he thought, and then ask. This was against his principles, but a cabinet minister was due at twelve. However, Mr. Rice did not have to do violence to his principles; after ninety seconds or so Sir John spoke.

"No doubt my letter surprised you?"

"To some extent," Mr. Rice admitted cautiously. One did not admit to clients that one had been surprised, as the tactician, Sir John, should have known. "You appear to have gathered a great deal of information in a very limited space of time," he went on, "and one or two items are of great interest."

He paused.

"It is all exceedingly plausible—"

He paused.

"Plausible?" Sir John cried, exasperated by this lack of enthusiasm. "It is conclusive."

"No," said the lawyer slowly, "no; far from it.. It is circumstantial evidence; and you have to remember that we are to set it up against a finding that amounts to flagrante delicto."

Sir John rose, and took a more commanding position. He never felt at his best sitting down.

"Circumstantial, yes," said he, "but how circumstantial! True, I did not discover any person who actually saw the murder committed, but I think that certain of my facts are not easily dismissed. For example the cigarette-case, with its tell-tale smear of blood."

He produced it from his pocket; Mr. Rice was not impressed.

"How do you know it is blood?" he asked. "Have you had it analyzed?"

"Of course it is blood," Sir John rejoined. "What else could it be? And my policeman, my false policeman? Why should a man dress up and come here in a policeman's clothes? Who drank the brandy? What of my broken basin, and the voices, which need no longer be considered those of two women, but may equally probably have been those of a woman and a man? What of all these things?"

"Yes, my dear Sir John," said the lawyer, "you have given us a number of very interesting questions. Unfortunately, you have not provided equally satisfactory answers. Let us see, now, what you have to offer a jury." He checked the points on his fingers.

"An ivory cigarette-case, owner unknown, with a dubious smear, which may or may not be blood. If it is, what is to prove that it is the blood of the dead woman? A policeman is seen, who walks away from a street disturbance not on his beat. (The policeman on the beat was Grogram, who appeared in due course. The other man did not interfere because it was not his business.)

"One of the actors in the company takes his stage clothes home with him to clean and press. He objects to having the clothes fingered by a child. (I cannot see that the broken basin has any connection with the affair at all.)

"The voices which Miss Mitcham heard may have been those of a woman and a man. But what man? Produce him. What man came into that house between the hours of eleven and three, except Druce, Markham and Grogram? You cannot prove any thing. Finally, you, and one or two others, are convinced that the accused is innocent; my dear Sir John!"

"Rice," said Sir John, "listen. Do you never for one instant cease to be a solicitor?. Do you never let your thoughts range skywards? Among these deeds in their tin coffins, dead deeds, do you never dream of deeds imaginary, rainbow-colored, living?"

"Not in my public capacity," said the lawyer, smiling, "and you are here this morning as a client."

"Be private for an instant," Sir John implored. "Rice, I beg you; just for ten minutes cease to be a trustee, a commissioner for oaths, a functionary without bowels—"

"Go on," said Trenny Rice. "As a mere tax payer, I'm listening."

"I begin," said Sir John, "with the assumption that Martella Baring is innocent."

Mr. Rice nodded. Encouraged, Sir John continued,

"Presumably, therefore, some other person is guilty. But what other person? Evidently someone in the company. A tramp, an outsider, would have stolen. Nothing was missing. Now, man or woman? The only other women of the company were Mrs. Markham, who was safe in bed, and two unimportant ladies, also in bed. It was a man, therefore; and here I am inclined to limit the possibilities. I am inclined to believe that our choice lies between the two young men who occupied the dressing-room with the broken basin, in which the cigarette-case was found. Both the young men had access to policemen's uniforms. To one of them the case belongs."

"Which one?" asked the lawyer.

"That," said Sir John, "is what I propose in the next few minutes, to discover."

"How?" asked the lawyer.

"Ah, that I shall leave to you," Sir John answered blandly. "Did I hear a bell?"

"Why should you hear a bell?" demanded Rice.

"Because it is half past eleven," said Sir John, "and I told, or rather, Markham told one of the young men, Mr. Ion Marion, to be here at that hour. We haven't yet traced the other."

Mr. Rice eyed the complacent knight with wonder, and some irritation. "My dear Sir John, of course I'm ready to do anything I can. But my time's not my own. I've got Hamilton Mainwaring coming at twelve."

"To make his will?" asked Sir John, unmoved. "Well, his political testament was proved long ago; chiefly legacies to servants, as I remember. My dear Rice," said Sir John, suddenly becoming human, "I know the value of your time. Believe me, if it were anything else—but it's the girl's life. I think she's innocent; and by God, while there's a chance, I'll fight!"

Mr. Rice hesitated, then went to his telephone. "Mr. Ion Marion, is he there? Yes. Very well. Send him up when I ring. Now," said he to Sir John, "what's your plan of campaign?"

"Ask him," said Sir John rapidly, "about his relations with Magda Druce. You remember that piece of information I had from Markham. Ask him why he went off so suddenly on the morning of the tragedy. Ask about the uniform. Ask about the cigarette-case. Bluff him. I'll help!"

"Thank you," said the lawyer, with a trace of irony. "The rest, and the manner, you'll leave to me?"

Sir John bowed.

"In that case," said Trenny Rice, "as you are near it, will you ring the bell?"

They both knew the type when Ion Marion entered the room. He was easy, well-dressed, confident; the man halfway to success. His quick glance recognized Sir John, but he was puzzled by Rice, until the lawyer explained himself.

"Good morning, Mr. Marion. Sit down, if you please. I don't suppose you remember seeing me in court at the Peridu trial? I am

Miss Baring's solicitor. You know Sir John Saumarez?"

Sir John acknowledged the introduction and effaced himself. Ion Marion sat down, adjusting the knees of his trousers.

"Yes," said he. "I believe I remember your face. Dreadful business. Extraordinary to think of it happening to anybody one knows."

"Quite so," said Mr. Rice. "Well, Mr. Marion, I wonder if you can help me in any way?"

"Glad to be of use, of course," Marion answered, "only I told all I knew, at the trial."

"Just one or two facts, however," said Mr. Rice, "are not clear to me, and for my client's sake I must make investigations."

"An appeal, you mean?" Marion asked. "Glad to hear it. What can I tell you?"

"My first question I believe you would be prepared to answer for your own sake. I may tell you that certain allegations have been made, which reflect on your—relations with the dead woman."

"What do they say?" Marion asked calmly. "That I was in love with her?"

"Something of the kind. That you were discovered by Mr. Druce togetherin—an attitude which was open to misconstruction, and that he did, in fact, misconstrue it."

"Who told you all this?" asked Ion Marion.

"I am not able to give you my informant's name," returned Mr. Rice very smoothly, "but I should be glad to know—and you may be glad of a chance to state—whether it is true or not."

"Not," said Ion Marion briefly. "I know the incident you're referring to. We were rehearsing, and Druce made a mistake. He's a fool, Druce."

"There was nothing of that nature between you?"

"No," said Marion. "You've never traveled in a company, Mr. Rice, that's obvious. We all saw quite enough of each other in the theater. We were all sick of the sight of each other. Love-scenes on the stage were bad enough, without going out of one's way to look for them off it."

"So there was nothing between you at all?" Rice persisted.

"No," said Ion Marion, and met his eyes squarely.

The lawyer shifted in his chair, and passed on to the next point with an admirable casualness, stretching his hand towards the box of cigars.

"By the way, Mr. Marion, do you smoke?"

"Thanks," said Marion, "only a pipe. I won't have one now."

"Not even a cigarette?"

"No," said Marion, "I hate the cheap brands, and can't afford the others, so I stick to a pipe."

"Ah," said Trenny Rice, "then you are not the owner of this—have you the case, Sir John?"

He put the ivory case into Marion's hands. Marion turned it about, opened it, looked inside, and said as he shut it again: "No, but I know whose it is. It belongs to a man called Fane."

"The Handell Fane who gave evidence?" said Rice. "You recognize it?"

"Oh yes, I often saw it on him. Where did you find it."

"The stage doorkeeper, I believe, found it on the floor of one of the dressing-rooms, and gave it to Mr. Markham."

"He must have knocked it down again," said Marion. "Fane, I mean. It was on the floor that last morning at Peridu and I picked it up."

"You picked it up?"

"Yes, and put it on the dressing-table in case he missed it."

"There's an odd stain on it," said Rice. "Did you notice that?"

"Oh that?" said Ion Marion. "No, I didn't. Looks like blood, doesn't it? It probably is blood."

"Why," Rice inquired, "should it be blood?"

"Because I picked it up just after I'd cut my finger," Marion answered, "on a confounded basin that got broken."

Sir John turned from the fire into which he had been gazing and came forward; he did not omit to glance triumphantly at Trenny Rice.

"A basin, you said, Mr. Marion? What basin was that? Forgive this inquisition. Perhaps you may have gathered that it really is not as trivial as it may appear. From smaller causes great events have sprung before now."

"Yes," the lawyer corroborated, "if we can get certain facts into line—will you tell us what you can remember about this basin?"

"I don't remember anything except that it was broken," said Marion, "and it was perfectly good the night before. Solid basin, too. Somebody must have jumped on it to smash it like that."

"And the cigarette-case, you are sure, belongs to Mr. Fane?"

"Quite sure of that. I've handled it often."

His interlocutors were looking at each other; in their expressions Marion read disappointment mingled with something of triumph. He came to a conclusion, and laughed as he voiced it. "So that's it. Well, I assure you I'm not the murderer."

"My dear sir," said the lawyer, "nothing of the kind has been suggested for a moment—"

"No," said Marion, "and if you'd ever seen Magda Druce it wouldn't have been thought for a moment."

He laughed again; and pulling down his waistcoat, added,

"Magda! She wasn't the sort a man would risk his neck for, or his career, either. Provincial, thirty-seven, and a deuced bad actress—however, de mortuis." He took up his hat and gloves. "Do you want me any more, gentlemen? Sorry to have to dispel your illusions. But really I didn't do it."

"There is nothing else, I think," said Mr. Rice, consulting Sir John with a glance. "Thank you for coming. Good morning."

"Good morning," Ion Marion responded, "and good luck to your appeal. Poor little Martella!"

He bowed to Sir John, who did not offer his hand; and departed.

"Well?" said Trenny Rice. "We're not much farther on."

"Insufferable cub!" Sir John responded, his thoughts busy with their visitor. "And the worst of it is, Rice, he'll be owning a theater before long. Anyhow," he went on, "we've cleared up the question of the basin."

"No," said Trenny Rice, "he only said that it was broken. We knew that before."

"And the cigarette-case belongs to Fane."

"You've only this man's word for it. Besides, where is Fane?"

"I'll find him," said Sir John fiercely. "Meanwhile, have we got anything to go on for an appeal?"

Trenny Rice shook his head. "No, there's nothing here. I tell you frankly, Sir John, I have no hope, unless we can get something more out of the girl herself."

"Why not?" said Sir John with enthusiasm, "Why not?"

"They didn't get much out of her in court," Rice reminded him.

"They didn't ask her properly," said Sir John, "not as an intelligent man would ask."

"You?" said Trenny Rice.

"Why not?" asked Sir John; and dared him with a look to put his thoughts into words.

"Well," said Trenny Rice, "I suppose it could be done—"

"Of course it can be done," Sir John responded. "The home secretary's wife is one of my first-night props and stays."

"An interview," Trenny Rice mused; "it's possible. There's the bare chance that we may get something more out of her. If I approach the ' right people—"

"Leave that to me," said Sir John, very grandly. "I'll see to that."

The clock struck twelve.

"Mainwaring will be cooling his heels," said Sir John. "I'll go. Make him a delightful will, Rice. Make death appear as attractive to him as you can. The country will thank you."

He went. Mr. Trenny Rice looked after him, quietly laughed, and moving to the fireplace, rang the bell.

CHAPTER XVI Martella

By Jove! I'll play the hunter for thy life
With all my force, pursuit and policy.—Troilus and Cressida

The two men were very silent on their way to the prison. For the lawyer the visit was a matter of routine; it did not occur to him to comment on the details of the journey, the reception at the prison, the observance of the usual formalities. To the actor, on the other hand, the experience was so novel that he had no time to talk. He was too busy observing, and pigeonholing his observations for professional use. Also, the air of unreality that overhung the prison, as it inevitably overhangs any bricks and mortar routine community, made him feel as if he were in some theater run by strict evangelicals for the performance of carefully bowdlerized plays by Strindberg.

The solicitor's room into which they were shown, with its sanitas-covered walls and massive mahogany tables and chairs, was more like the third act of a Galsworthy than was sane. Indeed, now that he thought of it, the place was crazy in its sanity, its dreadful sanity. That was what was the matter with it. Better the tyrannies of the bagnio with all its filth and torments, thought Sir John, than this unnatural mercy of law and order translated into terms of brick, whitewash, sanitation, and silence.

Besides, the decency, the strength of the place oppressed him. He felt his gay quixotic mood drop from him like a mantle. He did not feel sure of himself any more. The life-rope he was throwing out to the condemned woman no longer seemed a strong cable of safety, but the gossamer thievings of a stage Puck from the relentless spider Destiny. How could such a rope hold?

He began marshaling the evidence he had gleaned in the last two days to restore his confidence. The second policeman, Handell Fane's stage uniform, his anger, the original position of the poker, the confusing of Miss Mitcham, the basin, the cigarette-case, the pain in Martella's head, his own conviction of Martella's innocence.

It was little enough to go upon. If Martella could not help them, or preserved that sullen obstinacy that had wrecked them at the trial, England's leading actor-manager, who had gone out to shear, would come home shorn. Delia would not laugh at him, little Markham's allegiance would not be shaken; and Ruthven Traill would not so much as dream that he, Saumarez, had attempted the retort courteous; but he himself would know it.

His own allegiance to that ideal leading actor of England would be shaken. He would have to laugh at himself, a thing he had never done yet. He would have to laugh, and let Martella go hang—literally, go hang!

He shivered. He did not want Martella to hang; he wanted to take her back to the Sheridan in triumph, his new find, his new and magnificently advertised star, bound to him by fantastic ties of pure gratitude. She would be perfectly satisfied with twenty pounds a week, and—

The door opened and Martella and the wardress came in.

His hobby-horse hobbled away more swiftly than such toy beasts usually do as he looked at her, and left him afoot and very sober.

He had expected—what? Corday? Tosca? Sarah Siddons as the Tragic Muse? Something of the kind! An accentuation at any rate, of the dark lady defiant of the Peridu case.

Instead there came in a pale child in a stupid dress, who recognized him joyfully, though she waited for Trenny Rice to say: "This is Sir John Saumarez."

Then she put out her hand, saying shyly, "We did meet before. You will have forgotten it."

He said quickly, "It's because I haven't forgotten."

She looked round for the wardress, "May I ask them to sit down?"

The grave woman nodded, not unkindly, glanced round the room and withdrew.

"Won't you sit down?" said Martella. And they sat. But, seated, she waited for them to take charge of the conversation, quietly attentive, her hands folded in her lap; her dark eyes turning from one speaker to another.

"The home secretary has allowed us an interview," began Trenny Rice.

She woke up at that with a start. She said—with the oddest smile:

"When they said, someone to see me, I thought it was a hoax; I thought it was—the other thing," said Martella. And with her irrepressible instinct for the language of the hands, her hands flashed to her throat and circled it for an instant. Then they dropped to her lap again. "I'm half sorry it wasn't. You don't know what it's like, the waiting," said Martella to the two free men.

"We're hoping," said the lawyer hurriedly, "that if you help us as we—as Sir John thinks you can help us—"

"Does he?" she broke in.. "Why? What has it got to do with him?" Her tone was innocent of offense. It held only the most candid pleased curiosity. Watching her, each man thought to himself that she did not in the least realize her position.

"Sir John has taken a deep interest in your case," began Trenny Rice.

"Oh, have you?" said Martella. She looked at him gratefully.

"Sir John believes, and I am inclined to agree with him, that he has discovered sufficient grounds for an appeal."

"Appeal?" Martella caught up the word sharply and half rose from her chair. "D'you mean you can prove I didn't do it?"

"I hope so—" Sir John was beginning; but the lawyer broke in:

"I beg your pardon. It would not do at this stage to raise false hopes, but I can at least say this—it may be possible to get a commutation."

"I won't have that," said Martella. "I tell you I won't have that."

The two men stared at her. She had risen from her chair, and if her lips trembled, her voice was like flint.

"I knew that would be the next thing," said Martella shuddering. "I knew they'd try to get me off and think they were doing me a kindness. Imprisonment for life—why, a week of it has driven me half crazy. I tell you I won't have that done to me.

"If they want to hang me they can: and they will. I know that. I've fought it and I've faced it and I've got over it—except at night," said Martella. "It'd be no worse than the dentist; and I do believe in God; and He knows perfectly well it isn't in me to do such a thing when I'm myself," said Martella with a shaking voice. "And if I do have fits as they say, then I'm better out of the way. And—and anyhow I've made up my mind that I can stand it.

"But to be in prison all my life when I haven't meant any harm—that's too much to pay for an accident. Appeal? I won't do it." Martella turned sharply on Sir John. "You—if you were a friend to me you wouldn't suggest it. You lock yourself up for one day, only one day, in your own bedroom before you come and suggest things—suggest things—"

Suddenly as she had begun she ceased. Then, as if a frost had nipped her between a breath and a breath, she began to shudder, arms, knees, body, as she looked at them, smiling still.

"I'm sticking to it," said Martella, her teeth chattering, "because it's what I used to think, before—before it all happened; but I don't pretend I like it, being hanged. You must see that."

Sir John rose and came to her. He took her icy hands in his and rubbed them, as you rub a child's hands when it has run in to you out of the cold.

"If you do as I tell you," he said deliberately, "I'll have you out of this in a month."

"Be careful, Sir John," warned the lawyer in an undertone. "It's a mere assumption."

"Assumption be damned. I say I'll have you out in a month if you're a good girl. You wanted to join my company, didn't you? Well, I expect my company to believe I know my business, and do as I tell them. So now then—will you do as I tell you or will you not?"

"I'll do—anything," said Martella weakly.

"Sit down then, and answer my questions."

"I—"

"We don't want any arguing—there's no time to waste on arguing," said Sir John.

She sat down in the seat that he pulled toward her. Her body no longer shook. The color was stealing back into her cheeks.

"Now then, Rice, fire ahead—Act I, scene I."

"I beg your pardon, Sir John?"

"Ask your questions, man! She'll answer them."

He rose and strolled over to the window. The lawyer coughed, and drew toward himself the foolscap and pencil which lay, as at a committee meeting, upon the table.

"Let us turn to the main question first, Miss Baring. You refused in court—and no doubt"—Trenny Rice hurriedly anticipated his difficult client's probable outburst—"for reasons that seemed to you impeccable—to mention a certain name."

Martella pressed her lips together.

"The name of the person," resumed Rice, with an appealing glance at Sir John's back, "over whom you and er—Mrs. Druce quarreled."

"Not quarreled," said Martella. "It takes two to make a quarrel."

"Oh? Quite, but—"

"I wouldn't quarrel with her," said Martella. "I just held myself in and answered her quietly."

Sir John in the window strangled a cough. Trenny Rice resumed with elaborate patience, but not hopefully, "Let us say then that you did not quarrel, but argued."

"No," said Martella, "not argued. She tried to say poisonous things, but I wouldn't let her. I just put my fingers in my ears and kept them there."

Sir John spoke from the window: "Note that, Trenny! It's important. Why didn't you say that at the trial?"

"Didn't I? Oh, but I said I wouldn't listen. It's the same thing."

"Not quite. Why did you do that, Miss Baring?"

"Yes, why did you do that, Miss Baring?" said Trenny Rice, scribbling. "It was—er—unusual."

"Well, what was I to do?" said Martella. "She would talk; and

I wasn't going to listen to—to the sort of things I knew she was going to say. I hate scandal," said Martella impatiently. She paused. "Besides," said Martella, "I knew it already."

"Knew what?" said Trenny Rice.

"What she was trying to tell me."

Sir John swung round. "What was she trying to tell you?"

"I can't tell you that," said Martella looking at him.

"Now, why not?"

"Yes, why not?" said Trenny Rice. "We're your friends, your advisers."

"Because," said Martella patiently. "It would give the person we talked about away. I've explained that," said Martella wearily, "till I'm tired."

Sir John returned to the table. "D'you mean that the person concerned might be suspected of the murder?"

"Oh, good Lord, no!" cried Martella. "He hasn't the remotest connection—That's why it wouldn't be fair to drag his name into the case."

Sir John drew a deep breath—a breath of relief, of triumph—and, from behind Martella's chair, caught the lawyer's eye and touched his own lip significantly. The pronoun had escaped neither of them.

"Why wouldn't it be fair? Won't you tell us that? Other people's names were involved—Markham, Druce, Fane—Marion. They all had to give evidence. Why should it be a special hardship to this particular person to have his name mentioned?"

She looked up at him.

"Tell me!" said Sir John.

She continued to look at him.

"I wonder if I ought to tell you," said Martella.

"It's four walls."

"Is it?"

"Absolutely," said Sir John and Trenny Rice.

"I wonder if it would matter," mused Martella, weighing Sir John's assurance, and taking no notice whatever of Trenny Rice.

Sir John spoke: "Look here, Miss Baring—we accept your motive: and it's very decent and all that. We'll even say that you're right, and accept the fact of this person's complete innocence—"

"But of course he's innocent: he's nothing whatever to do with it," said Martella.

"Give me a minute! I say we'll accept his innocence; but the fact does remain that the mere fact of his innocence might lead to the discovery of someone else's guilt."

Trenny Rice nodded. "Very possible," he said.

"I wonder," said Martella.

"It's not your place to wonder," said Sir John tartly. "We're honorable men; we've assured you of secrecy. To hesitate is to—to impugn—"

"Oh, I never meant that," said Martella, distressed.

"I—er—we accept your assurance," said Sir John, and paused. Well he knew the value of a pause. He resumed at the right moment. "And now tell us, please, why it should be specially hard for this particular person to be involved in a—a criminal case?"

"Mud sticks," said. Martella.

"Why to his coat specially?"

"He had a—disability," said Martella slowly. "He wouldn't wish it known."

"Did he tell you so?"

"Oh no! He didn't know I knew it."

"How did you know it?"

"I—I could tell," said Martella uneasily.

"A disfigurement?"

"Oh no, nothing like that. It was something that nobody would realize in the usual way. But somehow or other Mrs. Druce must have found it out. I can't think how she did," said Martella. "But I'm sure she knew. Something she said made me know what was coming next. She was going to tell me. I knew the beastly sort of way she'd tell me. Well it wasn't her business, and I wasn't going to let her."

"And if this disability had been mentioned in court it would have affected this gentleman? It was a man, wasn't it?"

"Yes," said Martella unwillingly.

"An actor?"

"Why should you think—"

"If you both knew him. You would scarcely have mutual friends off the stage."

"You're quick," said Martella.

"Never mind my quickness. This—er—revelation would have affected his position?"

"To a certain extent," said Martella, choosing her words, "with certain people."

"Not with everyone?"

"Oh no, not with everyone." She hesitated. "With people who counted," said Martella, and hesitated again. And once more Sir John, unseen, made a warning gesture, and once more the lawyer refrained from speech.

"Well?" said Sir John at last, softly.

"I—" began Martella; and then in 'sudden decision, "No, it's not fair, I won't tell you," said Martella.

At this Sir John to his own surprise, lost his temper. Quietly, deliberately and imposingly flung his temper to kingdom come, and did not pause to watch where it fell.

"You realize the construction that will be placed on this—extraordinary consideration?" said he furiously.

"What construction?" demanded Martella, the gleam in her eye waking at the gleam in his.

"Why, that—that you're in love with the scoundrel," said Sir John Saumarez.

"Gently, gently," murmured Trenny Rice.

"Scoundrel?" said Martella, indignantly.

"I could find apter names if you like, to call a man who shelters behind a girl."

"He can't know that he was the subject of such a conversation," began Trenny Rice soothingly, but neither one of his difficult clients took the faintest notice of him.

"In love with him?" cried Martella wrathfully, as the accusation with all its implication soaked well into her consciousness. "Why, you must be lunatic—completely lunatic!"

"Why must I be lunatic?" demanded the owner of the Sheridan.

"But the man'sa chi-chi," said Martella, with her air of "Heaven give me patience!"

"Chi-chi?" broke in Trenny Rice clutching his head.

"Half-caste—a Eurasian," said Sir John quickly; and Martella added kindly, indulging his ignorance:

"It doesn't show. At least—you wouldn't notice. But if one's lived in India—"

"And his name?" said Sir John Saumarez.

She looked up at him. "It can't be necessary."

"His name?" thundered Sir John Saumarez.

"You know—honestly—" began Martella, "I don't think—"

"I'll do the thinking!"

"I—"

"Tell me!" said Sir John, and smiled at her.

"Handell Fane," said Martella.

Then the wardress came in.

CHAPTER XVII Acrobatics

These are the youths that thunder at a playhouse, and fight for bitten apples; that no audience but the tribulations of Tower Hill or the limbs of Limehouse, their dear brothers, are able to endure.
—Henry VIII

But for three anxious weeks nothing could be heard of Fane. "Find him for me," Sir John had said. "I'll know how to deal with him when I've had a look at him." The rest he had left to Markham.

Markham, and the helpers placed at his disposal by the Haroun al Raschid, Sir John Saumarez, patient, loyal, went the round of the West End agents with his inquiry. They remembered Fane, but he had dropped out, they said. They gave Markham his address. The address led nowhere. It was a lodging he had not used for a year.

Markham took another line: remembering Fane's versatility, his good voice, his athlete's training, he went to other agents, those who arranged music-hall bookings. In the third office, heavy with smoke and crowded with unnaturally cheerful photographs, he found traces of his quarry. Fane had changed his name and joined forces with a partner in an acrobatic turn. It was not a bad turn, the agents admitted—only Fane was too la-di-da. They were "on" that week at an outlying music-hall.

Back with his information went Markham to the Sheridan. Sir John thanked him charmingly, looked at the clock, and rang for his car.

"We shall be in time for the first house," Sir John explained. "I dislike having to hurry over my dinner. A glass of Madeira before we set out, Markham, to give you heart. This music-hall, no doubt, will be crude as life—as Tower Hill no doubt is crude. But after a glass of Madeira, life—and Tower Hill—may take on different aspects. 'Wine, that subtle alchemist—' You remember old Omar?"

They drank the Madeira without haste, entered the car and drove, still without haste, but at great speed, to the Hippodrome, Tower Hill.

It was some time since Sir John had last visited a music-hall. Indeed it was some time since he had entered any theater with the exception of his own. Officially his interest in the theater was great. Each year he ran a show at the theatrical garden-party; he sat on committees whose objects were the renaissance, encouragement, dragooning, and subsidizing of the drama; but actually his successes had left him little time to take a personal interest in what the drama was doing: and no time at all for music-halls.

He looked about him with interest. Disregarding the tenor vocalist who, for the time being, literally held the stage, gripping it with both feet like a cock as the top notes approached. Considering one by one the faces of the audience, Sir John decided that it would take courage to submit oneself to their judgment. These faces which in his own theater belonged to the gods of the gallery, here sat close to the stage, intent, in the intervals of eating, on having their money's worth of entertainment.

When, as sometimes happened, Sir John's own stalls did not receive full value, they never protested; they were too well bred and too well fed to protest. These stalls, who were neither the one nor the other, would not scruple to show their displeasure in the crudest manner. Here the casual art of the West End would not serve. This audience, which itself worked hard, demanded hard work of its entertainers, liked song to be noisy, dances to be restless, and jokes to be driven home like nails. Sir John could imagine no circumstances which would induce him to appear before it, and he feared for the vocalist, now intoning his last chorus:

"Dreaming, dreaming,
I long for you,
When I feel blue.
Just me and you,
Dreaming through.
So when my heart grows weary
When clouds are dark and dreary,
I seem to think I see your smile,
Dreaming through."

But this was the kind of song the audience understood, and could hum afterwards. The vocalist, moreover, was crimson with effort. Applause began before the last note, and was hearty enough to justify two reappearances of the singer, bowing.

He was succeeded by a bicycling turn—lady in pink tights, gentleman dressed as a drunkard—a comedienne in a red wig, whom the house welcomed with a roar, and whose only too comprehensible sallies were launched in a voice like a factory hooter. The conjurer who came after her was an anticlimax; he failed to interest, and when he retired the clamoring kettle-drums in the orchestra could not disguise lack of enthusiasm in the house.

Number six went up.

"Saltarelli Brothers," Novello murmured. "That's him. That's Fane."

Sir John nodded, and awaited with a slight quickening of his heart the lifting of the back-cloth with the view of Buckingham

Palace which had served as décor for the comedienne. It rose. The stage was set with two small platforms, a trapeze, and a succession of rings swinging from invisible battens. Other accessories lay on the floor, a hoop the width of a man's shoulders, a red silk handkerchief.

From opposite sides of the stage two men advanced and bowed; they were dressed alike in black tights with gold-spangled trunks; but while the face of the man on the right was unpainted, the face of the man on the left was grotesque, the mask of a clown. Sir John looked at Novello, his eyebrow lifted. Novello nodded toward the left; and Sir John, without comment, turned his attention to the face whose crude make-up was a defense against recognition or emotion.

The turn began briskly, with the two men swinging up each from his own platform by way of the horizontal bar to the rings. The clown, affecting incompetence, missed his grasp with one hand, and at once supplied its place with his foot, so that he hung awkwardly, his limbs in a tangle. His partner let himself down to a horizontal bar, gripped it, and swung to and fro to gather momentum until at last he turned completely over as though the bar had been the hub of a wheel and he the spoke. He made three or four complete revolutions, slowed, dropped to the ground, bowed.

It was Fane's turn. He came down from the rings where he had been suspended, watching with apparent amazement the slickness and ease of his partner's feats, and began to burlesque them. He took confident hold of the bar, nodded at the audience to assure them that the trick was nothing to him, and instantly, with an expression of surprise, fell flat, saving himself by his hands. He did a back spring to gather his wits, returned to the bar, explored it for the cause of his fall, and flicked a piece of fluff toward the wings, whence came a crash. The audience was familiar with this type of business, but it was the familiarity which breeds contempt; and, as it seemed to Sir John, Fane was too languid, too careless whether or no he pleased. His clowning was perfunctory, and a doubt intruded itself to which Markham gave voice.

"He's not up to it," said Novello. "You can't drop that sort of thing and pick it up again after ten years. He's playing the fool because he can't do the straight stuff."

"He's not getting it over," said Sir John, still intently watching.

The turn went on, close-packed, dangerous, but not showy. The competent partner twisted and swung himself with the facility of an ape, from ring to bar, from bar to stage again. He was a young Jew, strong but badly proportioned. Each one of his movements offered an opportunity for grace which his short-legged body denied. Fane, on the other hand, was slim yet rounded, with his muscles lying close to the bone; the pair, it seemed to Sir John, were wrongly cast: and if Markham were right, there lay the explanation. With this in his mind he watched the mechanical fooling, while his actor's sense registered the feel of the house.

"No, they don't like him," thought Sir John. "It's not going. Wonder how long that partnership will last?"

The two men were at the rings again now, Fane waiting, head downwards, his knees hooked through the rings, while the Jew worked himself backwards and forwards, gathered impetus and launched himself across the intervening space to be caught by Fane. Fane was not quick enough, or his hands' were damp; he missed the grasp, not completely, but enough to spoil the finish of the trick: and the Jew dropped to the ground landing neatly on his feet, but patently angry.

The house laid the blame where it was deserved by means of uncouth noises. The Jew beckoned Fane down to the stage, shot an inaudible sentence at him, and went on with the act alone. Fane stood on his platform at one side of the stage, slowly wiping his hands on the square of crimson silk. His partner was accomplishing unheard of dexterities, taking the act on his own shoulders, and physically, it was evident, a trifle distressed, since he had been obliged to miss the occasional few seconds' pause. When he dropped again to the floor, panting, there was a slight rattle of clapping.

He bowed twice; and signed to Fane to hand him the hoop. Fane gave it, and prepared to ascend the bar. The Jew cut him short with a gesture, and he halted at the edge of his platform uncertain what to do. The Jew, standing back, held the hoop above his head, showed it to the audience, turning it about so as to display both sides.

He, like the house, was totally unprepared for the next incident. As the hoop presented itself to him full circle, Fane leaped for it, hands out like a diver. It was not a yard in diameter, yet he went through it cleanly, without touching either shoulders or feet: and landed on his hands six feet beyond the astonished Jew.

It was a movement so quick, so clean, the grace of his arched body was so sure, that the house after an instant's silence, gave him reluctant applause. Drums augmented it; the two men acknowledged it; and the drop scene came down. It rose again a few moment later to reveal number seven—a gentleman seated at a table surrounded by concertinas of varying size.

Markham's eye inquired of Sir John who nodded. They rose, to the surprise of their neighbors, leaving the gentleman wringing a mournful intermezzo from his largest instrument. As they put on their coats in the vestibule Markham asked:

"What about it, sir? Would you like me to go behind?"

"I wonder," Sir John answered thoughtfully, and stood looking at the floor.

"He'd remember me," Novello went on. "It wouldn't look anything out of the way."

Sir John hesitated, then answered: "No. I think not. Leave it for today."

"But we may lose track of him," Novello insisted. "They can't have many bookings, a turn like that."

"We'll leave it," said Sir John with decision; and added deprecatingly: "You'll think it odd, Markham, but it occurs to me that I should enjoy a personal encounter with that young man. It would be disturbing; it might be surprising; but I have a curiously strong conviction," said Sir John, "that it would be worth while."

Knight and the squire stepped out together into the London street.

"The car's round the corner, sir," Markham reminded Sir John.

"Send it home!" said Sir John. "We'll walk. One can think walking. That is," said Sir John, "if you'd care to?"

The car slid away from them into streets that were dark as yew hedges. By the waterside, oblivious of dinner, silent, Sir John walked with his aide-de-camp. Their footsteps, after some adjustment on Markham's part, rang together, while their thoughts diverged, hovered above probabilities, dismissed these, and came at last into line.

"I think, Markham, d'you know, I'll send for that fellow."

"Yes, sir. Would he come?"

"Why not? How should he think that I suspect him? People respond, I find, as a rule," said Sir John, "when I ask them to come to the Sheridan."

"Yes, sir," Markham agreed fervently. "They do. But after all, he's been out of things in the West End for a good while now. They've forgotten him."

"People rarely see these things themselves with quite the same clearness," said Sir John; and left it at that.

They walked on for another hundred yards. Sir John avoided a dust-bin, and with a neat kick displaced a fragment of orange peel from its post of danger on the pavement.

"I believe," said he, "that it may be done through Foulkes. Foulkes was with Wakeling, you know, before he came to me. You said, did you not, that this young man was with Wakeling?"

"Yes, Sir John. Pre-war."

"Foulkes would remember. Foulkes shall remember. That's simple enough. He shall walk gladly into our parlor, Markham; and once there—" Sir John stopped in the middle of a stride and smiled down on the aide-de-camp. "Markham, are you familiar with a certain play—William's greatest to my mind, and one which as yet has found no adequate interpreter? The play which, for three hundred years, has offered a question and a philosophy to the world? You understand me, I see. Yes, the play of plays—'Hamlet, Prince of Denmark.' To the rest of the world it offers a problem; how if, for us, it should provide a solution?"

Markham choked down the inclination to tell Sir John of his ambition. It was not the moment. He answered only:

"Yes, sir! I know it. Every line."

"Then let me suggest for your consideration the series of events embodied in Act III, scene 2."

Markham stared at him.

"What? But that's the play!"

"Yes," Sir John confirmed, and began to walk on. "The play: do you happen to remember its title?"

"'The Mousetrap,' " said Novello, awed.

"Quite so," Sir John answered: "the Mousetrap. There will be three of us—three cats to one mouse."

For the first time Markham jested with Jupiter. "And the cheese, Sir John?"

"A fat part, Markham—a villain's part in a blood', and thunder. A part," said Sir John, stroking his chin, "that he will play, as I think we shall convince him, to the life."

CHAPTER XVIII Mr. Fane Reads a Part

We shall know by this fellow: the players cannot keep counsel: they'll tell all.—Hamlet.

For the fourth time Sir John looked at the clock on his desk. Twenty minutes to twelve, it said; the show had ended half an hour ago, and Sir John began to be restless, though he knew that the wait represented nothing more than a few drinks exchanged between Fane and Foulkes in the latter's office. He wondered if Fane had got wind of the plan; he wondered if somehow Foulkes had muddled it and let him go; he doubted the plan itself.

Walking up and down his room, halting by the window to watch the glittering advertisements, turning to question once more the face of the clock, Sir John, the imperturbable, was displaying all the symptoms of everyday stage-fright. It took time for him to realize this; but when at last he understood, he laughed and took the half-dozen deep breaths on which he had learned to rely. With the last of these came a knock.

"Come in!" said Sir John in his cool voice. "Is that you, Foulkes?"

"Yes, Sir John! Could you give me a moment?"

"Certainly. Who is that you have got with you? Ah, of course, I remember—this is the gentleman you suggested—"

"For 'Armytage,' Sir John. Mr. Handell Fane."

"Sit down, Mr. Fane, won't you?" Sir John was as grand a seigneur off the stage as on it. Actually he did nothing but look elegant; but his manner conveyed to the guest appreciation, hospitality and a sense of benefits to come. Outwardly, at least, Handell Fane was his match. The two men, each with a furious anxiety at his heart, though not the same anxiety, regarded each other with calm, and bandied courtesies. Mr. Foulkes, having introduced his protege and seen him installed in a chair with a cigarette, made for the door.

"Don't go, Foulkes," Sir John implored. "I may need you. I conduct these interviews so very badly," he continued, with his crumpled sideways smile, "and I leave out all the more important points. Perhaps I'd better begin with an explanation."

Handell Fane bowed, and Sir John proceeded to take him into his confidence. "I dare say Foulkes told you who is the author of the play in question?"

"No, sir. I understand you wanted it kept dark for a bit."

"You see Mr. Fane, how discreet he is? I can keep other people's secrets, but my own always escape me. Let us put the fact bluntly, without false shame. I wrote the play. That was simple enough. But it's proving astonishingly difficult to cast."

He swayed to and fro and looked at his guest as though for aid. Fane, well aware of the competence and other businesslike qualities that this helpless manner served to hide, smiled and answered:

"I can't understand that. You have the pick of London to choose from."

"There are so few actors now," said Sir John, gazing into remote distances. "People expect parts to be written for them, to express their own personality. I confess that as a rule they play themselves very well. But I deplore this device of setting a dog to act a dog. I think the first duty of an actor is to act. Don't you agree?"

"Certainly," said Handell Fane, amused. He recollected clearly Sir John's last three successes, in which Sir John had played himself with perfect fidelity down to the last waistcoat button.

"This part has a complete change of personality in the middle," Foulkes explained.

"Thank you, thank you," said Sir John, childishly grateful at being recalled to the point. "That's what I meant, but I can never express myself. The part, Mr. Fane, as Foulkes says, really needs acting. Now I had thought of Jocelyn Monk; but he's going to Australia; and I thought of Wetherby Langton, but he's got appendicitis. I was in despair until Foulkes remembered you. He told me your record—Manchester, wasn't it?"

"And one or two shows in town. I was with Wakeling—"

"Of course. Yes. Might I ask you to stand up for one moment?"

Handell Fane rose and Sir John surveyed him.

"Thank you. It's so difficult to appreciate the figure sitting down. D'you know, Foulkes, he looks, it. He looks it quite perfectly."

"That's what I thought, Sir John."

"I suppose," said Sir John wistfully, fingering a typescript, "you wouldn't care to read me a few lines—just to give me some idea—"

"Of course." Fane held out his hand for the papers. But Sir John retained them, frowning a little, and turning the pages as though reluctant to part with them.

"You see," he explained, "I've done something which you may think quite unjustifiable. Yet why? The greatest actor-manager of us all, Moliere, once said, 'I take my own where I find it!' The fact is, I have used for my theme a scrap of contemporary history. It's legitimate, I think. The Elizabethans permitted it. And such later masterpieces as 'George Barnwell' had their roots in reality. Let me see now—" He turned over a flimsy page or two only to break off and address Foulkes with some sharpness.

"This is illegible. Ask Waldron to come, will you? He's just next door. Ask him to bring the fair copy of Act I."

Foulkes opened the second door, disclosing the figure of a young man bending over a desk, to whom he spoke a few words.

"May one ask, Sir John," Handell Fane inquired, "what exactly is your theme?"

Sir John brightened under this encouragement, forgetting the sins of his typists. "You may question my taste," he replied, with an embarrassed if faint cough, breaking the awkward silence, "but as an artist you will understand the temptation. My theme, Mr. Fane," and he coughed again, "is the inner story of the Peridu murder."

"Indeed," said Handell Fane, and looked about him for an ashtray.

"Your indifference surprises me," Sir John continued. "Surely I understood that you were a member of Druce's company at the time."

"That is so."

"Then you actually knew both the women concerned?"

"I knew them well," said Handell Fane steadily.

The secretary and Foulkes came back into the room, the former bearing a typescript neatly bound in red paper. This he gave to Sir

John, who fingered it absently before he looked up with his inviting smile.

"Now we can begin," said he. "Will you have any objection to Foulkes and Waldron remaining? It makes more of an audience. Some people prefer that"

"I should prefer it," said Fane, again holding out his hand for the script. But Sir John had not done yet with explanations.

"I've had to alter it a little," said he regretfully. "One has to indulge the censor. Details, however, remain pretty much the same. The set, for instance, is a duplicate. We have the sitting-room divided from the bedroom by double doors. The sofa—I was present at the trial," said Sir John in soft aside, "and made one or two notes—the sofa runs across the corner, so. In front of it is the table on which the two women put their cocoa cups, and the flask of brandy which was, if you remember, offered by the murderess to the murdered woman, and refused. You know, Mr. Fane," said Sir John winningly, "I always wondered that nothing spectacular developed in connection with the brandy. Speaking as a dramatist, I can't help feeling that the brandy was not exploited with sufficient imagination! I should have drawn deductions from the brandy—and, of course, the poker. But the law has no sense of drama."

Sir John ranged the room as he spoke, shifting his admirable furniture to the order which had governed Miss Mitcham's bamboo table and her chairs.

"You'll be bored by me, I suppose," said he, with a characteristic lift of the left eyebrow that invariably indicated amused appeal. It would convince any audience that he could see a joke against himself. "And I'll admit it shows a certain lack of imagination, but I always find that if we have the actual set it helps me. The two fireplaces, now—the undisturbed front-room fireplace—and the second fireplace with its fender, and its harmful necessary poker, would both be on my left and your right, wouldn't they? Is that how you see the fireplaces, Mr. Fane?"

"Quite," said Handell Fane, and waited till the room was arranged to Sir John's liking and Sir John had returned to his writing-table and picked up the manuscript so recently condemned as illegible. Then:

"I believe," began Handell Fane, uncertainly, gathering up his hat and stick; but if he had intended a movement toward departure, Sir John did not see it.. He began to speak again; and Fane, after a moment's hesitation, laid down once more his hat and stick.

"I have thought it best," Sir John was saying, "to begin just before the actual murder. There is a short scene, between the women, which turns into a quarrel. I needn't read the whole of that. In the middle of it you make your entrance by the window, on the words—'Friends! I could tell you things about your friends that you don't know.' Just carry on from that point, will you?" And then as Fane turned from the desk and walked to the window, and with the subtle alteration of bearing that marks an actor attacking a part from an actor receiving his instructions, placed himself in position, Sir John's laugh rang out sunnily:

"But you've forgotten the script, Mr. Fane!"

"Oh—the script—" said Handell Fane; and the watching Sir John laughed again.

"You misunderstood me," said he. "Did you think I wanted you to gag? Oh no, Mr. Fane! At any rate, not yet. Later, perhaps, I may be grateful; but this part of the scene is already written out and cannot be altered. Here—" and he held out, open, the clean copy, bound in red.

For a moment Handled Fane stood without moving, framed in the square of night that was by day a casement, while the three men stared at him and Sir John's lazy hand made a gesture of appreciation. For the great electric sign of the Sheridan Theater was set at right angles to the open uncurtained window of Sir John's office; and the peripatetic light, shifting solemnly, monotonously, inevitably as destiny, from blood-red to unnatural green, to glassy white and so to blood-color again, turned the lithe, hesitating figure into Harlequin. Here was a haunted Harlequin with starved, high cheeks, flaring nostrils, and angry eyes, a Harlequin wavering yet poised for action, graceful as a cat, dangerous as a striped cat. It needed but the traditional wand to complete the picture of the traditional "odd man out." Sir John clapped softly.

"Charming, Mr. Fane, charming—all that I could hope. But you will need your script, and of course, the poker. Where are we? Ah, yes! I was just reading through the end of the scene between the women. Where is it? (You're sure you don't mind this? My methods are never very orthodox). Now—'Friends? I can tell you things—'" Sir John interrupted himself once more. "You're just behind the door by this time, Mr. Fane!" Then, patiently: "No, no, the other side. The heroine is standing on this side. She is the one you have to hit first. Besides, how about the poker—perhaps you could make a suggestion?"

"I think," said Fane, still deliberately, "you had better let me pick up the poker from the bedroom fireplace before I reach the folding doors."

"Splendid," Sir John agreed, and made a note with his gold pencil. "Now go on, please! You're behind the door. Try to imagine the man's state of mind—"

"Can I have a poker?" Fane asked suddenly.

"So sorry," Sir John apologized, "so very sorry. These are all electric fires."

He offered his pencil as a substitute. Fane made no movement to take it.

"Very well," said Sir John. "We must get on without it as best we can. Just let me see how you manage that entrance—the sudden rush from behind the door."

Fane's hands were trembling. To hide the movement he turned the page of the script he held. The three men heard a swift breath like a sob: and knew what caused it. The page at which he stared was blank.

"Yes?" Sir John inquired.

Fane let the papers fall and clenched his treacherous hands. "The script ends there," said he.

"Yes," Sir John answered gently. "I know. I had hoped that from that point I might persuade you to—collaborate!"

Fane's eyes searched the room. Foulkes leaned against the outer door. Waldron blocked the other. The window opened onto unknown depths. Having measured his chances and reached the only conclusion, Fane surveyed his captors and laughed.

"Well, why not?" said he.

They let that question pass. It demanded no answer.

"You've got most of it," he went on, "and you may as well have the rest. Clever to spot the brandy. Nobody else got that, though it was fairly obvious. I knew it was a risk, but I had to drink it or I couldn't have got out of the room. Blood makes me sick."

"So I understood," said Sir John, "from Mrs. Markham. Now, will you explain one or two points that puzzle me?"

Fane nodded.

"The policeman, for example," Sir John went on, "the policeman who came round the wrong corner?"

"If I tell you the whole story in my own way," said Fane, "that will come in."

"Very well," Sir John agreed. "But you'd better have a drink first. A bracer, Foulkes—no—not brandy," said Sir John reproachfully. "A whisky and soda, Foulkes."

There was whisky and soda on a table near the fireplace. Fane took the glass that was handed him and drank. They could hear his teeth chatter in the glass, yet he bowed to the three of them before he emptied it, gaily, almost with a flourish.

"Sit down," said Sir John.

"Thanks, I'll stand," Fane answered. "It won't take long. You know most of it and I won't waste your time. But you didn't get the main point. You don't know yet what made me do it."

"No," said Sir John suavely. "But for your own sake, Mr. Fane, it would be easier to tell us. Don't improvise, Mr. Fane!"

Fane flung up his head like a bull headed for the yard by pitchforks. "Improvise! God, I wish I could. I'll confess to that murder—yes, I murdered Magda—but this thing's different. It's something I've always hidden. It's what Magda Druce was going to tell that night. The words were almost out of her mouth when I stopped her."

"You were in the room?"

"Of course I was in the room. I'd been drinking with Druce, at the Red Lion. He'd had the proprietor in, jollying him; but he'd gone, and I was going too when Druce said, 'Oh, you may as well wait till Magda turns up.' I asked him where she was. 'Oh,' says Druce, 'the Baring girl asked her to supper, and I hope they get through supper together without another row. Magda didn't want to go, looks on it as humble-pie; but I put my foot down. Can't afford to lose the girl till the tour's over; and tantrum or no tantrum, I made Magda go. But I don't know that I'm wise,' says Druce, 'with Magda in one of her moods. She said she'd go, but she'd be damned if she'd be "musted." If the Baring tried it on, she'd make her sit up.' "

Handell Fane paused, hesitated, caught Sir John's eye, and resumed: "Ever been blackmailed?"

"Never," said Sir John blandly.

"Then you don't know what it feels like, to turn cold, cold—I knew well enough what Magda would be telling her once she lost her temper."

He stopped again, his face working—oblivious, it seemed, of his three watchers.

"What?" said Sir John at last, gently.

"About me. Magda always would have it that Martella and I—well, it was plain enough, I suppose, to a jealous woman, what the girl meant to me. But Magda didn't understand—didn't want to. She'd have known, if she'd cared to understand and watch; that Martella never looked at me—in that way. But there it was. I hoped, I schemed—Oh, have you never dreamed the impossible till it became possible to you? Till you couldn't believe facts when you, ran your head against them like walls? I thought she might alter in time, somehow, anyhow—so long, you see, as she didn't know."

"What?" said Sir John again.

"What Magda knew, about me. We—we'd lived together once," said Fane with that sallow flush of his. "She—she knew how to get hold of a boy. The war broke it; and I thanked God for the war. I loathed her. Cheap, she was. Well, after the war I came back. Nerve gone; couldn't get a job; ran into her in an agent's office, picking up suckers. She'd married that tippling fool Gordon; and I—I was out of a job," said Fane weakly.

"She was kind enough at first: But I hadn't been at Peridu a week before I found out what I was in for. She wanted money. Young Marion had taken her measure—the first man who ever had. She was in love with him. She—supplied him—or tried to! But Gordon Druce held on to his cash. He had that much sense. So Magda came to me, said she'd got me the job and wanted her commission—she called it her commission—and she'd get me sacked as incompetent if she didn't get it. I handed her over that week's salary, and half the next week, and the week after that. But then I began to have an answer.

"Martella, bless her sweet silly soul, saw the stafe I was in, and set out to rescue me, as she'd set out to rescue a—a galled horse," said Fane, with his bitter smile. "That's it—galled—galled!" He began to laugh noiselessly to himself: and Waldron, whose pencil had been racing over the paper as he took down Fane's words, sighed in momentary relief.

"Continue," said Sir John.

"Well, my answer was—that I wasn't so incompetent! Martella had put an end to that. I was getting my nerve back and I wasn't so easy to sack. So Magda changed her tune. If I didn't pay up she'd tell Martella what she knew, and there'd be an end of all dreams," said Handell Fane, and pushed back his lank hair with twitching fingers. "Only that night she'd issued her ultimatum. Ten pounds or she'd split to Martella.

"I thought it was bluff; she'd surely never kill the goose that laid her golden eggs. I'd forgotten that a woman in a rage doesn't care what she says or what she loses. But I'd heard no more from her that night, and I thought that for the night at least I was safe! There'd be another scene tomorrow, but—well, I was used to scenes! Then Druce tells me, d'you see, that she'd gone out to supper with my darling—against her will and in a damn nasty temper. Then I saw in a flash what was bound to happen if Martella lost hers. She had one, you know! Well, I had to act.

"I said good night, quiet as I could, and off I raced. I knew where Miss Baring lived and which rooms she had. Time and again I've wandered up and down, down and up, watching her shadow on the blind. It was an old-fashioned casement, bowed out into the street. You could be half-hidden in the angle between the bay and the wall, where the jasmine hung down. Often enough I'd hidden there to watch her. 'Charmed magic casements opening on the foam of perilous seas—' Perilous seas, my God! Yes, I knew her windows—oh yes, oh yes!"

The shrill tone was coming back into his voice.

"This is distressing for you. Won't you sit down?" said Sir John. His professional observation of the human passions was blurred by a human impulse of pity. But Fane continued his story as though he had not heard. He was looking into the past; the sounds he heard were three months old, and the room he saw was lighted by a single candle.

"Well, I got as far as the front door. I saw by the light that they were still in the front room. I could hear their voices. But then—d'you think I could knock? I didn't dare. The old stage-fright got me—paralyzing, deadly. But I knew the lay of the rooms, and I knew how Martella was about fresh air. I slipped round the back of the terrace. Window open. All dark. Light and voices behind the half-closed double doors. I swung myself over the sill, crouched by the fireplace, listened, heard what I expected—and Martella with that cool, courteous way of hers making it worse."

"Can you remember what they said?" asked Sir John.

"Remember?" He laughed. "Says Magda, 'You think you'll find it easy to get a job, don't you, when you clear out of here? You'll try London, I shouldn't wonder. And where do you suppose you'll get a reference?' And Martella says, 'I shan't ask you for one, Mrs. Druce, so please don't trouble.' Then Magda says, 'Oh, we all know you think you've only got to go to Saumarez! Friends at court, I suppose.' Says Martella, 'Yes, I have friends.' 'So've I,' says Magda, 'and I'll see to it that your behavior gets broadcasted wherever you try for a job.'

"'I shall be able to defend myself,' says' Martella. 'I may not have friends at court, but I have in the company.' 'D'you mean Marion or Fane or both?' says Magda. 'Oh, please—' says Martella. 'Because if you mean Marion,' says Magda, 'he's no fool to quarrel with his bread and butter, and if you mean Fane, I could tell you something about Fane—'

"'Oh, please—' said Martella again in that prim way of hers that always maddened Magda; and Magda was going on with 'Why, Fane—' sneering at me, you know, when I—I think I went off my head. I caught up the first thing that came to my hand as I crouched behind the fire-screen—on my honor, I don't know now what I meant to do—shout—knock down chairs—create some sort of disturbance—anything to stop that woman's tongue....

"But before I could move Martella said, 'I won't listen!' And I could see her through the half-open doors stuff her fingers into her ears like a child. Funny, it was—so funny that I actually laughed. Magda heard me; but Martella didn't, of course. She lifted her head and saw me behind Martella, creeping forward, and she called out,

'You—you dare!' and then to stop her I sprang at her.

"I caught Martella by the shoulder and dashed her aside. I didn't realize till afterwards that she'd caught her head against the table as she fell and was stunned. I didn't even think of her. It was Magda. I had to stop Martella knowing what Magda was trying to say. I had to, I tell you, I had to! I couldn't let Martella know."

"Know what, man? Know what?" shouted Sir John.

Handell Fane looked from one to another and opened his mouth. For a moment no sound came, then:

"I'm not white," said Handell Fane.

He waited for comment. None came. Fantastic motives enough had occurred to Sir John; but nothing so fantastic as this.

"My mother was a Eurasian," said Handell Fane. "'Where is Eurasia?' some fool asked once. Well, wherever it is I come from it. Half-caste, that's what I am—neither fish, flesh, fowl nor—"

"Steady," said Sir John, watching him intently.

"You say to me, steady"—Handell Fane's voice was shrill—"control myself, eh? Keep a stiff upper lip—British phlegm—public school tradition! White man's burden. Keep the flag flying and all the rest of it! Steady—even when you've murdered and are caught! Very proper and all that. But I'm not white."

"Just so," said Sir John. "And Miss Baring is still under sentence of death."

"Not now," said Fane, and drew in his breath as a man might who suddenly tastes freedom. "Not now: this clearsher."

"Don't pose!" said Sir John sharply. "You'd have let her hang."

Fane twisted his hands together.

"No," he said slowly. "Yes—perhaps—I don't know. Oh, God!" he broke out. "You can't understand what it is to be afraid."

"I should say your nerve's remarkably sound," said Sir John. "You all but got away with it."

"I'm afraid of contempt," Fane said deliberately, "and I'm afraid of dying."

"So are we all," said Sir John.

Fane caught him up. "Ah! You wouldn't let a woman be hanged when you loved her, because of a look."

"No," said Sir John, thinking it out: "I don't think—I say it in all humility—but I don't think I would save my own skin at a woman's expense. I hope not."

Handell Fane broke in: "I tell you I loved her. It was because I loved her, and because of a look I saw in her eyes once when a lascar brushed against her in the street. She can't help the feeling. She was born in India. She was brought up to look at us—so! But I love her. And if ever she'd looked at me—so! one of us would have died. As it was, that poor meddling fool of a woman died instead. She'd have let her know; and I'd rather she hanged than knew. Yes, when it came to that, I was ready to let her hang rather than let her know.

Then Sir John said gently—

"But she knew."

Handell Fane stared at him.

"She knew?"

"Certainly. She told me so herself. That was why she refused to allow your name to appear—she said that it wasn't fair when you were already ah—handicapped…."

Handell Fane's face—white, green, red, as the lights chased each other across it—suddenly twisted itself into a foolish clown's grimace of savage mockery—self-mockery.

"She knew? Oh, isn't that humorous, now? Isn't that good enough for a play? There's your third act, Sir John. You needn't ask me to collaborate. It's there already. So she knew. Makes you laugh, doesn't it? Fit to kill. It has killed too—Magda first—now me. I sell my soul to save her knowing, and all the time she knew. Ah, she was a good actress, my Martella—and sorry for me, don't you see, the poor fool, half-caste! So damned sorry for me that she never let on that it made her sick to play with me. 'Steady!' says Martella. 'Be kind to him—he can't help it—control yourself!' Yes—she had control—she was white. But I'm not white, and she knew it all the time. Now wouldn't you call that funny?"

Suddenly he flung himself down in the low chair by the window, and began to sob with an abandonment that made Foulkes shrug and Waldron turn away uncomfortably.

But Sir John watched, bright-eyed, unmoved. He had a very vivid recollection of Martella saying, "I don't pretend I like being hanged"; and he had no mercy whatever to bestow on Handell Fane.

"Pull yourself together, Mr. Fane," said Sir John coldly, at last. "If you wish to put right what you can, you must tell us the rest. The girl is still in prison."

Passion shook Handell Fane for the last time, as wind shakes an all but leafless tree, and left him. He straightened himself; he shrugged.

"The rest? What else is there to tell? I'll tell you anything I can."

"That policeman—" said Sir John Saumarez.

"Yes, I forgot that. When I saw Miss Baring lying on the floor I turned on Magda. She didn't finish what she was going to say.—It was pretty much as you've got it there!—She was frightened. No wonder. I still had the poker in my hand, and she kept her eyes on it all the time she spoke. She asked me what good I thought I'd done. Oh yes, she stood up to me. It may have been courage, or it may have been just fear.

"Well, I threatened her. I said that I had nothing to lose now, and that unless she swore to hold her tongue I'd kill her and myself too. At that, the fool, she began to scream. Oh, she did it well, too, the real Amy Robsart touch. She thought she had me, that I'd do anything to stop her letting out her silly peacock voice. So I would; so I did. Do you know what she called me? She called me a black beast. She called me a murdering nigger. I stopped her screaming then. Noises, yes, there were noises, little darkish noises, but she didn't scream again.

"I don't remember the feel of the blows, or how many times I struck her. The next thing I knew was seeing a dark oozy patch on the carpet near my left foot. I wanted to be sick, and—I had to get away. I didn't dare turn dizzy. There was a flask on the table, and I managed to get the last dram between my teeth. Then when Martella began to move—she was only stunned, I could see that—I got out as I got in, by the window."

"But you didn't go home at once," interpolated Sir John. "Why was that?"

"I was afraid. I knew the landlady would be in bed and asleep, and that it was Grogram's night watch. I could get in unnoticed all right; I had a key. No, it was that anyone who might notice me in the street, and wonder what I was doing at that hour, that scared me! And passers-by notice one another when the streets are empty. Besides, I had to wash my hands. The theater was a yard away. I hadn't a key, but I could climb."

"The basin!" cried Sir John; "the broken basin!"

"Ah! You spotted even that! It was easy enough to get in, but I'd forgotten the fixed basin under the window. I swung my leg over the sill and my foot went through it—wonder I didn't cut myself to pieces. Well—there I was safe for a minute. A little water cleaned me—but I had to get home.

"Then I had it. I'd been playing a policeman—there were four of us altogether—me and little Tichfield and the two supers—four uniforms—a protection, there being four. People might wonder what Handell Fane was doing at three in the morning, but no one ever wonders what a policeman's doing, no matter what hour they see him. Just as I slipped out again through a ground-floor window—the knocking began. Then I had a bad moment. It hadn't occurred to me that when they found out, a policeman would be needed; but I had enough sense to take the opposite direction from the row."

"Markham saw you," said Sir John. "So did his wife."

"Trust Doucie! Well, I walked back along Grogram's beat, playing the policeman literally for my life. I watched every step I took. I thought myself into the part as I'd never done before or since, and I got safe home."

"I see," said Sir John. "That puts it fairly straight, I think. Whatever happens now, Miss Baring's safe. You've been making notes, Waldron?"

"Yes, she's safe," Fane repeated. "She's safe. And now that's off my mind, I'm free too. I can make a fight for it."

"No doubt you'll have an opportunity in court," said Sir John coldly, and stretched out his hand to the telephone. The room was utterly quiet: the three men could hear the click as the receiver was taken off, could almost hear the operator's query. Sir John's voice, civil and smooth in answer:

"Scotland Yard, if you please."

And an instant later, in a shout that was neither civil nor smooth: "Stop him, Waldron! Look out, man! The window!"

There was a crash as the great standard lamp went over; the noise of feet—a grunt as two men's bodies collided. Against the shifting colored lights which the window framed, Sir John saw a dark shape loom and disappear. Foulkes, recovering, switched on the light at the door. Waldron was gasping, bent double over a chair. Sir John, rising from the floor, held one hand to his eye. Fane was gone.

CHAPTER XIX The Yellow Taxi

Scorn running with thy heels.—The Merchant of Venice

Sir John lost no time in trying to follow from the window the fugitive's movements. He knew his theater inside and out like the palm of his hand; and he knew that the electric sign, of which Fane had taken such unexpected advantage, afforded no halting-place until it ended on the flat roof just above the stage door. Thence to the ground was an easy drop for a tall man. Sir John's tie was askew; his eye pained him and already had begun stealthily to close; but the physical disarray did not extend to his wits.

"Foulkes, stay here," he ordered, "in case he doubles back. Waldron's out of it. I'll go after him."

"Let me come too, sir," Foulkes pleaded. "You can't tackle him alone. He's savage."

"Stay here," said Sir John, from outside the door.

The automatic lift was ready. Its leisurely descent was in strange contrast to Sir John's entrance and impetuous exit. Like a mad lamplighter Sir John coursed through his theater, turning on switches as he went, until he emerged at the stage door. The glare of a street lamp showed no figure on the flat roof, no figure climbing down the sheer side of the wall. When he was sure of this he ran along the narrow alley to its entrance, and twenty yards away saw a tall man with his foot on the step of a yellow taxi.

With his wind already coming short Sir John pursued; but the door of the taxi banged, the driver, seeing a clear run before him and urged by his fare, put on speed and drew away. There was no other cab in sight. Sir John, his elbows close to his sides, his one useful eye alert for a policeman or another vehicle, held on at a good ten miles an hour. His quarry was almost out of sight when it suddenly turned and disappeared altogether into a side street.

"Hell!" thought Sir John. "They'll lose me here!" But he followed, and almost at once was rewarded: a green taxi with its flag up emerged from the very street just as he reached the corner. Sir John leaped onto the box.

"What's the game?" said the driver, regarding him with disfavor and alarm.

"Did you pass a yellow taxi?" Sir John gasped.

The driver's silence gave consent.

"Go after it then!" said Sir John. "It's life or death."

"Doctor?" inquired the driver suspiciously. "Or police?"

"Police," Sir John replied, thinking to apply a spur.

The driver, whose hand had been on his gear lever, leaned back. "Not me!" said he firmly.

"For God's sake, get on!" Sir John implored, feeling for his notecase. "I'll make it worth your while."

"Not me!" the driver repeated. "I've seen enough of the police. I took that trunk wot 'ad the baby in it to St. Pancras Station, and the trouble I 'ad afterwards, you wouldn't believe."

Restraining an impulse to knock him off his box and take the wheel, Sir John produced from his case a five pound note and a card. These he handed to the driver who leaned out into the light to survey them. When he had mastered the half-dozen words engraved on the card he looked closely at the note, and equally closely, but with greater mistrust, at Sir John. The actor by this time had adjusted his collar: the light full upon his undamaged eye: summoning all his resolution, he met the taxi man's gaze with the smile his photographer knew, the smile for whose sake typists waited for hours in the rain, the smile which had never yet failed him. It did not fail him now.

"Cripes!" said the taxi man. "So it is!" And began to set the machinery in motion. He added, amid the jarring of gears: "My missus ought to be 'ere."

Sir John, his victory gained, abandoned charm, and became the despot once more, conscious that precious seconds were flying.

"Where does this street lead?" he demanded. "Which way did that taxi go? Did it turn off?"

"Couldn't 'ave," the driver replied. "There's only Coulson Street, and that's up at the far end."

"Get on then," said Sir John, but without much hope. Fane had five minutes' start. There might be half a dozen yellow taxis in sight when they reached the great thoroughfare. He felt resentful. It irked him not to come off best. He had the habit; he had been coming off best every night of his life for the past twelve years.

The taxi was advancing at a decent rate toward the intersecting street when the driver's voice roused him. "That's 'im!" said the driver. "Well—didn't know Coulson Street was up, I'll lay."

Sir John, with a forewarning of triumph at his heart, first heard, then saw, a yellow taxi coming swiftly round the corner. His own driver jarred on his brakes. They avoided collision by a couple of feet, and for an instant Sir John saw clearly the white face of Handell Fane. Then the taxi swung back in the direction from which it had come.

"After him!" said Sir John. "Don't lose him! We've got him now. He's wasted his start."

"Righto!" the driver replied, almost with animation, and turned his car to follow.

They raced up Kingsway. Sir John, straining forward as though by so doing he could increase the engine's power, kept an eye on his prey. It occurred to him that while he was doing his best to catch up the other car, he had not the slightest idea what to do when he caught it. He was no cinema actor. The prospect of leaping from one moving car to another did not please him. In a pause of his thoughts he became aware that the taxi had stopped.

"Get on!" said Sir John savagely. "What the devil—"

The driver indicated that the policeman's hand was up. Sir John swore, while a string of carts and trucks lumbered by on its way to Smithfield. The yellow taxi had already slipped through. The carts were top-heavily laden with crates. They set the pace, and the lorries crawled behind them. The eight or ten vehicles seemed to Sir John to take as long to pass as a lord mayor's show. At last the policeman dropped his hand, and the taxi wheeled to the right down High Holborn, past monumental shops with old houses sandwiched between them, past Staple Inn. Streets led away from the main road on either side, tempting streets which by night would be empty, and in which a man who knew his London might turn and twist like a hare. The driver, pursuing his way at an even pace, discouraged Sir John's notion of turning aside.

"What?" said the driver. "Down Leather Lane? Whatever for?"

"He might have gone in there," said Sir John, peering back at the cranny between tall buildings.

"Yes," said the driver, "and he might have gone down Chancery Lane, or Fetter Lane, or to Jericho' either, for all you know. Which way now?"

They had arrived at Holborn Circus where five ways meet. The yellow taxi was out of sight. Sir John, raising his eyes for guidance, observed the statue of some whiskered dignitary on horseback, who might have been, and indeed was, the prince consort. He was in uniform, and his feathered hat was held at arm's length pointing down St. Andrew Street in the direction of Ludgate Hill. Sir John accepted the omen.

"To your right," he ordered, and was obeyed. But. Ludgate Circus presented further difficulties. A. further embarrassment of choice. In despair, departing from his principles, Sir John asked a policeman standing on the corner, if he had seen a yellow taxi pass that way. The policeman took time to answer; he wore the elaborate helmet and red armlet of the city force to which he was new; and he had a tradition to maintain.

"Yellow taxi?" he repeated. "What number would it be?"

"How should I know?" said Sir John. "Surely the color's enough."

"Gent's got a bet on," said the driver, apologetically and in haste, well aware how touchy were the police, but also how human.

"Yes," said Sir John, taking the cue with practiced ease. "He's bet he can lose me in half an hour, given three minutes' start, and there are seven minutes still to go. If you could help me with any information, officer—"

Sir John's hand was at his trouser pocket. The constable looked tactfully away and responded with a clue:

"There was a yellow taxi down here a minute ago—near ran into a mail van—one o' these horse vans it was. Would that be the one, sir?"

"Yes, I think so," said Sir John feverishly. "Which way did he go?"

"Gentleman puts his head out of the window when they 'ad to pull up, and he shouts out to the driver, 'Straight on, you fool! Keep down toward the river!' Then the van went by and they turned off sharp making for St. Paul's, I should say. Thank you, sir! Good luck!"

On the word, Sir John and his taxi turned off too. There was a clear road before them, and they raced down it, down Ludgate Hill, down Watling Street, past the blank shops which by day sold food and underwear, linoleum and fountain pens, to the Royal Exchange. Here again was traffic, but this time luck served them, they reached the end of the queue as the policeman dropped his hand, and were in time to see a yellow taxi, which had headed the waiting line, disappearing down Cornhill.

Sir John, bumping sideways on the floor by the driver's box, began, despite discomfort and anxiety to feel an inner glow, a premonition that he was destined, once more, to come off best. In imagination Sir John gained on the yellow taxi, drew level, leaped for the running board, wrenched open the door, and in the darkness, with one blow or a series, avenged Martella's sufferings and his own black eye; but still the yellow taxi kept its lead.

"Bit of a change for you, this 'ere," said the driver, looking down at his fare. "Bit of a change from walking round in spats with a teacup."

"You've seen me play, then?" Sir John asked, distracted for a moment from imaginary fisticuffs.

"I've been twice with the missus," the driver replied. "She goes to a lot of these theaters. But what I say is, it's not my idea of spending money. Why, you can get a pint o' bitter for sevenpence, and not have to sit half the day on a camp stool for it either."

They turned a corner abruptly. Sir John, first craning forward to make sure that the quarry was still in sight, recovered his balance and continued the conversation.

"Questions of money apart," said he, "how did the performance strike you?"

"Performance?" said the driver. "Didn't see much performance the time I went. I seen some sea-lions do more performing that that at the Victoria Palace once. I'd rather 'ave sea-lions," said the driver with decision, "instead of a lot of young fellers in new trousers, following about after a lot of young women you couldn't 'ear what they said."

"That must have been 'Adolphus Dailies,'" said Sir John, interested, and feeling for the driver's opinion. But the driver maintained unbroken silence for a hundred yards or so, and his manner made Sir John disinclined to risk a direct question. He bent his mind once more to the task in hand.

They were approaching the river. A salty wind came from it, and an occasional scream from some small craft whose task is never done—tugs with a string of lighters following—police boats—barges. The fugitive, it seemed, was making for the docks, and might hope to baffle pursuit in the checkerwork of mean streets beyond the Tower.

"Get up closer, if you can," Sir John urged, a little breathless, for they were jolting over what appeared to be cobbled streets, and there was a penetrating smell of fish. "He'll try and shake us off here. D'you know this part of London well?"

Once more the driver did not answer, and once more Sir John did not press his inquiries. They turned out of the cobbled streets into a thoroughfare in which, even at this late hour, crowds sauntered: out of that into an alley: and off again at right angles. At the end of five minutes twisting and turning among streets indistinguishable from each other, they had lost the yellow taxi; at the end of three more minutes the driver halted. Words were not needed. Sir John wasted none, nor did he look about him for guidance. Policemen and statues were equally rare, as he knew, in this barbarous quarter.

"Straight on," he said at a venture, the glow which had warmed him fading.

The driver obeyed without enthusiasm or comment. At a laggard pace they entered some wider street, drove the full length of it, followed it when it adopted an alias.

"Damnation!" said Sir John suddenly. "This is a wild goose chase. It's no good going on; he's beaten us."

"I don't know these parts," the driver defended himself. "I got no call to know them. Talk about looking for a camel in a needle's eye, you'd lose a bloody elephant in this 'ere roundabout."

Sir John did not reproach him. As they slowed down he stepped to the pavement and walked a few steps, stretching and finding momentary ease. The driver, with an injured expression, slowly discovered a bent cigarette in some inner pocket, and lighted it with care. He feared recriminations; but Sir John's anger was directed against himself only: and he blamed himself that he had not left the whole business, with dignity, to the police. He had lost the murderer; but at least, as he remembered with relief, he had secured the confession and Martella's freedom. It wasnot, after all, absolute defeat. Still—with a sigh he opened the door and put his foot on the step. As he turned to give his order, the words left his mouth and he stood motionless; the yellow taxi, its flag up, was coming at a meek pace toward them.

CHAPTER XX For Lack of a Nail

Vaulting ambition, which o'erleaps itself
And falls on the other … how now? What news?—Macbeth

Sir John hailed it, both arms extended.

"Where did you drop that gentleman?" he asked without preliminary.

"Gentleman, you call him?" responded the driver of the yellow taxi—and without a trace of amusement, laughed.

"Where is he?" Sir John persisted.

The driver fumbled at length in a side pocket of his coat, and produced some coins which he held out in his palm beneath Sir John's nose.

"Look 'ere," said the driver. "That's wot 'e give me. Eight and sixpence! Eight bob and sixpence! That's all I get for dodging about London like a blooming mechanical hare, and fair shaking the guts out of my old engine!"

"Which way did he go?" Sir John interrupted.

"Eight and six on the clock it was," the driver continued, "and this hour of the night too! Catch me taking a fare without a hat again. I thought 'e'd been having a wet night, and they're free with their money generally speaking. I never said nothing to him neither. I tell you, you could 'ave knocked me down with half a brick when I looked at the clock and saw 'ow it was. Just as well for 'im he made off quick. Eight and sixpence!"

"So you didn't see which way he went?"

Sir John clung like a burr to the main point of interest, and his persistence was rewarded; for the driver, after a further jarring laugh, answered his question more fully than he had dared to hope.

"Ho!" said the driver. "Didn't I? Didn't I sit there like a stuffed monkey watching after 'im till I got my breath back? I see which way 'e went all right; and I don't 'know wot you want 'im for, but if it's to get back five bob 'e borrowed off of you, you're wasting time."

His own driver joined them at this point, and immediately entered on a conversation with the driver of the yellow cab, wherein the words eight and six-pence made their appearance with the fidelity of a recurring decimal.

"Look here," said Sir John, cutting them short, "you've got to take me on to where you left him."

He leaped onto the box, a proceeding which his own driver regarded without approval.

"'Ere!" he said, but without truculence. "Won't you be wanting me no more, guv'nor?"

"Murder?" he repeated after Sir John.

Dubiously, Sir John eyed him. The thought of "sea-lions" assailed his mind, and his look grew stern.

"I'd like to be in on this," said the driver forlornly. "It ain't the money. I've 'ad my fiver and thank you for it. Fact is, I miss the war. 'Tisn't often these days you get the chance of something doin'."

"Come on then!" said Sir John, with one generous gesture dismissing the sea-lions.

"Right-o, guv'nor!" the driver responded gratefully, and jumped for the running-board as the engine started.

One long street—one right turn—one left turn—and the cab began to slow down.

"That 'ouse it was," said the second driver, pointing to a wizened door which bore the number twenty-three.

Even as they looked, this opened, and a tall man, hatless, unmistakable, emerged. He looked right and left, perceived the taxi with its load, and began at once to run. The driver, Sir John's driver, and Sir John, venting their excitement according to their different traditions and vocabularies, made after him.. But the chase this time was not long; for at the first corner Fane encountered disaster. As he raced blindly round it, a policeman strolling in the opposite direction, a policeman trained to sudden emergencies by long association with that beat, put out a long leg and tripped him. The fall knocked the wind out of Fane. He was surrounded before he could regain it, and the very opportune policeman was questioning his pursuers.

"Murder?" he repeated after Sir John. "Near by 'ere, was it?"

"It happened some months ago," Sir John explained, "the murder at Peridu."

"Peridu's murder's been convicted," said the policeman. "What are you getting at!"

"No, I assure you," Sir John began.

"I can't take this man up on a charge what's already been proved against somebody else," said the policeman reasonably. "You couldn't expect it."

Crestfallen, inwardly condemning the etiquette of his country's laws, so helpful to criminals, so baffling to the righteous, Sir John with a glance consulted his allies. It was the driver of the yellow taxi who rose magnificently to the occasion.

"I got a charge," said the driver of the yellow taxi, red with inspiration. "I got one. I give him in charge for not paying me my legal fare. Two bob short it was. Ten and sixpence on the clock, and eight and sixpence 'e give me: and then off down the street same as now."

This simple expedient was altogether successful.

"That'll do," said the policeman. "You come along!" he addressed them both—the driver and the prostrate figure that lay flat yet supple as a cat on the pavement at his feet. Fane rose. The fight was out of him for the moment, and the three men pressed on him closely. He did not protest against the driver's lie, but obeyed the policeman's hand at his shoulder; and the procession moved on, the first driver, still avid of excitement and envious of his compeer's resource, following at Sir John's heels. The blue lamp of the station came in sight.

"I suppose," said Sir John to the constable, "your people will have a telephone? I think perhaps I ought to let Major Traill know at once."

Impressed, the policeman answered respectfully: "Tel-ephone? Yes, sir! You from the Yard, sir?"

"'E ought to be," the forlorn taxi driver chimed in. "Picked up the scent in Holborn like a bloodhound. He's one—" said the driver admiringly.

They entered the station and the presence of the sergeant in charge. This officer sat at a high desk in a fair-sized room, lighted by three staring electric bulbs and a skylight above the door. Near the door the desk stood at an angle. The sergeant looked without much interest at the group, and noted the formal charge. His expression changed with the policeman's next words.

"Gentleman"—indicating Sir John—"like to telephone, sir, to the Yard. Superintendent Traill."

"Yard, eh?" said the sergeant, taking in all the contradictions of Sir John's appearance.

"And if I may, to my secretary," Sir John answered, taking a card from its case. "This matter goes deeper than the question of an evaded fare. It will interest you, I think, inspector—"

The sergeant did not correct his misapprehension. He listened to Sir John's story, which was supplemented by the two drivers. He believed. He offered the use of the telephone on his own desk: and they all listened as Sir John's voice for the second time that evening, said civilly, smoothly:

"Scotland Yard, if you please."

This time Fane did not interrupt. He was haggard in the strong light, and his mouth had a trickle of blood at one corner. He still stood straight, but the reality of the situation had begun to overwhelm him. This room and Sir John's elegant study were two very different things. He had not taken the latter seriously; he had considered it as a stage set whose walls of lath and canvas could not effectively hold him in. He had slipped from the window with as much confidence as though there had been a net stretched beneath to catch him if by chance he should fall. Sir John, his manager, and his secretary were clever, but they were not professionals like these policemen. Fane did not fear individuals; he feared the system: the unimaginative, logical succession of precautions, surmountable one by one, together unassailable. He reminded himself that he had nothing to lose, and used his eyes while Sir John conversed at the telephone.

"Is that you, Ruthven? Saumarez speaking—John Saumarez. My dear fellow, I'm afraid I've brought you out of your bed. Forgive the indelicacy. So very sorry. I'm speaking from some police-station or other—"

"Orange Street," the sergeant prompted.

"Orange Street police-station. D'you know where that is? You do? You're astounding. Well, I've got a personage here for you—the Peridu murderer. I assure you I'm quite serious.. His confession is probably neatly typed by this time. My secretary was attending to it while I left. Yes, I allowed myself to hope you'd be interested. Will you really? How good of you! How very good of you! If you cared to ring up Waldron, or send a man round to my flat I'm sure you'd find the document quite in order. Witnesses? Certainly—three deep. You will? Splendid. Splendid. So glad to have been of use."

Sir John replaced the receiver and smiled at the sergeant.

"Coming without delay," he confided, "and bringing a warrant. That's good news, isn't it? Meanwhile two imaginary shillings stand between your guest and his freedom."

His voice lost its mockery as he spoke direct to Fane. "That's odd, you know. I believe just for the moment your nerves got out of hand. You'd shown extraordinary coolness all along. You'd allowed for every contingency; and yet at the end, when everything depends on making good your advantage, you pay a taxi his exact fare. If it hadn't been for that, we'd have lost you. We had lost you. I was turning home when I saw this fellow coming. Why, in heaven's name," said Sir John, with the dispassionate rage of an artist who sees a work of art bungled, "why in heaven's name didn't you give him a pound?"

"Think of a very good reason," said Handell Fane.

The naive Sir John stared, unable to conceive any very good reason for not tipping a taxi.

"Because I hadn't got it." Fane went on. "I had eight and sixpence, and that was all."

"I see," said Sir John slowly. "I wondered why you accepted the charge just now. Half a crown would have settled it."

"That was why," said Fane. "I hadn't got half a crown. But it's not important. You could have found another charge." He indicated Sir John's black eye, and continued, "Assault, for example."

"Lord!" said Sir John, amused. "I never thought of that. It went clean out of my head. But I'm not going to waste it. I'll find a use for it."

The voice of the sergeant in controversy with the two drivers interrupted their duologue.

"You be off!" he was saying. "You're not wanted here. I've got your names and addresses. You go and get your beauty sleep."

"We got a right to give evidence," said one driver, loath to miss the chance of a new sensation.

"That's right," the other confirmed, and added a little hazily, "We come 'ere of our own free will."

"Well, you leave of your own free will," said the sergeant threateningly. "You go along and find your cabs. Somebody's taken them to the pawnshop by this time, I shouldn't wonder."

This argument was not without its effect. They moved off; but at the door the driver of the yellow taxi turned and accosted the astonished Sir John.

"What about my fare," he inquired.

"Get along now!" said the sergeant. "Don't try to come that caper twice!"

"I tell you I haven't had a penny out of him," said the driver excitedly. "It'll be up on my clock; and I got to account to the guv'nor for what's on my clock. Stop me in the middle of the street, he did. I never arst him to, did I? I never arst him to get out of his own cab into mine, did I?"

"That's right, mate," the other driver agreed, secure in the possession of his own five-pound note.

With the first words of the exhortation, Sir John's right eyebrow had begun to lift. Deliberately it rose, arching like a bow; and when it had reached its maximum tension, the eye beneath launched at the driver a glance like an arrow. The driver faltered. He had ceased to speak even before Sir John's hand requested silence.

"You are to drive me home," said Sir John; adding after a tiny pause, "If you will be so good?"

"I'm out o' petrol, guv'nor," said the driver, intolerably confused, and struggling feebly to escape from the toils.

"Had you not better get some?" Sir John suggested. "I shall not require you for half an hour or so."

The driver abandoned the struggle; as others, more especially those who had known the honor of being produced by Sir John, had abandoned it before him.

"You have a card of mine, I think," said Sir John charmingly to his own driver. "Just let me have it, will you?"

Reluctantly it was handed over. The gold pencil which had figured that evening in an earlier scene scribbled a word or two beneath the line of engraving. "And your name?" Sir John asked.

"Reddiman," said the driver. "Albert Edward Reddiman."

"Thank you," said Sir John, and wrote this too on the card before he restored it. "If you care to present this at the box office—" He left the rest of the invitation unspoken.

The driver took the card, read it carefully, secreted it, and turned to his fellow colleague. Three sentences exchanged between them in the passages reached the ears of all in the charge-room.

"Oo's the bloody marquis?"

"Actor. Acts in a theayter."

"Cor! Got an eye like a referee."

Their voices died away, leaving behind, like an echo made visible, the smile of appreciation which Sir John could not restrain, and which even twisted Handell Fane's mouth, so as to set blood flowing again from the corner. He put up his handkerchief instinctively, and at sight of the dark stain upon it, grew livid and swayed.

"Hold up!" said the nearest policeman, taking his weight.

"Put him on the bench!" said the sergeant. "No reason why he shouldn't sit down."

He stepped down from his desk, and surveyed the prisoner closely. He was used to the stratagems of the intelligent criminal, but Fane's ugly pallor reassured him.

"Get him some water!" he ordered a subordinate. "No need to bring the doctor out to him at this time of night. And fetch a chair for the gentleman!"

"I understand it's a weakness of his," said Sir John. "He can't stand the sight of blood."

"Funny weakness to go with a charge like that," said the sergeant shortly. He looked curiously at Fane, and continued: "Ah well, they're always finicky. The way I've heard some carry on in the cells because of the bunk being hard, or a spot of grease in the soup—"

"Odd!" said Sir John. "Human nature. One is constantly baffled—"

"I don't know so much," said the sergeant. "You'll find the same three or four reasons for crime all the world over."

"Tell me!" said Sir John, interested.

The sergeant arranged his thoughts, and issued them slowly like so many warrants.

"First is—wanting something or other you haven't got. Second—

not wanting something you have got. Third—showing off."

He paused.

"That leaves out the unintentional criminal," said Sir John.

"I hadn't finished," said the sergeant. "Fourthly—temper. Fifthly—losing your nerve. That about covers it."

Sir John agreed. He did not look at Fane, whose temper once had mastered him so completely, and whose nerve had broken at the sound of a woman's voice in anger. He sat at ease on an unaccommodating wooden chair, while the guardian constables eyed him with unwinking interest, memorizing every detail of his appearance to tell their wives. He did not smoke, nor did he fidget. He merely sat, offering remarks from time to time, as much at home in that angular liver-colored room as the officials whose local habitation it was. As the huge clock above the sergeant's desk showed twenty minutes to two, the telephone bell rang. The sergeant attended to it, grunted once or twice, and put the instrument down.

"Send Cox in here!" he ordered.

One of the guardian constables left the room, and presently returned with another, wearing the expression of one whose collar had only recently been fastened.

"Get down to Lassiter Street!" said the sergeant. "Where's Bailey?"

"Gone sick, sir!"

The sergeant grunted. "Well, get down as quick as you can. Sheenies at it again."

The constable departed.

"Rough neighborhood, inspector?" Sir John asked.

"Tough lot of foreigners, sir," the sergeant answered. "And there's trouble sometimes with the men off the ships. Lascars and the like. But that's nothing," said the sergeant, tolerantly. "They don't know our ways and they don't like 'em. You can't blame them for it."

"I should like to send my young actors here to you, to study the objective outlook," said Sir John; and translated a moment later, "You take life here as it comes."

"Yes, I see meself looking after a pack of actors," said the sergeant sourly. "Newspaper men's bad enough. But with actors it'ud be a regular monkey house. No offense to you, sir!"

Sir John smiled; but inwardly he was a little chilled. He was accustomed to consider his profession a noble one, whose members unsparingly labored to educate and amuse the every-day world. He had taken for granted that the every-day world was grateful for his labors, and esteemed them as he did. It appeared, however, that to the official mind actors were no more than the irresponsibles of the fourth estate, no more than the unpaid versatile acrobats of the zoo. It was a shock to Sir John, whose contact with his public was indirect, mellowed by footlights. He allowed the subject to drop, and, crossing his legs, gazed abstractedly at the clock.

The sergeant, perceiving the conversation to be at an end, began to study the book that lay on the desk before him, to turn pages and tick off entries. The guardian constables still stared unwinkingly. Sir John sat, once or twice putting a hand to his eye, which, now that he had leisure to observe it, was beginning to pain him. In this silence and tedium of waiting, the excitement died down which for two hours had sustained him: and the whole affair, the interview, the chase, the capture, appeared to him in a different light—as an impulsive display whose object was not very clear.

The chase, in particular, seemed futile. The confession was the thing, and that had been attained in the first twenty minutes. Fane's escape was an extra, something not contemplated, which a wise man would have allowed to pass with a shrug. After all, the capture of a criminal, his crime once proved against him, was the business solely of the police. But the primitive Sir John had, in the shock of the moment, overpowered the wise man, who now sat on a kitchen chair fingering a painful bruise, and conscious, not of duty done but of having been deceived by an impulse.

Another development presented itself; this would mean a further appearance in the courts for Martella. She would be an essential witness; she would have to tell of the old semifriendship that existed between her and Fane, on which Fane's counsel would put God knows what construction. It would not do, thought Sir John. One such appearance, followed by triumphant vindication, made of her a clean woman wronged, in fact was good publicity; but this second affair, the suggestions of intrigue, the suggestions of complicity unacknowledged—no reputation could stand it. That would be notoriety, a very different thing, It would not do for his theater.

Made uncomfortable by these thoughts, Sir John shifted in his chair and in round terms cursed his own officiousness, coupled with his own efficiency; heartily wishing that he had left the whole thing in the hands of the police, where, as he told himself ironically, it would have been safe. His brooding was broken by the sound of a car drawing tip outside.

"That'll be them," said the sergeant, rising.

"Ah!" said Sir John: and rose too. Traill and a second personage—of importance, as Sir John, watching the respectful bearing of his immediate allies, concluded—entered the room together.

Major Traill, who was still sleepy, made no attempt to disguise this fact, or the condition of his temper as he addressed Sir John.

"Confound you, I've just been hearing all about it from Waldron. Extremely useful and all that, but why the devil couldn't you stage the frame-up at some reasonable hour? And why not have arranged to have one or two of us there? He nearly gave you the slip, Waldron said."

"He did," said Sir John. "However, all's well. I congratulate you, my dear fellow."

"Don't be a fool!" said Major Traill shortly. "'There's no credit to me."

But as he looked he perceived that the accustomed face was not symmetrical, and on the perfect dinner-jacket there was dust. He swung Sir John to the light, and a moment afterwards burst into a great whoop of laughter.

"By Jove!" said Major Traill between explosions, "it suits you. Walk down Bond Street tomorrow morning and you'll start a new fashion. Look at him, Towser! There's a tough for you! Oh—by the way—Towser—Inspector Towser—Sir John Saumarez!"

Inspector Towser finished reading his warrant before he turned and acknowledged the new acquaintanceship.

"It was a neat piece of work, sir," he said.

"Just what I was thinking. Looks as if it had been put on with grease-paint. Much too good to be true."

"I wasn't referring to the injury, sir," the inspector continued heavily. "I was referring to the way Sir John handled the confession. It's not a method I'd care to employ myself—"

"No, Towser, quite," said Major Traill.

"But there's no doubt it was a success. Puts me quite in mind of the French methods."

"You'll notice I don't pay any tribute, Johnnie," said Major Traill. "Not that I don't think you've pulled this off well. But you're getting too old to be sucking in flattery. It's time you were weaned."

"Should one ever be weaned from the milk of human kindness?" Sir John asked plaintively.

"Well, anyhow," said Major Traill, closing the conversation. "Towser's grateful."

Inspector Towser shook Sir John's proffered hand. "Yes, sir," said he, "I am. Mind, I don't say the Yard couldn't have done it, given the time."

"Time? Ah, yes," Sir John answered absently. "The law's delays. Have you ever tried to unhang a hanged woman, inspector? No? Ah! well, if you won't think me rude—"

He began to take his leave.

"Good-by. Sorry we haven't got a band," said Major Traill. "And Johnnie, I'll say this much—It was a far, far, better thing you did than any you have done."

Sir John laughed and moved toward the door against which the sergeant leaned. He did not reach it.

Fane had been huddled on the bench, his hands between his knees holding the empty glass. Now he bent forward to put this on the floor; and thus, with his feet well under him and hands touching the ground, was in the very attitude of a sprinter waiting for the pistol. For an instant, in the movement of Sir John's departure, no one regarded him. In that instant he measured his chances, and took his incredible course. He was across the room in a flash, leaped at the sergeant's desk, onto it; thence, as from a diving board, upward; and went through the skylight above the door as cleanly as though it had been a paper hoop.

CHAPTER XXI Exit a Runner

… This my hand will rather
The multitudinous seas incarnadine,
Making the green one red … —Macbeth

For the final adventures of Handell Fane, that swift runner, his pursuers had to rely on outside sources. The amused Sir John, the raging Traill, the solemnly excited sergeant—Fane, by the fog's aid, had eluded them all and was lost; but from the accounts of eye-witnesses, which trickled in, they could make a sufficient guess at the manner of his escape.

First there was the story of the police constable Dennis Albert Duty, who at two-twenty-five on the morning of the nineteenth observed a hatless man come lurching round the corner of Eel Street. The constable had supposed from his gait that the man was drunk. Seeing him, the man had broken into a stumbling run, and almost immediately turned down a narrow passage known as Coram's Alley, which led from Eel Street to the water. The constable did not follow, being of opinion that he could come to no harm on the mud. An hour later, repassing this passage on his beat, he went down it from curiosity, and observed on the pavement a dark smear that looked like blood. He went right through the archway and onto the cobbles that led down to the water; but there was no more blood and no further sign of the hatless man.

Two other witnesses were Henry Doggett, skipper of the tug Alice, and Stanley Harris his mate. They had set out on the turn of the tide with four barges in tow from Chelsea Borough Wharf to Tilbury. Just after passing the North fleet lighthouses Harris went along to the rearmost barge to extinguish the riding-light, which had been left burning. As he reached it a man rose up almost from under his feet and dived overboard. Harris shouted to Doggett and started to climb back over the barges to tell him to slow down—it would have been awkward, in fact impossible, to put about—but seeing that the man was a good swimmer and in no apparent danger of drowning, Harris did not take any further trouble, beyond telling Doggett of the incident. It was not unusual for a man to cadge a lift on the barges. This man was thin and had black hair. He seemed to have cut himself, for there was blood on the tarpaulins where he had been lying.

As for the captain of the Bonita, the Spanish fruitship, which sailed from Gravesend on the morning of the nineteenth, his story did not reach the police or the newspapers until the Peridu murder had long ceased to be news.

But the most circumstantial witness of the flight of Handell Fane was a woman—Ethel Clover—who was brought into Orange Street police-station as the result of a notice which had been circulated to pawnbrokers. She had attempted to pledge a watch with the inscription on the back "M to Him." She refused at first to answer any questions, but at last, after persuasion, relented; and one incident of the escape was fully revealed.

She had been sitting just inside Coram Alley, on the stones, with some idea of putting an end to things once for all. She had taken no money for two days, was hungry and had nowhere to go. Her state was evident from her appearance: the cracked patent-leather shoes had no stockings beneath them; her yellow hair was tousled; the paint on her face must have been put on days ago. She said that as she sat there on the cobbles making up her mind, she heard someone come running down the alley, and that she half got up in case it should be the Police' who, as she said, didn't like to see a person sitting too near the water, and were always shoving their noses in.

But it was not a policeman who emerged from the tunnel into the wavering light of the gas-lamp. It was a young man, tall and dark, with sweat running down his face. He stopped when he saw her, and made a kind of sound as if he had seen a ghost. He said "Magda" or some such name. But her name was Ethel—always had been—christened so in Wapping Church. Then he seemed to get a hold of himself, and she said to him—"What's up, dearie? Cops after you?" He said yes, that they were after him; but he thought he'd fooled them.

He gave her a funny look that frightened her. She knew what he meant. He thought she was going to give him away. Not her! She'd had enough of the police. She knew what they were, always so nosey, and on to a poor girl if she so much as stopped in the street for a minute to speak to a friend. So she was going to tell this man not to worry, when he out with his watch and put it into her hand. She remembered his very words. She could remember fast enough if she wasn't hurried. He said:

"Take it! Sell it! I give it to you. I haven't got any money. Take this instead, because you haven't seen me. You understand—you haven't seen me!"

And before she had time to say so much as a thank you, he was into the water and swimming. She stood watching until she couldn't see his head any more or the ripples he made. There were steamers going by at the time; he might have got on one of those, or on a barge; there were always barges going by.

With the watch—and it was a good one, a watch that you might get anything up to two pounds on—she turned out of Coram's Alley. She was afraid if the police were after him they might come and find her there, and take away the watch the gentleman had given her with his own hands. Just like the police, that would be. A poor girl hadn't a chance with them, always spying and nosing round. If she'd known she'd never have gone to the pawnbrokers; she'd have taken it to a gentleman a friend of hers knew, who gave you a fair price and didn't ask no questions. This was what came of trying to go straight for once....

The rest of her evidence was not relevant. When a slightly expurgated version reached Major Traill at Scotland Yard, he tossed it across to Inspector Towser and said:

"Another link! No use to us now though. He's got clean off by the look of things. Well, speaking unprofessionally, I'm not sorry. That fellow was a sportsman. Remember the jump he made? By Jove, that took some nerve. Why didn't he train for Olympic Games instead of taking to crime?"

Inspector Towser, who was quite unable to regard the matter unprofessionally, and whose pride had been hurt, made no reply.

Thus the story of Handell Fane's escape reached the police. And wires ran round the world for a little while, but without avail. The head bobbing in the river, swimming for dear life from very death, was the last appearance of the Peridu murderer among his father's people.

CHAPTER XXII First Night—Last Chapter

The lady shall say her mind freely, or the blank verse shall halt for't.—Hamlet

Sir John Saumarez, black and white against the forget-me-not blue curtains, smiled at the packed house. He did not bow, he stood; he looked; he smiled. He knew the house would do the rest of the work for him; and the house did. The new play, before the morning papers could say so or the libraries do their deal with the lesser elegance of Herbert Foulkes, was good for a year.

And yet the play was not in the least what the public expected. For weeks the public had been thrilled by accounts of how Sir John had played the hero in real life, with the same rare finish that graced his every rôle, upon the stage. The recital, though true, was as exciting as a serial by a practiced hand, as glamorous, almost as glossy. The chase of one shambling taxi by another yet more decrepit took on all the fire and grace of a Derby finish. Fane's leap for freedom became the salto mortale of the spangled acrobat of fiction. While Sir John's eye had not darkened by vulgar contact with knuckles, but had blossomed in the course of the struggle delicately as any pansy.

Despite all this the public was still curious. The public that is to say, quite frankly wanted to see Sir John's black eye. Sir John sympathized with that touch of nature which made his gallery and his boxes kin, and was prepared to permit the exhibition of his black eye—blue pencils are cheap—for at least nine months; but in his own way! He elected to display it behind a monocle. For Sir John, with his unerring perception of the difference between what the public thought it wanted and what the public actually did want, had revised his theatrical plans for the season.

On the day following the escape of Fane, and in close consultation with the pike-jawed Foulkes, Sir John had waved aside such dramatic studies of the sixth commandment as, "Hark from the Tombs," "Who Hangs," "The Spiders and the Fly," "The Gallow-Gird," "Ishmael," 'Daughter of Cain," "This Woman," "The Weaker," "Vengeance is Mine," "The Urge," "Subliminal," and "The Rest is Silence," and directed little Novello Markham to ring up the author of "Griselda's Garter."

The author of "Griselda's Garter" had made a profound study of Sir John Saumarez. He knew that any part written for that great man, must contain, if it were to do him justice, opportunities for tender humor, casual strength, wit, wistfulness, and his smile.

With these requirements in his mind, he produced in a month's time a light comedy concerning a grand duke who, with whimsical determination, had become chauffeur to a lady of uneasy virtue and recent fortune. In the course of this association he succeeded in the difficult task of improving her manners without strait-lacing her morals. With one of those flashes of insight into Sir John's mental processes which endeared him to Sir John, who disliked explaining himself as much as he disliked being misunderstood, the author labeled his comedy "Bracelets," and the public, with handcuffs in its mind, flocked to see Sir John's black eye.

Anticipation, however, varied with the price of the seats. The stalls, for example, while deriding his late exploits as a press stunt of overwhelming magnitude, secretly were amazed, and came to stare at this different person whom Sir John's suavity had so long concealed. The dress circle came unquestioning, worshiping, much as it was accustomed to go to church. The amphitheater too came to adore, but only if the play would permit; for the amphitheater was critical and expected full value for its three and sixpence. The gallery came with its enthusiasm barely contained, with a sense of ownership and pride. Sir John touched the pockets of the stalls most nearly, but the gallery's heart.

The inexorable gods of the gallery, the critical demons of the pit, and the mere eartheners of the circle—ecstatically recognizing and applauding suns, moons, planets, comets, meteors, meteorites, nebuli, thunderbolts, constellations, and galaxies, as well as the fixed stars of the first nighters' heaven—yet failed to recognize, retired in a dim corner of the stage box, the shape that had so recently rocketed across the front and back pages of the daily press, more lurid in its brilliance than any star.

Martella Baring's release had sent a curious wave of sentimental thankfulness across the breakfast tables. The odd, frank bearing which at her trial had lost her all sympathy established her—now that her innocence had so excitingly made plain—as more than a popular heroine. She was once more—the breakfast tables declared it—a nice woman. It was part of her reward for a certain uprightness of bearing that nobody said or wrote, and few whispered, the word advertisement, when it became known that Miss Baring did not intend to retire into the traditional obscurity of wronged innocence, but proposed ("If I can get a job," said Martella) to continue to earn her living upon the boards, as she had done before tragedy had overtaken her.

For, as Martella told her protectress, "My own people won't look at me: and I've got to live somehow, and I do like my job. Why should I stop acting because people said I did do what I didn't do? Why should I stop working because poor Magda—because Handell—"

She paused; she shuddered.

She had been calm since her conviction. She had taken her release with equal calmness, save for one indignant—"Pardon? Why should I be pardoned for what I never did? I ought to pardon them for convicting me for what I never did." She had left the prison a justified, independent woman, free to live again, to earn her own living again, yet with such terror in her soul as only an independent woman cart feel when the world is hostile and her employment insecure. She had left the prison, still with the habit of obedience to any authority upon her, left it to enter a limousine she had never seen before, and had been purred forward over velvet streets to a house she had never entered. A kindly woman—nurse, maid, wardress? how was she to know?—who had sat beside her in the confused drive, had shepherded her upstairs to a warm room of soft reds, crimsons, and purples, lighted by a flickering fire. She had been greeted—oh, bliss!—by a woman of her own class. She became the guest of some incarnate kindliness with gray hair, perfect clothes, and the groomed speech that reminded her of—whom?

She had said blindly, "Why am I here? Did Sir John—" and had broken off, flushing. John Saumarez had saved her, she knew that much; but what, the impulse of humanity apart that makes any stranger save any drowning woman, had a Martella Baring to do with a Sir John Saumarez?

Said the kindliness, delightedly:

"Ah, you recognized me! We are alike, aren't we, Johnnie and I? Johnnie doesn't much care to have it pointed out. It's all very well for a man to be like his mother; but for a man to be the living image of his aunt—I don't know why they don't like it, but they don't. Yes, Johnnie thought you'd better stay with me for a little, till you've had time to rest and look about you. But you needn't talk of the future now, not till you've had your tea and a hot bath. Nothing like a hot bath."

But later there had ensued that talk about the future, and it was then that Martella—grateful for her harborage, so anxious not to be a useless ship in harborage, and asserting her right not to stop working because poor Magda had ended tragically—had had a sudden swift vision.

She had seen, as a child sees in a kinetoscope, the last six months unreeled, from the summer days in that town "straight out of Mrs. Gaskell," the mimic, comic warfare in that company "straight out of Dickens," the abrupt and awful change from rehearsed horrors to the unrehearsed horror of poor dead Magda—poor dead Magda's silly, stiffening face, the incredible policeman, the ridiculous policestation, the trial itself, the condemned cell, the incredulity, the horror, the final, unutterable yet still incredulous despair, and then its sudden banishing.

"Oh, oh! I wish it all hadn't happened!" cried Martella in that hour, and wept in the friendly arms the first tears she had shed since that dead night in the little town of Peridu. And as she wept, remembered the one break in those reeling weeks of horror.

As a child wakens from nightmare to a happy dawn, and breathes more easily, only to fall back into the fag end of nightmare till true day comes to flood away the darkness for good, so the strange interview with John Saumarez had aroused her out of nightmare. She had clung to the memory of his look, his words to her, so nearly a stranger; even his sharp dragooning speeches had heartened her, so friendless, so unadvised as she had been. Now, remembering that lightening of the nightmare, she clung to this second stranger—"so like Johnnie"—and listened to all good advice, and wept, and obeyed, and was comforted.

And the advice was so easy to follow: "Stay in bed and rest till I tell you to get up! When you feel fit we'll go about a little, get some new clothes, face people, take the plunge. You've got to let yourself be seen, my dear, get it over. Of course they'll stare at you. But after all it's your profession to be stared at. Let them stare and they'll be kind."

Miss Simmonds was right. People were kind; inquisitive, tactless, but very kind. But kindest of all was Miss Simmonds. Martella was taken to lunches, teas, little dinners. She found it easier than she had believed possible to get back to the life to which her childhood had accustomed her. She found it easier to like people, to be liked by people. Old friends came to see her—Lady Plumptre wrote—she saw nearly everyone she had any liking for.

She did not see Sir John. She had written to him; she had had no answer. Sir John was exceedingly busy with the production of his new play. After all, why should she see Sir John? As it was she had enough to make her happy.

Yet she was not happy. She missed—and found it difficult to believe that she could so miss it, after the havoc it had brought in her life—the little company at Peridu; the herd life; the theatricalities; the simplicities; the nightly facing of a crowd.

"Born to it!" said Miss Simmonds, in one of her brief colloquies with her nephew at his flat above the theater. For it was agreed between them that when he was in one of his Noah's Ark rushes they should not lose touch with each other; but she went to see him, not he her. "Born to it! The shock's not budged her. She's aching to get back. One day she'll be thankful for all this business. It's made an artist of her."

"I'm not interested in the artist," said Sir John beautifully.

His aunt laughed. She knew well enough how inextricably mingled were his interest in the artist and his interest in the woman, and that he would never have permitted himself to take seriously any person that did not do his judgment credit. But she did not attempt to analyze him to himself aloud.

She said instead: "When your first night's over."

"Are you coming? I'm keeping you a box."

"Of course. It'll be a great night."

"We've turned away eight hundred already," said. Sir John casually.

"Of course," said Miss Simmonds.

"Shall you bring—"

"Why not?"

"She'll be recognized."

She looked at him shrewdly. "Of course. But you realized that. She must be prepared for that."

"I don't like notoriety for her," said Sir John fastidiously.

"Rubbish! She is notorious, poor child. She must make a virtue of it, make an asset of it. She could become something much more permanent than notorious, if guided."

"She is not easy to guide," said Sir John, with a vivid recollection of a white stubborn-faced girl in a hideous dress crying: "I won't let you appeal! Prison for life. I tell you I'd rather, rather behanged."

"I find her easy," said Miss Simmonds.

"Has she—er—referred—er—to my share?" He actually flushed, as his aunt noticed, though she made no comment, but answered:

"Not in so many words, but she recognized me instantly from the likeness to you."

"Did she now?" said Sir John, not quite sure if he were pleased.

"And, so far, is guided by me—as well as I can judge—purely on the strength of that likeness."

"Hm! Well, look here, Aunt Delia, after the show is over—" He outlined his arrangements.

"I'll think about it," said Miss Simmonds, and did not think any more about it, till the excitement of the final calls were dying down. These were vociferous, and answered at last by Sir John in person. At sight of him the clamor stilled to a rustle. Ladies stood with their resplendent cloaks half on, half off to catch what the voice from the stage was saying.

"Ladies and gentlemen," Sir John began, "I must ask your forgiveness if I do not this evening make the customary first-night speech. It is usual on these occasions, and, I think, commendable, to thank everybody, from gallery to stalls, from box-office to stage-door. But I believe that at last we have reached a point, you and I, where we may trust each other, where I may take your enjoyment and you may take my gratitude, my wholehearted gratitude, for granted."

Sir John paused, smiling at his audience, which smiled back, delighted with him. They knew that first-night speech—inevitable, delicately fulsome—and recognized the justice of the change of tone. It was no longer Sir John the actor-manager, the lead, the manikin, speaking; but Sir John the actor upon their own stage of the world, lead no more, but leader. They hushed indignantly when a voice from the gallery inquired, apparently without relevance:

"'Ey, Sir John? What price sea-lions?"

Sir John lifted his glance to the gallery, and unhesitatingly, but equally without relevance as it seemed to the wondering stalls, replied:

"What price? I should say at a guess, eight and sixpence!"

A roar answered him from that part of the gallery where Albert Edward Reddiman and his compeer had spent the intervals joyously retailing in detail the most sensational event of their lives. Sir John resumed:

"Forgive the interruption, ladies and gentlemen! It refers to an incident—a private matter—"

He gently, and as it were absently, put a hand to his darkened eye. The house guessed at the nature of the incident, and laughter broke out mingled with a cheer or two. Sir John waited, and when quiet was restored, spoke his last lines:

"I will not keep you; it is already late. But even though I do not thank you in so many words, I think I may fairly offer you my congratulations. It is the audience, not the playwright or the players, that makes a success. Ladies and gentlemen, we on this side of the footlights are your debtors."

He bowed finally. The forget-me-not blue curtains fell in suave folds to hide him; and he was free to be the pivot and center of the crowd which swelled upon the stage.

Then Miss Simmonds in the stalls checked her companion's movement.

"Let them get past us, my dear. We don't go their way. We'll go through the pass door. My nephew wants us to go to supper. Didn't I tell you?"

"No," protested Martella.

"Then I suppose I didn't," returned Miss Simmonds airily, as she groped her way through coveys of stage-hands round the wings, between a back curtain and the walls of the set, and so by way of the insecure door that had unspeakably irritated Sir John earlier in the evening, arrived, followed by the white-faced and panicked Martella, upon the crowded stage itself, where several stars and innumerable star-dust surrounded the small company who surrounded Sir John. As his irreverent aunt remarked to an entirely inattentive Martella:

"To watch him would be an education to the Prince of Wales himself."

But Martella's attention had been claimed by Miss Doucebell Dearing, in more than Persian attire of gold tissue, with a turquoise head-band and a furry jacket-wrap of a dubious white, whose turquoise-blue fringe and knotted cords did not altogether disguise the fact that it had in its day "half-lined" a tweed traveling coat. Doucie, in her jacket-wrap, bowed gallantly at anyone who looked her way. But she was a little frightened none the less by her own glory, and very glad indeed to see Martella, very eager to tell her that Novello was Sir John's right hand in the new show, and that Sir John had made such a point of Doucie's joining the supper-party after the show that Doucie hadn't liked to refuse.

And Doucie spoke the truth. That unimpressed and winged recorder of the humors of a Sir John may perhaps wipe out the records of several spectacular gestures in order to give good space to that invitation. Sir John had not wanted Doucie at his party; but he had a heart. Perhaps his supreme sense of his own sympathetic insight and generosity, however, did on the whole reward him for thus recklessly marring his reputation as a mixer of cocktails and men.

And as if to reward him, the gratified crowd did melt away quickly and contentedly under his skilful direction till there remained but the leading lady, the leading lady's husband, a viscount who had become a film star of the second magnitude, an actress who had married a baronet, a cabinet minister, a vivacious male dressmaker, a playwright, the playwright's betrothed, the editor of a woman's paper, three feminine effulgences from Shaftesbury Avenue theaters, a leading man, a publicity agent, the Markhams and the inevitable Foulkes. As Sir John said, with real relief, as he greeted Miss Simmonds, "At last we're by ourselves!"

He turned to Martella, skilfully detached from Mrs. Markham by his invaluable aunt.

"It was kind of you to come."

"It was kind of you to ask me," said Martella fervently.

He waved his guests forward, and they filed up stairs and down corridors to the lift, while, lingering a little, as he rounded up his party, his eyes roving as they passed along upon such evidences of neglect or disorder as the open dressing-room doors afforded, he said to Martella indulgently—

"And did you enjoy the play?"

"Yes," said Martella heartily.

"And did you—" Nothing would have induced Sir John to add, "Did you enjoy my acting?" but it was what he meant. He said, however, as they waited for the lift which had already hoisted the rest of the party upwards. "You must tell me, you know, exactly what you thought of it—of us—of" he laughed—"of me. It's so helpful to get impressions at first hand.

"I'm not one of those people who can't bear discussion of their work. On the contrary, I welcome it, I seek it! For example …" He explained to her, lightly, the joke about the eight and sixpence and the sea-lions. It was not quite the same story as the taxi-driver had told to his neighbors in the gallery, but it was a very good story indeed. Martella admired him for liking criticism even from a taxi-driver, and was only too glad to tell him, as he really seemed to want to know, the one thing about his acting which had always irritated her.

"Well, I have noticed—" said Martella charmingly, and hesitated.

"Tell me," he said indulgently.

"It's nothing much, of course," said Martella. "I don't suppose people would notice it unless they were professionals. But—"

"Well?" said he, a little less indulgently.

"Well," said Martella, frowning with interest, "you always look past a person when you speak to them. It doesn't show much from the front, of course," said Martella consolingly, "but—"

"But what?" said Sir John, who was not looking past her at the moment. "Do go on!"

She did, willingly. "It must make you very difficult to act with," said Martella.

"Possibly," said Sir John.

"There was a man in the last company I was in," she began.

"Handell Fane?" said Sir John viciously, and stopped dead because Martella had cried out:

"Oh—oh, how can you?" and then woefully, "I suppose you have the right to remind me."

They looked at each other. She had the ready tears in her eyes, and he was uncomfortably red. He was ardently hating himself, and disliking the novel sensation.

"It was unpardonable," he murmured. "There is no excuse. It was one of those things one says, and must blush for ever after. You'll never forgive me. I haven't the courage to ask you to."

Nor did he in words, though there was a little gesture of the hand which implored her, and which she disregarded. The hand dropped to his side as he repeated, "No excuse!"

"None," said Martella, bright-eyed—and waited for the excuse. She was twenty-three. She was penniless. She was a jail-bird. She was his aunt's protégée. She owed him her life, her reputation, her present comfort. Her professional future, they were both aware, was in his hands, to make or mar. Nevertheless, he quailed, and in his dismay, told the exact truth about himself, for the first time in his personal and professional career.

"Frankly," said Sir John, "one can say this to you—I—I—dislike criticism."

"I see," said Martella. Her dark eyes awaited—what? Further apology? He did not know, he hesitated, he was at his wit's end. He was very much upset.

His liftman, despairing of the two passengers ever leaving the lift, stood in the little archway holding back the curtains, with the sculptured resignation born of long experience. Sir John, as he knew well, might stand with one foot on safety, the other on the frail flooring of the lift, for another five minutes, 'for another fifty minutes.

"You see—" Sir John began again, doubtfully and his eyes roamed past her and swept the little hall, the alcove, the impassive servant, the glimpse of brightly lighted supper table. He did not know what he sought, but, as a matter of fact, he was missing his audience.

"There," said Martella calmly, her eyes recalling his, "that's what I mean."

"Oh, oh, I see!" said Sir John.

Then, outgeneraled, shaken, deserted by his reserves, in despair, he called out the old guard of his personality, and Martella encountered for the second time the direct assault of his smile. It was not the smile his photographer knew, not the smile that endeared him to typists; it appealed, it deprecated, it was a little unsure. And it had its effect, but not the one he expected, for she smiled back with such sudden friendliness, such disarming submission, that he felt himself once more beaten, amateur or no amateur, by a superior technician.

"It's absurd for us to talk like this," said Martella, with her alarming directness. "Of course you know more about acting than I'll ever know even when I'm as old as you are. But you did ask me; and I said that, stupidly, because my mind was elsewhere."

He looked at her helplessly. Minds did not usually roam in his presence. He felt that she was a phenomenon with which he was totally unfitted to cope; and, with one of his famous emotional decisions, made up his mind then and there that he only was capable of coping with her, that she was the most moving thing that had ever happened to him, and that professionally, with proper training, if, that is to say, he trained her himself—

"You see," Martella was saying, eagerly, "I've been wondering how ever, when I did get a chance, I was to say thank you for all that you've done for me. What haven't you done for me? You saved my life. You've got me back. You—oh, you know well enough what you've done."

He made the gesture that could so easily have stopped her if she had wanted to be stopped; but when she went on he did not repeat it. For after all he had exerted himself to a considerable extent, and he knew that he deserved all the thanks that she gave him; and she gave them too with an earnestness that enchanted him. Except in the looking-glass he had never seen anything so expressive as her smile. He literally could not bring himself to stop her.

"Well," said Martella. "I can't talk about it."

"I don't want you to," said Sir John regretfully.

"No, you wouldn't," said she, directing upon him her candid, admiring gaze; and he realized with an extraordinary sense of exhilaration that, though she might criticize his acting, she was more completely his partizan than anyone he had ever met in his life.

"She discriminates," he marveled. "That's what it is; she discriminates Astonishing! Not like the rest of them." And he continued to listen, rested.

"You never would," said Martella, "that's why, if I say thank you, I don't say it for the big thing that you know you've done for me. I say it for the little thing, that you don't know you've done for me. It's absurdly little to you, of course," said Martella, flushing anew, "but—do you know when I began to be grateful to you?"

"No," said he.

"Well," said she, "you'll have forgotten it, but you gave me an interview once. You said that I was most promising and that I could write to you when I'd been on tour for a year or two and got experience."

"Oh, my sons, my sins!" cried the actor-manager, remembering how many nymphs he had thus sent empty yet comforted away. But Martella did not perceive the implication.

"Well, it did encourage me," said Martella. "Of course I haven't toured for as long as you said; but I have had experience; and you did say I'd make an actress one day; and they said I was one in the courts. So—oh, you've done enough for me, I know. But I have tried—Will you do something else for me? Will you give me a job? You did say you would when I'd had experience; and I have had experience," said Martella, "all sorts of experience."

He looked at her hard. Serenely she returned his gaze. Sir John made up his mind.

"Experience?" said Sir John, "H'm! Your experience and my experience together—"

"Together?" breathed Martella, her eyes alight with excitement.

He smiled at her, but not as he smiled upon the stage. "It would be a new experience," said he, "for both of us."

"Oh—" said Martella enchanted.

"So," said he, taking her hand, "you consent?"

"Consent?" cried Martella, shaking it heartily. "Of course I consent. But goodness," cried Martella jubilantly, "I didn't think that would happen for another five years at least."

Sir John wondered if the lift were sinking under him. He brought his right foot into safety, but still the dazed feeling persisted. He could find no answer but the single, unintelligent query, "Didn't you?"

"No," Martella confirmed. She moved nearer. "I'll tell you something, shall I? We're not strangers after all this. D'you know, I had a photograph of you. I took it with me wherever we went. I used to put it on my mantelpiece in all my bed-sitting-rooms."

Sir John's world began to move back into perspective; she was, after all, not so unlike the others. But Martella had not done.

"And I'd absolutely made up my mind—I used to sit looking at it in the evenings—and I'd say to myself, 'I will—I will play leads for him some day.' "

Sir John's career had given him an eye for a comedy situation; and this, though ill-timed, was comedy pure. Spontaneously and with real appreciation he laughed. Martella's face clouded.

"You didn't mean it," she said reproachfully. "Then I don't think you ought to have said it. It wasn't fair."

"No," Sir John answered, recovering. "I did not mean it. At least, not primarily. What I was trying to suggest was a—a different sort of experience."

"I don't know what you mean—different," said Martella, all astray.

"Don't you?" said Sir John.

For the second time he held out a hand toward her, a sensitive hand that explained his entreaty. For the second time Martella disregarded it.

"I give you my word, I don't know what you're talking about," said she—reluctantly, for she hated to be thought stupid—"unless—oh, are you going into Shakespeare? I always hoped you would."

"Not Shakespeare—matrimony."

"Matrimony? Oh, but—matrimony?" Then her charming face broke up in immense amusement and surprise. "What, with me?" cried Martella.

"Certainly," said Sir John tartly.

"Well!" said Martella. She was certainly staggered, but she showed no signs of displeasure. "And I thought you meant Shakespeare. Well, I was a fool." She paused; she perpended. "But whatever would people say?" she began, half laughing, yet with the familiar frown deepening on her forehead.

"Say?" said Sir John. "Let 'em say! Come along and tell 'em, and then we'll find out."

"Oh, not yet," Martella begged. "I haven't said—we haven't thought."

But already the inward glow had begun to warm Sir John. Once more he was in his element. He was irresistible in his sudden realization that here too, despite unexpected sallies and forced strategic retreats, he was about to come off supremely best.

"Martella," said he, "be good enough to do as you're told. I forbid you to argue."

She had the last word, however.

"Argue?" cried Martella indignantly. "I never do!" and slipped her hand through his arm. They went together into the room and Sir John's man closed the door behind them. The liftman, observing this, sighed and sank earthward.

The assembled guests screamed welcome to the couple in a well-bred manner; and the financier, who was nearest, perceived that the moment had arrived for a little wholesome fun. He slapped Sir John's shoulders, crying archly: "Well, where have you been, you old swashbuckler? Let's hear all about it! Planning another campaign, eh?"

"Not exactly," Sir John answered, and inclined his head toward Martella. "Merely an engagement."

Silence ensued; then babel. The leading lady, her husband, the viscount who had become an actor, the actress who had become a baroness, the cabinet minister, the vivacious male dressmaker, the playwright with his betrothed, and her sister, the editress of the woman's paper, the three female effulgences, the leading man, the Markhams, and the inevitable Foulkes, each had something to say, and loudly said it. Only one, the press agent, was mute: and he, using his elbows ruthlessly to make his way between white arms and black coat sleeves, at last reached Sir John's side, Arrived, breathless, he asked one question:

"For publicity?"

'Naturally!" replied Sir John Saumarez.

THE END

"Now, Miss Baring, where were you on the night of September 27?"

www.ingramcontent.com/pod-product-compliance
Lightning Source LLC
Chambersburg PA
CBHW070628310726
48982CB00001B/204